Als
Agatha No
TAG

Praise ~~*for Death*~~

"*Tagged for Death* is skillfully rendered, with expert characterization and depiction of military life. Best of all Sarah is the type of intelligent, resourceful, and appealing person we would all like to get to know better. Hopefully, we will have that opportunity very soon!"

Lynne Maxwell, *Mystery Science Magazine*

"A terrific find! Engaging and entertaining, this clever cozy is a treasure—charmingly crafted and full of surprises."

Hank Phillippi Ryan, Agatha-, Anthony- and Mary Higgins Clark-award-winning author

"Like the treasures Sarah Winston finds at the garage sales she loves, this book is a gem."

Barbara Ross, Agatha-nominated author of the Maine Clambake Mysteries

"It was masterfully done. *Tagged for Death* is a winning debut that will have you turning pages until you reach the final one. I'm already looking forward to Sarah's next bargain with death."

Mark Baker, *Carstairs Considers*

THE LONGEST YARD SALE

Sherry Harris

KENSINGTON PUBLISHING CORP.
http://www.kensingtonbooks.com

KENSINGTON BOOKS are published by

Kensington Publishing Corp.
119 West 40th Street
New York, NY 10018

All Kensington Titles, Imprints, and Distributed Lines are available at special quantity discounts for bulk purchases for sales promotions, premiums, fund-raising, and educational or institutional use. Special book excerpts or customized printings can also be created to fit specific needs. For details, write or phone the office of the Kensington special sales manager: Kensington Publishing Corp., 119 West 40th Street, New York, NY 10018, attn: Special Sales Department, Phone: 1-800-221-2647.

Kensington and the K logo Reg. U.S. Pat & TM Off.

ISBN-13: 978-1-61773-019-1
ISBN-10: 1-61773-019-X
First Kensington Mass Market Edition: July 2015

eISBN-13: 978-1-61773-020-7
eISBN-10: 1-61773-020-3
First Kensington Electronic Edition: July 2015

10 9 8 7 6 5 4 3 2

Printed in the United States of America

This book is dedicated to Bob Harris.
You inspire me—you know what I mean.

ACKNOWLEDGMENTS

Many thanks to my agent, John Talbot, and my Kensington editor, Gary Goldstein, for helping me turn a longtime dream of being published into a reality. I'd also like to thank the talented team at Kensington who remained behind the scenes but were indispensable to the production of this book.

To Sergeant Patrick J. Towle of the Bedford Police Department, thank you for patiently answering my questions. As they say, all mistakes regarding the police work in this book are mine.

Barb Goffman is not only an amazing editor but a wonderful friend. Thank you for your help with details big and small, your support, and hand-holding!

Clare Boggs and Mary Titone not only read *The Longest Yard Sale* but cheered me on. Thank you for your keen eyes. I'm so glad to call you friends.

I'm fortunate to be a member of two awesome chapters of Sisters in Crime—the Chesapeake chapter and the New England chapter. The members of these two groups are fabulous.

Where would I be without my fellow Wicked Cozy Authors—Jessie Crockett, Julie Hennrikus, Edith Maxwell, Liz Mugavero, and Barbara Ross? Shudder—I don't even want to think about that. You are wonderful authors, blog mates, and, best of all, wicked awesome friends.

Thanks to my husband, Bob, for helping me get the military stuff right, and for answering most of my questions, and for always making me wonder what you know when you say, "I can't answer that." I wish you talked in your sleep—not that I mind the snoring. I'm sorry I didn't write an entire page explaining why someone would be in a hyperbaric chamber—your explanation was fascinating. If any of you are curious, give Bob a call.

To Lieutenant Richard Hickle (Ret.) of the Des Moines Police Department, a long time ago you decided I wasn't actually trying to commit a crime and answered my questions. Thanks for your help and guidance! Forgive me for any errors.

CHAPTER 1

My personal D-day had arrived. While I wasn't going to storm the beaches of Normandy, hopefully by day's end the invasion I'd planned would also be a huge success. I tucked a map, marked with strategic locations and weak points, under my arm. I grabbed the ridiculous earpiece and lapel mike the town manager deemed essential for our communications. In a few hours, I'd launch New England's Largest Yard Sale.

In April when my landlady, Stella Wild, mentioned that her Aunt Nancy wanted to attract more tourists to Ellington, Massachusetts, my adopted hometown, I'd casually suggested throwing New England's Largest Yard Sale. I didn't realize that offhanded comment would result in me being hired, at a hefty fee, to run the event. But here I was, up early on a Saturday morning, energy thrumming through my body like the beat of a rap song.

For the past five months, I'd planned, promoted, and argued with the enemy. Okay, enemy might be a bit strong; naysayers would be more appropriate. The main naysayer was my ex-husband, CJ Hooker, police chief of Ellington, and therefore along with him the entire police department. They'd voiced concerns about traffic, crowd control, and riffraff coming to town. But Nancy Elder envisioned publicity, money in the town coffers, and maybe a political career beyond town manager. She'd beaten the police department into submission. That was before we unleashed the full glory of our plan.

Not only would there be the main event on the town common across from my apartment; we'd cajoled and coerced over 50 percent of the population into having their own yard sales at their homes on the same day. Churches and community organizations jumped on the bandwagon, adding their own events, car washes, book fairs, and bake sales. I'd been writing a column about organizing yard sales in the local paper. It had been picked up by a few other papers around New England. Nancy had been interviewed by the *Boston Globe*, the Boston television stations, and the Nashua, New Hampshire, and Lowell, Massachusetts, newspapers. She was very pleased. This would be the biggest event in Ellington since the start of the Revolutionary War, and would hopefully go off without any bloodshed.

After scooping up a jacket and my purse, I closed the door to my apartment, one of four in an old colonial home, with a quiet click. The apartment next to mine sat empty.

I crossed the foyer to the steps, trying not to wake Stella or the Callahans, who lived below me, as I left. I crept down the staircase but stopped halfway. A man stood with his hand on the knob of Stella's door. He was thin and tall, with one of those two-days growth of beard that under other circumstances might look sexy.

Scenarios zipped through my mind as I scrambled to figure out what I should do. Scream? Run? Attack? Between fight and flight was the rarely talked-about freeze, those few seconds of hesitation in which I was currently trapped. The man turned just as I opened my mouth to scream. I quickly swallowed the scream.

"Bubbles?" I asked in astonishment as I trotted down the last few stairs. Thoughts of being quiet evaporated with the shock of seeing David "Bubbles" Jackson standing outside Stella's door. CJ and I had been stationed with Bubbles years ago. I hadn't seen him in a long time.

Stella's door jerked open. Stella looked from Bubbles to me and didn't look surprised to see either of us. Which surprised me. Stella wore a slinky, silk robe of the palest green. It set off her olive, Mediterranean skin and deep green eyes. Her hair was messy and her skin a bit flushed.

It took me only a couple of seconds longer to put two and two together, or in this case one and one. "You know Bubbles?" I asked Stella.

"Bubbles?" Stella widened her eyes.

I gestured up and down at Bubbles as much as

I could despite having the map tucked under my arm and carrying my purse and jacket.

"It's my call sign," Bubbles said. He had deep brown eyes that always showed his emotions and dark lashes that framed them. Right now they sparkled with fun and satisfaction.

Stella looked mystified.

"It's a nickname," Bubbles said. "From the air force."

I snorted. "That's a bit of an understatement." I looked at Stella. "It has something to do with an incident in a swimming pool and a bit of gas."

Stella glanced between us as if trying to decide if this was a joke.

"I know. It's a bit gross," I said. "CJ's call sign is Hooker; his last name sufficed as a joke." Until CJ had retired last year, he'd served for twenty years in the air force with the security forces.

Bubbles grinned. "Sarah, why are you lurking around on the steps?"

"I live upstairs. Stella's my landlady."

"When Stella told me she had a pain-in-the-neck tenant upstairs, I never dreamed it would be you. Small world, huh?"

Stella opened her mouth to protest. Bubbles winked at her as he hugged me, enveloping me in his arms for a brief second. Then he held me away from him. "You look great."

I had to agree. I looked pretty darn cute this morning in my favorite jeans tucked into boots I'd probably later regret wearing and a long-sleeved, sky-blue V-necked T-shirt. Even my blondish hair cooperated, swinging sleekly just below my shoulders. I'd managed not to stick the mascara wand in my eye, quite an accomplishment at six AM, or really, any time of day for me.

"You're looking good yourself," I said. "But what are you doing here?"

"Leaving," he said.

"I don't mean here in the foyer. That seems pretty obvious. I mean in Ellington," I said.

"I got stationed at Fitch a few months ago." Fitch was the air force base bordered by Ellington, Bedford, Concord, Lexington, and Lincoln. CJ and I had lived there for two years. Last December he'd been getting ready to retire and take over as Ellington's chief of police when a young enlisted troop member falsely accused him of having an affair with her. The accusation led to CJ retiring quickly—and to our divorce.

"We met at karaoke. At Gillganins," Stella said before I could ask, not that I would have in front of Bubbles.

Gillganins was an Irish pub close to the base. Not only was Stella my landlady, but we were both in our late thirties and about five-six, and we were becoming friends.

"I've got to run." I held up my map, purse, and jacket. The earpiece and mike dangled from my fingers. At least we didn't wake up the Callahans, who lived across the hall from Stella. They must have taken their hearing aids out.

Bubbles brushed a kiss across my cheek, laid one on Stella, and walked out with me.

***

Bubbles and I parted ways on the wide porch. He climbed in a dirty, old beater of a pickup truck and left with a wave. I took a moment to look over the town common's wide expanse of lawn. It was broken by a long sidewalk that meandered the city block from the Congregational church on one end of the common to Great Road on the other. The town common was a hub of activity for Ellington—the apple festival in September, an ice rink in the winter, and my favorite event in the spring, Prom Stroll, when most of the townspeople lined the sidewalk as each couple attending prom was announced and paraded their sparkling dresses and sleek tuxes as photos were snapped and people applauded.

For the moment all was still as the sky lightened. The sun would rise in about fifteen minutes. I breathed in the crisp fall air, tinged with the scent of fallen leaves. As I trotted down the porch stairs and crossed the narrow street, Nancy's shrill voice called out.

"Sarah Winston, where have you been?"

I glanced at my watch. It was six thirty-one. Yeesh, we'd agreed to meet at six-thirty, but that was Nancy for you. She had the precision of a drill sergeant, only she was more demanding. She marched across the town common toward me as I picked up my pace to match hers. The Congregational church, four stories of white wood plus a steeple, loomed behind her. It always spooked me a little at night, with its wavy, glass windows staring blankly out, but in the early-morning light it glowed. Nancy's brown hair bobbed around her ears as she came toward me.

"Why isn't your earpiece on?" she asked when we met near the church steps.

I sucked in a sigh and smiled. None of the vendors had shown up yet. The event started at nine. I put everything down on a table Nancy had set up near the entrance to the towering church. I slipped on my jacket and slung the long strap of my purse across my body so I wouldn't have to hold it. Nancy clipped the lapel mike to my jacket. I dutifully adjusted the earpiece as I wondered again where she'd procured equipment that seemed worthy of the Secret Service.

"Nice equipment," I said.

Nancy nodded. "Let's do a sound test." She walked a few feet away. "Testing, testing," blasted into my ear. I hoped this thing had a volume control. I answered with a "testing" of my own.

"It works," she said. "Testing done." Once she returned to my side, she handed me a cup of Dunkin' Donuts coffee from the table. The broad entrance of the church would serve as a stage for various musical and dance groups that were scheduled to perform during the day. We spread out the town map and the diagram I'd drawn showing each vendor's space on the common.

"Thanks for the coffee," I said.

"Walk me through the events again," Nancy demanded.

I winced at her tone and reminded myself that Nancy—well, the town—paid me a lot of money to run this event. I'd just have to bite my tongue for another twelve hours. At this rate, I'd have one very sore and swollen tongue by the end of the day.

Even though Nancy must surely know all this by heart, I led her around the common, pointing out where different booths would sit. I pointed out the kiddie area, where there'd be apple bobbing, face painting, and storytelling, among other things. I walked her through the schedule.

"Do you think we can pull this off?" she asked.

I almost dropped my cup of coffee. Nancy rarely showed a vulnerable side. She was one of those women whose look was always polished. None of her clothes were ever wrinkled, torn, or stained. Even at an event like this, she had on a red power suit and pumps. At least she'd be easy to spot in the crowd, even though she was half a head shorter than me.

It was a little late to be questioning our plans now. "It's going to be a huge success," I said. I hoped I was right.

"And the weather?"

It wasn't like I had any control over that. "A postcard-worthy autumn day in New England." Good thing I'd checked before I left the house.

"What about the noon flyby of the F-15s from Barnes?"

My jaw dropped. Flyby? Barnes was the air national guard unit in Westfield. Had I dropped the ball on something? My heart pounded harder than the feet of the Irish step-dancing troupe I'd watched practice for this event. I started flipping through notes on my phone, my hand shaking. "I'm sorry, Nancy, but I—"

"Gotcha. No flybys," she said with a smile before going over to refill her coffee.

"Ha," I called after her. "Very funny." I patted my chest, and my heart finally settled back into a more normal rhythm.

By seven, most of the vendors were jockeying for parking spots close to their booths. White canopy tents dotted the lawn. Early birds arrived and plucked items out of the backs of the vendors' trucks, trying to make a deal before the stuff hit the stands. I flew from vendor to vendor, helping where needed, exhilarated by the energy in the air. I texted Stella when I spotted a vendor with beautiful old sheet music, some with hand-colored covers that would be fabulous framed. I fired off a few more texts as I spotted things my friends collected—vintage tablecloths, cobalt glass, and silver spoons.

At nine o'clock, the town common was packed, and the surrounding streets were at a standstill.

Nancy stood on the steps of the church, mike in hand, trying to get everyone's attention. No one stopped what they were doing, though a few did glance over when the mike squawked. Two seconds later, Nancy screeched through my earpiece.

"No one is paying attention to me," she said.

Big shock. This was a yard sale, and an enormous one at that. "I tried to explain to you that this isn't the kind of event where people will want to stop and listen to someone speak. They're afraid someone else will find a hidden treasure or make a better deal if they stop to listen." At least I'd convinced her not to do a ribbon cutting. What an argument that had been. "The newspaper and local-access TV people are here. Go ahead and give your speech. They'll record it, and no one will ever know you don't have a huge audience."

She gasped into my ear. "You're right."

The mike squawked again, and Nancy plunged into her speech. A few people applauded politely when she finished. Nancy beamed her mega-watt, mega-white smile for the photographer. A rock band took over as soon as she'd finished speaking.

I roamed around, wishing I had time to barter for things for myself—a red purse, an antique chair, a chenille bedspread. Nothing pumped me up like making a deal. I consoled myself by remembering my apartment was small enough that I didn't have room for much else, anyway.

I spotted a vendor with beautiful old prints and boxes of empty, antique frames.

"I hand-color the prints," the vendor told me.

"I'm going to let a friend of mine know about all these frames." I sent a text to my artist friend Carol Carson, who owned a store, Paint and Wine. It was located on Great Road at the end of the town common in a line of storefronts. A few months ago I'd introduced her to the joys of garage and tag sales, and now she was always on the hunt.

I spent the next few hours monitoring the vendors, helping lost tourists, reuniting kids with parents, and settling the occasional argument that broke out when two people wanted the same item. I saw lots of people I knew but never had time to stop and talk to them.

"You have to do something about the traffic." Nancy's voice boomed through my earpiece.

I don't know what she thought I could do. I turned and looked over my shoulder at Great Road. I'd done my best to ignore it up to this point. If I'd thought it was jammed at 7:30, what it looked like now would have done New York City proud. The good news was that lots of people milled about, visiting the shops and restaurants along Great Road.

Carol's shop looked packed with people, and my favorite restaurant, DiNapoli's Roast Beef and Pizza, had a line out the door. A faint whiff of roast beef drifted over to me, and my stomach growled in response. My earpiece crackled.

"Chief Hooker just called, and he's not happy. Great Road is slow on either end of Ellington, all the way from Bedford to Carlisle."

"We both knew there was a possibility this could happen." This probably wasn't the right time to remind her I'd suggested having people park at the high school and run buses back and forth between there and the town common. "It means the event is a big success. Didn't you authorize some overtime for traffic control?" I asked. I could hear horns honking as people became impatient with the wait on Great Road. I hoped I could avoid CJ for the next few days until he got over this.

"Yes, of course I did," she said. "With all this traffic, it really will be New England's Largest Yard Sale. I wasn't sure you could pull it off."

I couldn't believe Nancy had thought I'd fail. She'd hired me, after all. But it was her political career that was on the line if something went terribly wrong.

"I'll tell CJ to get his officers out there and keep the traffic moving," Nancy said.

She could tell CJ that until she was blue in the face, but the truth was Great Road was a main cut-through from the 95, which connected Maine to Miami, and to the 495, which circumvented Boston. (The locals always made fun of my California speak, which had me using the word *the* before 95 or any other road number I referenced.) It was going to take more than a few police officers to get the road going again. I turned my back to Great Road and looked up at the church steeple reaching toward the bright blue sky. The weather was perfect. The trees were changing, the meteorologists had gotten it right, and I couldn't ask for a better New England autumn day. I focused on all the positives.

At some point, I'd turned down the sound on my earpiece. Nancy's voice droned on and on, more annoying than a gnat relentlessly buzzing my ear. After a few minutes I realized she'd quit talking—that it had been a while since I'd heard her say anything. "Nancy?" I asked several times. She didn't answer. I shrugged. I was too busy to worry about what Nancy was up to.

Sirens began to wail. First one, then others joined, in increasingly large numbers. I couldn't pinpoint where they were coming from or going to. Fire trucks crept out of the station a block up on Great Road, with some going left and others to the right. People quit shopping to look around. The band stopped playing.

I smiled at people as I hurried across the common to the church. "It's okay," I said over and over, desperately hoping it was. I tried to reach Nancy and turned up the volume on my earpiece in case I couldn't hear her over the crowds and the sirens. I motioned to the band and got them playing again as I scanned the crowd, looking for Nancy.

People took that as a good sign and began to shop again. Thankfully, the sirens headed away from the town common, but that many sounding at once couldn't be good.

I rushed back over to Great Road, hoping to catch a glimpse of what was happening. But all I saw were long lines of traffic.

My earpiece crackled to life. "What's going on?" Nancy's voice blasted my eardrum.

For once, I was happy to hear her voice in my ear. I'd been more worried about her silence than I'd realized. "I don't know." I craned my neck as I looked up and down Great Road. CJ, in his chief-of-police SUV, inched along. I knew that wasn't good. CJ pushed his Ray-Bans up on his forehead. We locked eyes for a second. From this distance, I couldn't see the pale blue of his eyes or the way he narrowed them when he was mad. He pounded his horn and hit the siren in frustration. Traffic was slow to get out of his way. Where could they go on a narrow New England road? His glare said it all—this is your fault.

"Where are you?" I asked Nancy.

"At the church. Meet me there."

I plunged back into the throngs of shoppers as Nancy came around the corner next to the church. She jerked her head toward a side entrance, and I followed her in. The noise level dropped instantly.

"We might have to shut this whole thing down."

I stared at Nancy. "Why?"

"There's an arsonist on the loose."

CHAPTER 2

I stared at her. "Why do you think that?"

"I just spoke with the fire chief. There's a series of small fires smoldering all around the area."

Shock and relief swept through me. The thought of an arsonist on the loose was awful, but at least the fires had nothing to do with my event. "Where?"

"One's near the start of the Rails to Trails path."

The path was only a few miles from the town common. It runs from Ellington to Cambridge and is heavily utilized by bikers, runners, and Rollerbladers. A biking magazine recently named it one of the best paths in America because of the ancient trees shading it and the easy access it provided to historical sites.

"How bad is it? Is there any damage?"

"I don't know. I'm waiting for a report."

"Where are the other fires?"

"One near the old missile silos on that land Harvard owns. A bigger fire at the old chicken

coops on the VA property in Bedford. And one
near the high school football field. The brand-
new *millions*-of-dollars AstroTurf field." Nancy
emphasized the word *millions* as if I didn't know. It
had been years in the making and a hotly debated
topic around town.

"How could one person start that many fires so
far apart from one another? Especially on a day
like today when the roads are clogged." As the
crow flies, the sites weren't that far apart, but on
the narrow, crowded roads they were.

"I have no idea." Nancy's face was creased with
worry. "If the fire damages the high school's
AstroTurf field, I'm holding you accountable,
Sarah."

I looked at her, thinking she must have lost her
mind. "How could I be responsible? This is the
work of a very sick person."

Nancy glared at me for a moment, then her
faced relaxed. She patted my arm. "I'm sorry. It's
just so terrible. The police department is overwhelmed with traffic direction, crowd control
near the fires, and actually helping put fires out.
The chief isn't happy," Nancy said as if I somehow had the key to the chief's happiness. On
reflection, that might be true, but this was not
the time to think about that.

"It's too bad CJ's unhappy. But this has nothing to do with our event, and there's no reason to
shut us down." Even as I said it, I wondered about
the timing of the fires and what, if anything, they
might have to do with the yard sale.

One of the vendors called to me, so I left Nancy. I worked the event, putting out fires—bad choice of words—and solving problems all across the common. Two hours later, Nancy instructed me to meet her at the side of the church again.

"The fires are all out. The creepy old chicken coops were slated to be torn down for low-income housing, anyway. The few officers left at the police station ran over to help put out the fire at the football field."

That made sense. The police station and the football field were separated by just a small park and some basketball and tennis courts. Many of the department's employees had kids that attended Ellington High School. They'd be highly motivated to make sure the fire was out and next Friday's football game was on.

"The other fires were minor and quickly extinguished."

"That is good news indeed," I said.

The official end of the yard sale was five PM. By six only a few stragglers roamed the common. All the canopy tents and booths had been taken down. The last of the sun's rays lightened the sky to the west. The church cast long shadows across the common. The event had been a huge success. Euphoria circled through me, and I wanted to celebrate.

Vendors had asked me if we were going to do this next year and could we add a day. They had little to load back into their vehicles. Most of the tourists didn't realize anything had gone awry. I heard reports that local businesses had boomed today, that the individual yard sales had good crowds, and that the car washes and other events packed people in. As long as I dodged CJ, life looked good.

Nancy strode up to me as I picked up some trash on the lawn. "How can we make next year's event even bigger?"

Inside my head, I did a fist pump and danced a jig. In spite of the fires, Nancy was happy with the event. "Some of the vendors mentioned doing a two-day sale," I began. "We could add a pancake breakfast with local maple syrup from New Hampshire, a clambake in the evening, an organic farm stand, an animal parade with organic treats as prizes." Who knows what I could dream up given more time? "I have a friend who's a horologist."

Nancy's mouth dropped open. "A what?" she sputtered out. "What's a horologist?"

"She makes clocks. I could have her make a special one to be auctioned off for a local charity."

"Whew. There for a minute I thought you were talking about some kind of illegal adult entertainment."

It was probably not the first time someone had thought that about my friend.

Nancy smiled. "Exciting ideas. I'll check my calendar so we can start planning for next year. I'll call you."

"Have you heard anything new about the fires?" I asked.

"I think it was someone trying to ruin our event. Some of the people in the other towns around here were quite jealous—mad they didn't think of New England's Largest Yard Sale first."

It was quite a leap, I thought, from jealousy to arson. "Where were you midday? You went radio silent for a couple of hours."

Nancy opened and closed her mouth. She waved a hand around. Interesting. This was the first and only time I'd seen her at a loss for words.

She finally lifted her chin and stammered out, "As town manager I have multiple duties—unlike you, who had only this event." She made a sweeping gesture with her arm as though this event had been no big deal. Nancy turned on her heel and headed off, looking a bit like a steam-roller. Tourists beware.

One of the local Boy Scout troops picked up trash as part of a service project. I helped. As I headed back to my apartment around seven-thirty my phone rang. I thought about ignoring it—I'd already ignored a couple of calls from CJ. But I saw it was Carol Carson. We'd met in Monterey and known each other for almost twenty years. We were thrilled when we both ended up at Fitch Air Force Base a couple of years ago after a long while of being stationed at opposite ends of the country. Last December we both moved to Ellington, for different reasons. Carol had her business, and her husband, Brad, after retiring from the air force, took a job at the Veteran's hospital in Bedford. CJ and Brad were almost as good friends as Carol and I.

"What's up?" I asked.

"Can you please get over here?" Carol said. Her voice had an edge to it I'd never heard before. "Right now."

"Are you at the shop?" I asked, but Carol had already disconnected. I glanced across the common at Paint and Wine. Lights blazed. I reversed direction to see what had put such a frantic note in Carol's voice.

CHAPTER 3

I looked through the beveled-glass window that filled the top half of the old wooden door. Tables topped with small easels filled the room. Stools were tucked neatly under them. Paintings lined the walls. No one was in the shop. I tried the knob. The door was unlocked. "Carol?" I called out as I stepped into the shop.

"Back here. Hurry," Carol said. She appeared at the door that separated the public space from her private studio. Tall and slender, Carol wore jeans and a tight-fitting sweater that showed off her ample chest. It wasn't that I was a washout in that department, but Carol had an enviable figure.

I hurried past the tables and easels, where her clients could create a painting in a couple of hours using Carol's unique teaching method. Carol led me to an easel holding a blank sixteen-by-twenty canvas.

"What?"

"Someone took my painting," she said, pointing at the easel. A large canvas tarp sat crumpled on the floor beside it. Her face was pale, her eyes wide. She twisted a strand of hair around her finger. "Right before I called you, I took the tarp off. The blank canvas was there, and my painting was gone."

"Oh, no. Did they take anything else?"

I looked around. She'd lined most of the walls with pegboard. Old frames and assorted canvases hung in neat rows. A table was covered with a neat array of paints, arranged by color. Brushes stood in brightly flowered vintage biscuit tins. A chaise lounge sat in one corner with a stack of art books beside it. The room smelled like turpentine and paint.

At the back of the studio, vintage curtains we'd found at a garage sale divided the working area from a small storage space and a door that led to the alley.

"No, just the painting."

"Nothing else is missing? No money?"

Carol shook her head. "It's worse than money. It's a catastrophe."

"Why?"

"It's a copy of the Patrick West painting at the library." She pointed to a computer monitor next to the easel. The picture of a recently fought battle glowed with its bright reds and blues contrasting with ashen faces, gray stone walls, and rolling spring fields.

"You were copying *Battled*?" *Battled* was Ellington's beloved painting by native son and Revolutionary War hero Patrick West. He'd first sketched a drawing at the end of the first day of the Revolutionary War. After surviving the war, West had used the sketch and brought the scene to life in an oil painting that depicted the anguish and triumph as the colonials chased the British soldiers from Concord back to Boston. He'd gone on to have a highly successful career as an artist. Some of his works hung in the National Gallery of Art.

"Yes. It was done—except it needed to finish drying. Here, I took some pictures of it." Carol clicked on the keyboard. Her hand shook as she scrolled through pictures of the painting in various stages.

I was shocked. I'd known Carol was talented, but only an expert would be able to tell that this was a copy. "It's beautiful. Was it for you?"

"No, a client."

"Who?"

"That's not the issue. I have three more weeks before my client needs it, but I'm sure I can recreate it in that amount of time."

It worried me that Carol didn't answer my question about her client. "When did you realize it was missing?"

"Just before I called. I'd draped the canvas

over it last night because I knew we'd be busy today, and I didn't want anyone to see it."

When Carol had painted a painting for me she'd done the same thing. She didn't like people to see her work in progress.

"So it could have disappeared anytime between last night and now?"

"Yes."

"Did you call the police?"

"No."

"Do you want me to call CJ?" I asked. Being close to the chief of police came in handy on occasion.

Carol took a shaky breath and thought for a moment. "No. It's okay. You know that copying paintings is a little shady. As long as it's for use in a private home it's not so bad. I was planning to sign it after the paint dried."

"Is there any chance Olivia moved it?" Olivia was Carol's new assistant, an art student who wasn't all that reliable. Carol had called me more than once to help out when Olivia was a no-show.

"I did a quick search, but will you help me look again? Maybe I somehow overlooked it."

"Sure." We started in the public space, going through cupboards and looking in corners. There weren't many hiding spaces out here. We quickly searched Carol's studio before moving to the small storage space. A stack of canvases, some finished, some waiting to be completed, yielded nothing. Shelves held cans of paint thinner, turpentine, and lots of tubes of paint. A couple of wooden boxes filled with a jumble of frames sat on the paint-spattered concrete floor.

Carol pointed at them. "Those are the frames I bought today at the yard sale." She smiled for a brief moment.

"Wow. That's a great haul." I opened the door to the small bathroom. An aromatic waft of scent came from a vase full of dried lavender sitting on a shelf over the toilet. A sink and wastebasket were the only other things in the room. I checked the wastebasket, just in case. It was empty.

"Did you ask Olivia about the painting?" I asked.

"I sent her a text, and she said she thought it was there when she left. We were really busy today with all the tourists. Olivia was only here until one because she had a study group for a class she's taking at Middlesex Community College."

"Did she know what you were painting?" I asked.

"She might have. I usually kept it covered during the day and worked on it when the shop was closed."

"What can I do to help? You know I can't paint," I said.

"You're better than you think. But I'll just have to give up sleeping."

"I have a couple of garage sales I'm organizing for next weekend." Organizing a garage sale for Carol last spring had led to a series of other people asking me to set up garage sales for them. "If I can help here or run your kids around, let me know." Carol had eight-year-old twin boys and a six-year-old daughter, all of whom participated in lots of activities.

"Thanks for coming over. I thought it would magically appear if you were here."

I paused as I watched her face the blank canvas on the easel, worry lines etched on her forehead. My rumbling stomach set me back in motion. I couldn't think of the last time I'd eaten. I headed down the block to DiNapoli's Roast Beef and Pizza.

Just as I arrived, Rosalie switched the sign on the glass door to CLOSED. I started to turn away, but Rosalie spotted me and opened the door.

"Sarah, we were just going to eat. Join us."

"Is she paying?" Angelo shouted from the back of the restaurant.

"Of course I will," I said.

"No. You want her to pay for leftovers, Angelo? Have you lost your mind?" She turned to me. "I think the crowds today wore him out," she said, her voice lowered.

But behind her Angelo winked and smiled at me. His bald head shone above a fringe of hair. Rosalie tried to whisk me over to a table where they would eat, one in a row of tables positioned on the right side of the restaurant. A low wall separated the eating area from the kitchen. That way Angelo could keep an eye on things while he cooked. No fancy tablecloths—or, for that matter, any tablecloths at all—covered the odd assortment of wooden tables. The tables and chairs were mismatched, not because it was trendy but because Angelo didn't want to buy new ones. Of course, if asked, Angelo would claim he started the trend. These days, when something broke, I found its replacement.

"I'll set the table," I said, shooing off Rosalie's attempts to stop me.

Soon dishes of pasta, pieces of pizza, an antipasto platter, and warm garlic bread with olive oil for dipping covered the table.

"Want some cooking wine?" Angleo asked with another wink.

"Yes, please," I said.

Rosalie served me Chianti in a kid's cup with a lid and a straw because they didn't have a liquor license. Anytime I looked around the restaurant and saw adults drinking out of kid's cups, I knew they were sipping wine and were close friends of the DiNapolis. It amazed me that they weren't able to get a liquor license while Carol had one for Paint and Wine. It burned Angelo as well, so two of my favorite people hadn't warmed to each other.

As we ate, we talked about all of the tourists and the success of the sale.

"We were swamped all day," Rosalie said, but her warm, brown eyes still sparkled with energy. Her brown hair was in place, as always.

"What do you know about the fires?" Angelo asked me.

It didn't surprise me that Angelo already knew the news. His restaurant was a hub for gossip in Ellington. Policemen and firefighters frequented the place.

"Not much. A series of small fires were started around town at about the same time. All were put out without too much damage, although those old creepy chicken coops out at the VA burned to the ground." I pushed my plate away and sipped my Chianti. "Nancy told me that if the fire damaged the new football field she'd hold me responsible."

Angelo waved his hands in the air. "That woman—she thinks she knows more than the rest of us." In Italian, *Angelo* meant messenger of God, and he took that role to heart, which meant he butted heads way too often with the town powers that be. "You let me know if she pulls something like that again. I'll take care of it."

I worried about what Angelo's method of "taking care of it" would be. I'd seen him nose-to-nose with a traffic officer when he didn't like the way traffic was rerouted. I knew Angelo had a cousin who was a lawyer for the Mob. His letters to the editor in the local paper were scathing if he didn't like something the town was considering. I hoped he was joking.

Rosalie set a tray full of cannolis and Italian cookies on the table. Minutes ago I'd thought I couldn't take another bite, but Rosalie's baked goods were irresistible. I picked a cannoli filled with chocolate mousse. The ends were dipped in mini chocolate chips. I must have made some kind of happy noise when I bit in because Rosalie smiled at me.

I left a few minutes later with one bag stuffed with what we didn't eat, plus another full of Italian cookies. As I left, Rosalie tucked the unfinished bottle of "cooking wine" under my arm.

My legs ached as I walked back across the common. I'd been on my feet almost all day. As I'd predicted this morning, boots with heels hadn't been a smart choice. But at least the fall air was still warm. When I stopped for a moment in the middle of the common to stare at the stars popping out, weariness settled over me. A bath, with a glass of wine and some decent blues playing in the background, sounded like the perfect ending to the day.

As I got closer to my building, I saw a figure sitting on the porch, arms on knees, head down. I hoped it was Bubbles waiting for Stella or one of the Callahans' kids. But soon enough the figure shifted, and I could tell it was CJ. I thought about ducking into the shadows of the church and sneaking around the back way. But CJ spotted me and stood.

I had a minute or so to decide, as I walked the rest of the way across the common, whether to invite CJ in or keep him out on the porch. Talking on the porch would shorten our visit and get me into the tub sooner. But I'd hurt CJ's feelings so many times recently that inviting him up might be the more diplomatic thing to do. I hoped he wasn't here for a relationship talk because I was too tired to fight.

I held the food between us when I reached the porch. "Want to come up for some leftovers?"

CJ took the food from my hands and swooped in for a kiss. I kept it to a brush on the lips, even though part of me longed to fall into his arms, lean into his chest, and surrender. But there was too much unfinished business between us to allow myself to do that. I stepped back, hoping the dark would hide the blush on my face. It wasn't dark enough that it hid the disappointment on CJ's.

In my apartment, CJ moved carefully through the living room so he didn't hit his head on the side of the ceiling that slanted down. CJ's light brown hair was a bit longer than when he had been on active duty in the military. I set the wine on the counter and pulled out a plate so CJ could eat. We settled at my small kitchen table, another barrier I'd used to good purpose on more than one occasion. CJ unpacked the food and took a bite of a meatball before it even hit the plate I slid in front of him.

"Their meatballs are the best," he said, wiping a bit of tomato sauce from the corner of his mouth. He stabbed a fork into a piece of Italian sausage. "And their sausage is blissful. You don't usually get sausage."

"This is food that was left over at the end of the day."

"I rarely get their food."

"I thought all was forgiven."

The DiNapolis had taken my side nine months ago, during the separation and divorce, when we all thought CJ had slept with a young woman. CJ, who befriended everyone, had been hurt by that.

"So did I, until I went in a few months ago. I don't think anyone actually spit in my food, but the glare and the chill made me realize I'm still persona not grata in there. Why is that?"

I shrugged, but I knew. I grew up in Pacific Grove, California, right next to Monterey. My family still lived there and were mystified that I stayed out here in the snow and ice. Ellington felt like home to me, and the DiNapolis were like my family. They not only filled my tummy but also my soul by listening to my woes. "They think you're pressuring me."

I stood and grabbed the bottle of wine off the counter. The cork slid out easily. I busied myself pouring two glasses of wine, hoping CJ would drop the subject, regretting we'd gotten to it in the first place. I sat back down and passed him one of the glasses.

"We have a closed-container law in Ellington," CJ said. Trust him to notice I'd walked across the common with the open bottle under my arm.

"Arrest me, then."

"I wouldn't mind cuffing you." CJ grinned.

Another blush coursed up my face.

"DiNapoli's doesn't have a liquor license," CJ said.

"Cooking wine."

"What are you planning on cooking?" CJ asked with a half smile that always melted me.

"Beef Wellington?" I had no idea if it needed wine or not. A talent for cooking eluded me. But the last thing I wanted to do was get the DiNapolis in trouble, and I wanted to forestall whatever it was that CJ had showed up to talk about. I didn't think it could be anything good after the day he and the police department must have had. "I ran in to Bubbles today. He was coming out of Stella's apartment as I left for the yard sale." Darn, I didn't mean to venture into that topic, either. "Did you know?"

"That he was seeing Stella? No."

I gave CJ a look, letting him know that wasn't what I meant.

"I did know he was here. He's been here for about six months."

"What's he doing here? I thought he was wing commander for one of the missile bases out west."

"He got caught up in the whole scandal with the missileers cheating on their tests, sleeping on the job, and not securing the vault."

Missile launch officers were tested constantly to make sure that, if the time came, they could turn the key without thinking about it. I didn't know how the tests were administered or what kinds of questions were asked, because all of that was classified. I did know the pressure to score 100 percent on every test was intense. If they missed one question on either of two monthly exams they weren't eligible to advance for a year. Not good for a career.

It wasn't a glam job like flying fighter jets. Since the end of the Cold War, the career field led nowhere. The best way to get a promotion was to get into another field, which wasn't great for morale. Missileers worked varying shifts, going out to the missile sites, then deep underground, where huge, steel blast doors locked them within a dingy space full of noisy equipment and speakers that continuously blasted codes. They spent the night with a crew partner, taking turns sleeping. Since the early '90s, crew partners didn't have to be the same sex. I had a friend who joked about her husband spending the night with another woman a month after they'd married. It was his crew partner, but more than one crew team had ended up in a relationship.

"Did he know his officers were cheating?"

"He says he didn't. I believe him. But since he was at the top of the food chain and the troops were his responsibility, he got the blowback."

"Was he fired?" Being fired in the military wasn't the same as being fired in the civilian world. It usually meant being removed from your current position and sent to another base with less responsibility. It almost always ended any possibility of future promotions. CJ had always said Bubbles was a fast burner—meaning he was getting promoted "below the zone," or early. He'd made colonel early and was on the fast track to becoming a general.

"Yes. Now he'll never make general."

"He must be really disappointed."

"He's had a great attitude. He started a financial planning company with a civilian he knows from Hanscom. They both have a couple of months left until they retire."

CJ, of all people, knew how disappointing it was to have your career end under a cloud. He'd retired quickly and quietly after one of his troops accused him of fraternization and said she was having his baby. By the time the truth came out, CJ was already out of the air force and the chief of police in Ellington. A lawyer had approached CJ about suing to get back in, but CJ was content with his new job.

"How'd he end up here?"

"He wanted to come. His kids are with his ex-wife, Jill, in Nashua. His parents are in Maine. Bubbles had planned to come back to this area eventually, anyway."

"At least something worked out for him."

"I didn't come here to talk about Bubbles," CJ said.

I grabbed the bottle of wine and poured the rest of it into my glass. "I'm sorry about the traffic." I took a drink. "No. Actually I'm not. It was a great event, and Nancy was really pleased. There are other events that cause traffic problems in Ellington. It just goes with the territory, right?"

"It was a great event. I'm happy for you. But that's not why I'm here. I want to talk about us."

Damn, I was afraid of that. "We've talked about us. You agreed we'd date. That we'd date other people. That we'd take this slow."

"For how long? That was six months ago. We were happy."

"It's me, CJ. I have to figure out why it was so easy for me to turn my back on nineteen years of marriage. Why I wouldn't even listen when you said you didn't sleep with Tiffany." I stood, slamming the kitchen chair into the cabinet behind it. CJ followed me into the living room. I plopped into my grandmother's rocking chair so I didn't have to sit next to him on the couch. It sat by the window that overlooked the town common. "Until I figure that out, I can't come back."

"Are you really pulling the 'it's me, not you' crap on me?"

"I don't want to hurt you again."

"You are hurting me."

I looked out the window over the common toward Great Road. The lights blinked out in Carol's store. "I'm sorry. It's the best I can do right now."

CJ studied my face. "Okay, then."

CJ wheeled around, knocked his leg on the corner of the trunk I used for a coffee table, cursed, and left. He didn't slam the door, but he pounded down the steps out to the porch. On the sidewalk, he looked up at me for a moment before striding down the sidewalk toward Great Road. Something about the way he said "Okay, then" had sounded so final. I tried to convince myself that my stomach hurt because of all I'd eaten at DiNapoli's and not because of what had just happened with CJ.

Last April, after a wacko almost killed me, CJ and I had spent the night together. I'd felt so safe after the scariest day of my life. But in the morning, CJ launched into logistics. Should he give up his apartment and move in with me? Or should I move in with him? Better yet, let's find a new place for a fresh start. I'd said no. The look on his face as he'd said good-bye that morning would never leave me.

I curled my legs up in the chair and tilted my head back against the solid oak. My phone rang. It was Seth, a temptation I had no energy to deal with now. I ignored it, skipped my planned bath, and flopped on my bed fully dressed.

CHAPTER 4

Someone pounded on my door. My bedroom door. I leaped up, still dressed in my clothes from last night. Only two people had the key to my apartment, Stella and Carol. I flung my bedroom door open. Carol stood there with her hand raised to knock again. Her face was about the same color as the blank canvas at her store, only stained with tears and mascara—a Jackson Pollock painting come to life.

"What are you doing here?" I asked. I glanced at my alarm clock, which read seven AM. I'd slept through the night.

"Come with me. Please." Carol turned and ran through my apartment, stopping only briefly at the top of the steps to make sure I was following her. I don't think she'd have noticed if I was buck naked. She, on the other hand, had changed from what she wore yesterday into black leggings and a red sweater.

I hurried to catch up with her on the town common. "What's going on?"

"It's awful," she said.

"What?" I asked. Carol shook her head. A shiver went through me. I hoped she and Brad were okay. We stopped at the front door of her shop. She pulled out her keys. Her hands shook worse than mine had the night Stella tricked me into singing karaoke with her at Gillganins. I took them from her and unlocked the door. I flipped on the lights as we went in, scanning the place.

"Is this about your painting?" I asked. Nothing looked any different than it had last night.

Carol shook her head "no" as I trotted after her through the shop to her studio. She stopped so abruptly I almost plowed through her.

It took me a minute to process what I saw. A man on his back sprawled across the floor wearing jeans and a blue dress shirt with French cuffs and gold cuff links. Around his face was a frame, a dark, heavy frame.

"Oh, my god," I said, looking away. The man was dead. Really, really dead. "Who is that?"

"I was hoping you'd know," Carol said.

I steeled myself and took another look at the guy. His sandy-colored hair appeared recently trimmed. He wore a gold wedding band. His long, denim-covered legs were askew. He didn't seem to have any wounds other than some bruising on his neck. His square-jawed face was mottled.

"I have no idea who he is," I said. I had no idea

why Carol would think I did. "He looks like he's
been framed. Picasso's blue period."

Carol's eyes widened in shock at my wisecrack.
I chided myself for how heartless I sounded. But
I'd spent a lot of time around military cops
during my marriage to CJ. They had the same
dark sense of humor civilian cops did.

"Have you called the police?" Obviously she
hadn't, since I didn't hear any sirens and no
officials were here, but my brain wasn't function-
ing on all cylinders. "Call 9-1-1. I'll call CJ." I'd
rather CJ hear this from me. I knew he'd come,
and I wanted him to know I was here before he
arrived, especially after last night.

"They said we should wait outside," Carol said
after we made the calls.

"CJ said the same thing." But neither of us
moved. I continued to study the room and stole
quick glances at the body, as if one activity or
the other could answer the multitude of questions I had.

I focused in on the frame around the guy's
neck. It was black and about two inches thick,
with carved curlicues. "Isn't that one of the frames
you bought at the yard sale?" I asked. It looked
like one I'd seen in the box of frames when we'd
searched the place yesterday.

"A man is dead on my floor and that's what
you're worried about?" We took another step
toward the man. "How do you think he died?"
Carol asked.

I looked around again. Anything was better

than looking down at that blue-faced body. "Nothing's knocked over or seems out of place. You didn't move anything, did you?"

"No," Carol said.

"So there wasn't a big brawl in here. No rope hanging from the ceiling, so it doesn't read suicide, but what do I know? I can't tell you what happened, but I can guess."

Carol continued to get paler as we talked. "What do you think happened?"

"Someone strangled him." Saying it out loud made me go from not-so-cool observer to involved. That man was someone's son, brother, husband. The thought punched into my soul.

"Why'd you think I'd know him?" I asked.

I looked at Carol. She was so calm. Maybe she was in shock.

"You know so many people," she said. "Should we look through his pockets for an ID?"

"No. The last thing we need to do is mess up the crime scene. You didn't touch anything, did you?"

Carol shook her head. "I saw him and ran to get you."

We heard sirens and hustled outside as a fire truck pulled up.

A couple of EMTs ran into the shop but came out quickly. As they did, the first cop cars showed up, with CJ not far behind them.

"You two okay?" CJ asked as he hurried by, barely waiting for our affirmative responses. But he did a double take when he realized I was dressed in the same clothes as yesterday. He opened his mouth to say something, but someone called to him from inside the shop.

If I could have shut out the noise and forgotten that terrible blue face, it was another lovely morning—rosy sky, dew glimmering on the grass of the town common, the sun lighting the steeple of the church.

"Why'd you come get me?" I asked in a low tone. Police officers and technicians scurried in and out of the store.

"I panicked. You felt safe and were close by." Carol shuddered. "I don't even know how he got in," she continued. "The back door was locked when I came in, and the front door was locked when I came to get you." Other than the large plate-glass window in the front, the half window on the door, and some skylights scattered throughout, there wasn't another window to crawl in through.

We entwined our arms, clinging together.

"That frame was positioned so perfectly around his neck. It must be a message of some kind," I said.

"A message," Carol squeaked out. "Who's the message for? What kind of message is it supposed to be?"

"I'm not sure. It's just a thought." I shouldn't have said anything. But thoughts flew around my brain like hummingbirds seeking nectar. The two most puzzling were why the frame and why in Carol's store.

The chimes at the Congregational church rang out. Before long, people would start showing up for church and wonder what the heck had happened.

"Do you think this has anything to do with the missing painting?" I asked.

Carol shrugged. She started to say something but cut off her comment when two officers arrived and separated us.

Scott Pellner escorted me to his patrol car. "Get in," he said, holding the front passenger door open for me. We didn't trust each other but had made an uneasy peace over each of us knowing the other's secret. Mine had to do with a night with Seth and his with lying to his wife about his application to be the chief of police. She liked the idea of the status Pellner would have as chief, but he'd withdrawn his application without telling her. He wanted to stay out on patrol instead of being stuck behind a desk.

"Walk me through what happened," Pellner said. He had dimples that softened an otherwise severe face. They flashed even when he wasn't smiling, which he certainly wasn't doing now.

I tried to be as succinct as possible. After Pellner quit asking me questions and taking notes, he looked me over. "Yesterday was a goat rope. You created a lot of work for us."

Goat rope. Yeesh, I'd forgotten Pellner had served in the military and sometimes used the lingo. He might think yesterday was a mess, but I didn't. I clasped my hands together. "The city created the work. I just implemented the town manager's idea."

"Not what I heard. I heard it was your idea. Thus your goat rope."

"CJ didn't have any complaints." At least not about the yard sale, although I remembered his glare as he'd fought to get down Great Road.

"The traffic problems, the fender benders. A brawl broke out during one of them."

"Poor you, having to do your job while I brought tourists and tax dollars into town."

"Then there were the suspicious fires. We're damn lucky nothing more serious happened and no one was injured."

"I thought the fires were small."

"The one out at the chicken coops got pretty big. Bedford called for backup."

"Nancy thinks they were set by someone trying to ruin our event."

"That someone was pretty darn sophisticated. They found timers at three of the fires. The ashes out at the chicken coop fire are still too hot to sift through."

I wondered why CJ hadn't mentioned that last night. I must have wondered out loud because Pellner snorted.

"The guy would do anything for you. And you don't even appreciate it. You're running around with Seth."

"CJ and I agreed to take things slow. To see other people."

"But he doesn't know you're seeing Seth."

"No. And it's not your business."

"It is when I see a great guy like Chuck mooning around because of you."

I hated it when people called Charles James Hooker "Chuck." CJ was not a Chuck. I climbed out of the car and firmly closed the door. Pellner might have considered it slamming, and one of the technicians jumped. I looked over at DiNapoli's. Rosalie stood in the window, motioning me in. I was surprised to see her there so early on a Sunday morning.

I shook my head and mouthed "later," not sure if she understood me or not. Carol stood on the sidewalk next to another officer. Her eyes looked glazed, and she stared off, maybe at the church steeple. But I don't think she saw it.

I went over and whispered in her ear, "Did you tell him about the painting?" just as CJ walked out of the shop. Carol shook her head "no."

CJ planted his hands on his hips and barked, "You two come with me. Now."

CHAPTER 5

We followed CJ up the block a little ways. He rubbed his face. "Something else is going on. What is it?"

Carol and I exchanged glances. Carol clamped her lips together in a firm line but moved her head in a "you tell him" motion.

"Carol called me last night. Someone stole a painting from the store," I said.

"You knew this when we were together last night?" CJ asked.

Carol's eyebrows popped up as she looked back and forth between us.

"Yes," I said. I looked at Carol. "He doesn't mean *together* together. I fed him, and we talked."

"I know neither of you filed a police report," CJ said, "because I don't remember hearing anything about it at the station."

I nudged Carol with my elbow. "It's your story."

She didn't look too happy with me. Carol

explained she was painting a copy of *Battled* for a client, that it appeared to have been stolen, and that she'd decided to start over instead of worrying about what had happened to the copy.

"How far along were you?" CJ asked.

"All the way done. Except for signing it."

CJ studied Carol's face. "Did you forge West's name on it?"

"No!" Color rose in her face for the first time that morning. "I'd never do that. I was going to sign my name," she said.

Carol stared back toward the store when she said it. I wondered if there was something she hadn't told me last night and wasn't telling CJ now.

"Have you told your client?" CJ asked.

"No. I have another three weeks. It's enough time to recreate it."

"Who's your client? Any chance he wanted it unsigned?" It was the the same question that I'd asked last night and that Carol had ignored.

Carol paled again as she thought about that. "No. He said he wanted it for his home. That he was a revolutionary war buff."

CJ looked at her, waiting for Carol to answer his other question.

She looked down at her nails and picked at a fleck of paint on her index finger. "I'm not sure who my client is."

CJ rubbed his face again. "How can you not know who your client is?"

"We talked over the phone," Carol said. "He

paid a deposit with a cashier's check that he mailed from a PO box in Boston."

"Did you call him to tell him about what happened?"

Carol blew out a long stream of air. "I don't have any way to contact him."

"How can that be?" I asked.

CJ glared at me with one of those "stay out of this" looks.

Carol turned toward me and grabbed my hand.

"He said he wanted to stay anonymous. When he called, a number didn't show up. It said 'private.'"

"You didn't ask why?" CJ asked.

"I did in the beginning, but the terms were very generous—if I didn't ask a lot of questions."

"That didn't worry you? Seem odd?"

"Not really," Carol said, but she gripped my hand tighter.

"Why you?" CJ asked.

Carol dropped my hand. "Why not me? I have a good reputation in this area. I'll start over and get the job done. There's a bonus involved if I complete the project in the time he gave me."

"So somewhere out there is a very good unsigned fake of *Battled*?"

"You're making it sound like I've done something criminal. I haven't. I wasn't going to forge West's signature on it. I made it very clear—in fact, I insisted that I would sign it with my name."

"The voice on the phone didn't sound familiar?"

Carol took her time answering. "No. I'm sure it isn't someone I know."

"How were you going to deliver the painting?" he asked.

"The guy told me he'd be in touch near the deadline and arrange for pickup then."

"Did he know it was almost finished?" CJ asked.

Carol shook her head. "I haven't talked to him for a while." She twisted her hair around her finger. "When can I reopen the store?"

"We'll have to get search warrants. It will be several days," CJ said.

"I don't have several days. I need to paint, and I have classes scheduled."

"You can sign a form giving us consent to search. That will speed things up." CJ looked around the shop. "We'll do everything as quickly as we can. I've got to go."

CJ left. We heard voices coming from Carol's store and strained to listen.

"ID says Terry McQueen. Heard of him?" a female voice asked.

We looked at each other, but before we could say anything, Pellner stuck his head out the door. "Come on, clear out."

We slid off our stools and followed him out.

"What's going on, Pellner? Where'd CJ go?" I asked.

He gave me his best cop stare, one that a few months ago would have had me shaking in my boots if I'd been wearing them. It didn't intimidate me anymore—not as much, anyway.

"Can we go?" I asked.

"Mrs. Carson needs to sign this form first,"

Pellner said. He handed Carol a clipboard with a document on it. She moved to sign it.

"Don't you need to read through it first?" I asked. "Or have a lawyer go over it?"

"I trust CJ," Carol said, as she signed.

Pellner took the clipboard back. "Don't tell anyone what you saw in there." Pellner tipped his head toward the store.

"Was he serious?" Carol asked as we walked down the block.

"He was," I said. "Do you know Terry McQueen?"

"No. I've never heard of him." Carol looked like she was about ready to throw up. "Do you know him?"

"I don't think so. Could he be one of your clients?"

"No. I *don't* know him."

"You told CJ everything you knew, didn't you?"

"Yes. I'm going to go talk to Brad. I don't want him to hear this from someone else."

"Does he know you were getting paid to copy *Battled*?" I asked.

"No. I don't tell him how to run his department at the veterans' hospital, and he doesn't tell me how to run my business." She sounded more confident than she looked as she bit her bottom lip.

I stopped in front of DiNapoli's. "Want to come in?"

"I've got to run. Besides, they aren't open."

I smiled. "They are for me. Call me if you need me."

* * *

Rosalie hurried around the counter and unlocked the door to the restaurant. I stepped in and breathed in the aroma of rising dough and tomato sauce. She glanced at my outfit and raised an eyebrow.

"It's not what you think," I said, not wanting her to think I'd spent the night with Seth. I'd told them about Seth one night when they were asking about how things were with CJ. "I fell asleep in them. Then Carol rousted me and didn't give me a chance to change."

Rosalie nodded. While she wasn't happy that CJ pushed me to get back together, she didn't necessarily like my relationship with Seth. I plopped down at a table, weary beyond what I could imagine. Angelo brought over a large cup of inky-looking dark coffee. "Here, this will help."

I wrapped my hands around the white mug, warming them. I hadn't even realized I was chilled until now. The mug was sturdy and serviceable. A lot like Angelo, it could be counted on to fulfill a need. I took a sip and gave a little shudder. It was good, and the perfect temperature. Angelo's coffee was always the perfect temperature. I'm not sure how he did it, and he never answered me when I asked.

"It's not any of that sissy coffee you find out there." Angelo waved his hand in the general direction of Great Road. "Carmel whatevers and flavored this and that. It's ridiculous."

Rosalie put a hand on Angelo's arm before he really got going. "Let Sarah talk or rest if that's what she wants to do."

I took another sip of my coffee. It was bracing, and right now I needed bracing. Rosalie disappeared into the back and came out with a thick shawl and put it around my shoulders. I wrapped it around me until I was swaddled tighter than a baby. Then I realized I couldn't reach my coffee, so I loosened it just a bit.

"Somebody died at Carol's shop," I said. My voice shook. I gripped the mug tighter.

"Natural causes?" Angelo asked.

He must have known otherwise, what with all of the hoopla going on out on the street, although in a small town, without a lot of crime, almost any event created hoopla.

"I don't think so. But I don't know for sure." Even without Pellner's admonishment not to discuss the circumstances of the death, I knew better than to give away any details that could possibly undermine the investigation, even to two people I trusted.

"Are you okay?" Rosalie asked.

I pulled the shawl tighter around me before answering. "I'm okay." I'm pretty sure no one believed that, but they didn't press me.

Rosalie stood and patted my shoulder. "We

have to get ready to open. But you sit as long as you want."

I huddled into the chair, sipping my coffee until I could face going back to my empty apartment.

CHAPTER 6

After a long shower and another cup of coffee, I headed over to Stella's other aunt's house for an appointment. Gennie Elder was a cage fighter, as Stella called her, or a professional mixed martial arts fighter, as most of the world called the sport. Her professional name was Gennie the Jawbreaker. I'd met her only once, but she'd hired me to do a garage sale for her. She owned a large colonial north of Great Road and was thinking about downsizing. I rang her bell and heard a deep gong resonate inside the house.

Gennie opened the door dressed in workout clothes, a tank top, and gym shorts. A white towel hung around her neck. Gennie took one end and swiped it across her brow. She stood about five-seven, so met me almost eye to eye. Even though she was Stella's aunt, they were about the same age. Stella had told me Gennie had grown up knowing she was the "mistake."

"Come on in." Her body was firm and so muscled

it would make nails seem pliable, quite a contrast to my curvy, somewhat-in-shape figure. Her hair hung down her back in a thick braid.

"I pin my hair up so no one can grab it in the cage," she said when she saw me studying it. We stood in the foyer of a typical colonial house: a center staircase was placed within a long hall with several rooms off of it to the left and a room with the door closed to the right. If every room was as sparsely furnished and lacking in décor as the entrance, it would be one small garage sale.

"You still fight?" I asked. She must be in her early forties. I'd looked up mixed martial arts on the Internet, and most of the women fighters looked young.

"I only do a couple of fights a year now. Let me show you around," Gennie said. She flung open the door on the right, and we entered a room that shattered any notion of what a cage fighter's decorating style would be. I'd been expecting sleek leather and modern abstract paintings. But this room was filled with delicate Victorian settees, lace-draped chairs, and bric-a-brac appropriate for the period.

"I love collecting things. Each room reflects a different era," Gennie explained. I followed her around the first floor, exploring rooms that ranged in style from Art Deco to midcentury modern. Each room was filled to the brim with pristine examples of the furniture and decorative touches from a particular era.

"This is the last of it," Gennie said as we stood in the midcentury modern room.

"Why stop with the fifties?" I asked, still stunned by all I'd seen.

"I couldn't stand doing a sixties room with beads, lava lamps, and beanbag chairs. The whole country, shabby chic thing never appealed to me, either. After the fifties, it seems like everyone just started taking elements from some other era and putting them together in a different way. Nothing new or original about that."

I'm not sure I agreed with her, but she was the client, and the customer is always right. "Any thoughts on when you want to have the sale?" I hoped she wouldn't say next weekend.

"I'm not in a huge rush."

"I'll have to take a lot of pictures and research the value of a lot of the items. I might even need to reach out to a few experts for some of the pieces. This isn't a typical garage sale. You might want to contact some estate sale experts instead of using me." I didn't like to turn away business, but this was a significant undertaking. "I could recommend someone."

"I want you to do it. Nancy called me last night, raving about what a great job you did yesterday. Come on into the kitchen. Let's get something to drink while we talk terms."

I stopped in the center of a room that by the

looks of the crystal chandelier was supposed to be a dining room but instead was a trophy room. A black-and-white photograph took up most of the far wall. The only color was the red blood trickling from the nose and mouth of a young, knocked-out Gennie.

Gennie gestured at the photograph. "My first professional fight. I lost badly. That picture appeared in the paper the next day. I kept it tucked in my wallet at first. Then I printed an eight-by-ten and kept it on the nightstand of every hotel room I stayed in. When I bought this place, I had that made."

"Why?" I asked.

"Reminds me of what losing felt like. I never wanted to feel like I felt that night again." Her eyes looked teary, but she blinked them back.

"You must be pretty good. I hear your nickname is 'the Jawbreaker.'"

That brought a smile back to Gennie's face. "I got beat again but never knocked out. And it's a lesson for the kids I teach who think they're invincible or think I'm invincible."

The rest of the room was filled with belts with giant buckles, gleaming trophies, and signed photos of Gennie with lots of men and women fighters.

I pointed at one of the photos. "Wasn't that guy on *Dancing with the Stars*?"

"Yes. That's Chuck Liddell. Next to him is Tito Ortiz. He was on *Celebrity Apprentice*." She stopped in front of another photo. "Randy Couture is an actor now. He's in the *Expendables* movies."

We went into the kitchen and sat at a gleaming granite-topped island. Light reflected off the stainless-steel appliances and glass-fronted cabinets. Gennie set out two glasses of iced tea and a bowl of lemon slices. "Need sugar?"

I shook my head and sipped the tea. I hated discussing how I charged people for my service, but it had to be done. "The way my business works is I take a percentage of what you earn at the sale."

"So if I don't make anything, you don't?"

"That's right. It's a powerful incentive to make sure I price things correctly and negotiate a good price."

"You'll have to spend a lot of time pricing," Gennie said.

"With any business there's a lot of work that goes on in the background."

Gennie nodded. "Okay. It works for me."

"Why are you downsizing?"

"I haven't told Nancy or Stella this yet, but I bought an old office building in Dorchestah."

She meant Dorchester. I found it charming how people from this area used the 'r' sound, dropping and adding it to their words. Gennie's accent seemed particularly strong.

"They won't like my idear, but I'm opening a studio there. I plan to live above it, to be a part of that community. I figure if I can motivate some of those kids, I'll have done something important—beyond beating the crap out of people for the past twenty years."

Dorchester wasn't the Boston area's best neighborhood, but I admired Gennie's philosophy. Although if she didn't like beating the crap out of people, why did she want to teach others to? As I turned to her, I knocked over a pile of mail that was stacked next to my left elbow.

"Whoops."

"Hand that to me, and I'll get it out of the way."

I scooped up the mail, but stopped handing it to her when the stack was in midair. The return-address label of the top envelope said "Jackson Financial Planning."

"What?" Gennie asked.

"Jackson Financial Planning. Do you use this company?"

Gennie had a funny expression on her face. Oops, sometimes I'd forgot I was dealing with reserved New Englanders instead of more open Californians. Even though before I'd moved here, I'd always heard about the Yankee reserve, I didn't usually notice it. I think my openness made others more open to me. But every once in a while, it was a conversation stopper.

"I didn't mean to pry," I said. "I know Bubbles, Dave Jackson."

"It's okay. Dave knocked on my door a couple of months ago. Friendly, sharp guy. I like to support our troops, so I invested some money with him. So far I've been getting great returns."

"Oh, good." I gulped down the rest of my tea.

"I need to come back with my good camera to take some pictures. I'll develop a timeline for when I think I can get everything priced, and then we can have the sale."

"Sounds good," Gennie said.

I went home for a quick fluffernutter sandwich. I might be the only adult in the commonwealth to eat this delicious combination of Marshmallow Fluff and peanut butter. I'd never heard of it until I moved to Massachusetts, home of the fluffernutter. There'd been a contentious debate in the state house several years ago when some legislator introduced a bill suggesting that fluffernutters weren't nutritionally sound and should be banished from school lunches. I'm all for kids eating healthy, but banning the flutter-nutter would be like banning cheese in Wisconsin, potatoes in Idaho, or corn in Iowa.

When I'd finished my sandwich, I grabbed my laptop. The name I'd overheard in Carol's shop, Terry McQueen, had been rolling around in my head all morning. I opened my computer and typed in "Terry McQueen." An article from the *Fitch Times*, the local base newspaper, popped up, along with a photo. The man in the picture bore some resemblance to the body in Carol's shop—lean build, same sandy hair. But unlike the dead man on the floor, the man in the picture wore a suit and a big smile. I studied the photo. It was hard to tell if it was the same man, but I bet it was.

According to the article, McQueen had recently won a Civilian Category II of the Quarter award, which meant he wasn't in the air force but worked on the base. It also meant his boss liked him enough to take the time to write up a nomination for the award and submit it. I wondered what Terry did on base; that wasn't mentioned in the article.

I called my friend Laura Nicklas. She lived on Fitch Air Force Base, and since her husband, Mike, was the wing commander, she was plugged into what was going on there. After a brief conversation, I arranged to meet her at four at the base thrift shop, where she volunteered.

I napped until three-thirty and fixed myself another fluffernutter sandwich. Full of fluff and peanut butter, I drove over to Fitch. Since the divorce, I no longer had a military-dependent ID, so Laura had to sponsor me on base. I stopped at the visitors center, where I had to show my driver's license, registration, and proof of insurance. The security guard handed me a piece of paper that had to be displayed on the dashboard. It said where I'd be and for approximately how long.

I drove around the large iron barriers that reminded me of giant jacks. They were in place to make it difficult to run the gate. I pulled up to the security shack and guard. My face was eye level with the gun on his hip. It was intimidating, but I guess that was the point. I knew some of the guards, but not this guy. He took my pass and driver's license, and studied the photo and then me. Finally, he stepped back so I could continue on.

Military bases are set up to be self-sufficient, like small towns. As I headed to the thrift shop, I passed the base chapel, a white clapboard building with a tall spire topped by a cross. The chapel held services for many different faiths, including Protestant, Catholic, Jewish, and Islam. CJ and I had attended a lovely wedding there last fall when we were still happy. He'd held my hand as the couple recited their vows.

I came to a T intersection. The gym, tennis courts, and baseball fields were straight ahead. I'd spent time at each—at the baseball games purely as a spectator. I turned left and then right onto Travis, the main street of the base. I headed up a hill, passing the gas station, library, and outdoor rec, where you could rent equipment for outdoor activities or sign up for an event at Tickets and Tours. It was a beautiful day, but the base was fairly empty. During the week, lots of people who worked on the base were out taking walks. In New England, people didn't waste good weather by staying inside. So probably half of the base residents were out leaf peeping or exploring one of the many charming towns in the area.

Laura was standing behind the register, checking out a customer, when I arrived. The thrift shop took donations but also let people associated with the base consign things. It was a popular shop and benefited from all the moving to and from assignments.

Laura was a slightly taller version of Halle Berry, and her smile, along with her deep brown eyes and long, curly, god-given lashes, always dazzled me.

"Give me a minute," Laura said as she typed codes from tags into the register. While I waited, I roamed around, chatting with the volunteers I knew as they reminded the remaining customers it was closing time. The shop had moved to this building last April after a murder had occurred at the old facility. This space was lighter and centrally located. From everyone's demeanor, I realized that no one knew that someone who might have been associated with the base had been found dead that morning.

"I'm done, and we're closed," Laura said as she bagged the last of the stuff and handed it to the woman at the register. She locked the door behind the woman and took off a blue apron. All the volunteers wore them. Women called good-byes to Laura and me as they headed out.

I followed Laura to a scarred leather couch that was for sale. She plopped onto it, and I sat on the other end.

"I haven't seen you around much lately," Laura said.

Even though CJ and I'd divorced and I had no official standing on the base, I'd continued to volunteer at the thrift shop. They raised money for scholarships for military kids and for other good, base-related causes.

"I've been so busy with the community yard sale in Ellington, I haven't had a lot of spare time."

"I went. It was wonderful. If you do it again, the thrift shop should have a table."

"I left a message about it, saying you could have a space for free. But whoever called back said it wasn't worth it to take stuff into town when it sold well here."

Laura frowned. "That's ridiculous. It must have been Beverly, our new manager. We hired her a couple of months ago to try to give the shop some continuity rather than being managed by people who'd have to move when the military saw fit."

"How's that working out?"

"She's really kept the inventory moving. The sorting room isn't a death trap anymore. She's selling some of the better stuff on eBay." Laura yawned and stretched. "She also got the idea that we should be open once a month on Sunday afternoon. Not everyone is crazy about the idea."

"It looks like you had a lot of volunteers." That wasn't always the case.

"We did today. I strong-armed them into it. I'm not sure about the Sunday thing."

"Is she here? I'd like to meet her."

"No. She had a church thing this afternoon." Laura yawned. "Beverly's also an accountant, so the books are up to date. Anyway, what's going on? It sounded like you wanted to talk about something when you called."

"Do you know Terry McQueen?" I asked.

Laura drew her knees up under her. "Yes."

I waited, hoping she'd volunteer more. Something must be going on or she wouldn't be so reticent. "I saw he got a Civilian of the Quarter award, but I didn't recognize his name."

"Do you usually know the award recipients?" Laura asked.

Rarely. How was I going to get out of this one without mentioning that he might be dead and having Pellner and CJ on my back for blabbing?

"Sometimes. I saw his picture in the base paper and thought he looked familiar." Whew, I didn't have to lie.

"He hasn't been very popular on base lately," Laura said.

"Why not?" Maybe the reason he was killed had something to do with the base, and I wouldn't have to worry about Carol being accused of murder. Oh, no. I tried not to have any physical reaction to that thought. I realized it had been lurking around the back of my brain since we'd found the body.

"Are you okay? You look a little pale." Laura's big eyes looked concerned.

"I'm fine. Just a little tired after the yard sale yesterday." I turned on the couch so I was facing Laura and tucked one leg under the other. "Are you going to tell me why Terry hasn't been popular?"

Laura sat for a minute staring at the front door of the shop. "Do you know Dave Jackson?"

That wasn't what I'd been expecting. "CJ and

I've known Bubbles—Dave—for a long time. I didn't know he'd moved here until yesterday morning."

"So you know about the missile scandal and that Dave was fired?" Laura asked.

I nodded, wondering what this had to do with Terry.

"Dave and Terry started a financial planning company, and some people on base are none too happy."

I stared at Laura, surprised by this bit of news. "I just heard about the company yesterday. I didn't know Terry was involved, though." If people were unhappy with him, it might be why he was murdered. It didn't explain why it happened in Carol's shop. I hoped Bubbles was okay. I'd check with Stella when I got home.

"Terry's a great guy with a mind for numbers. He was a shoo-in to win the civilian of the year award."

"But he isn't now?"

Laura plucked at an errant thread on the seam of the couch.

"Have a lot of people on base invested with them?" I prodded.

"I don't know for sure. We did."

It felt to me like Laura was holding something back. "Are people upset about the financial planning company? Isn't it doing well?" That was the complete opposite of what Gennie had said, but maybe someone on base was disgruntled.

"No. The people I know who've invested with

them are happy. I know we are." Laura shifted. "You know how the base can be. Some people are mad that Dave and Terry started the company. Says it takes away from their real jobs. That Dave is ROAD and Terry is the civilian equivalent of that."

Uh-oh. ROAD stood for retired on active duty—a derogatory term used for people who, in their last year or two before retiring, slacked off or were lazy. "It's never good if the perception is that he isn't doing his job anymore," I said.

"Some people have whined about Dave taking time to get all the licensing he needed. But he started before he left his last base, and he's on terminal leave now, so he can do what he wants."

Terminal leave always sounded scary to me, but it was just the period of time when you were finished with your official air force duties but could use your accumulated leave before your official retirement or separation. "Bubbles probably knew that, once the cheating scandal broke, he wouldn't get promoted again. It makes sense that he'd start preparing for what's next." Most military people lined up or at least looked for jobs before they were officially retired. CJ had already been hired to replace Ellington's retiring chief of police before the scandal with his subordinate last spring. Even after the scandal broke, Nancy insisted he could still have the job. She deemed that one blemish on an otherwise stellar career wasn't enough for the town to go through the search process again.

"I wonder why he decided to set his business up here," Laura said.

"CJ told me Bubbles grew up in Maine and his ex and kids are in Nashua." Nashua was a thirty-minute drive up the 3 depending on the time of day. Lots of military people lived up there because New Hampshire didn't have any state sales or income tax. "Since he's been in the military, he knows what military members' investment needs are. It all makes sense."

"Some people just don't like it when others are successful." Laura studied me for a minute. "Why do I get the impression there's something else going on that you aren't telling me?"

This is why Laura knew so much about what was going on around the base. She was either an astute judge of character or she just asked everyone that question, and in a fit of guilt everyone coughed up whatever they knew. Either way, it didn't hurt that the wing commander's wife stayed on top of what happened on base.

I shook my head. Laura would find out soon enough and probably be mad when she figured out I'd known when we chatted. But at least I had an out—I didn't know for certain that the victim was Terry McQueen. I wondered when I would.

CHAPTER 7

When someone knocked on my door at six that night, I panicked. I'd already washed my face, and my hair was pulled back in a headband. I was braless and wearing a tank top and yoga pants. I didn't want anyone to see me now, unless it was CJ; he'd seen me look worse. Besides, I'd left multiple messages for him, so maybe he'd decided to drop by. Although because of the way we'd left things last night, I hadn't thought he'd be stopping by anytime soon. I whipped off the headband and gave my hair a shake.

I opened the door, and there stood Seth, in a beautifully tailored custom suit. His crisp white shirt was unbuttoned at the neck, and a red silk tie peeked out of his right suit-coat pocket. He held a bottle of wine in one hand and a pizza box from DiNapoli's in the other. I slammed the door in his face. I didn't want him to see me looking like this. Although I guess he already had.

Last spring, not long after I'd met him, a magazine had named Seth "Massachusetts's Most Eligible Bachelor." He usually dated models, which made me wonder why he'd be interested in me. Two weeks ago, we'd argued when Seth asked me to go to some hoity-toity soirée at his family's compound on Nantucket. I'd refused. He'd called me stubborn. Which I was, but that wasn't the point.

The last I'd seen or heard of him was in an article in the *Boston Globe*. He'd been pictured at the event with a super-thin Victoria's Secret model. She glowed on his arm, dressed in a gown that probably cost more than I'd spent on clothes in the past five years. Seth looked a little stiff in the picture, or maybe it was my wishful thinking.

"Open up, Sarah," Seth yelled through the door. "You won't even eat a pizza with me now?"

I didn't want him to cause a scene—not that he would—but that was my excuse for opening the door and letting him in.

"Where should I put this?" he asked, raising the pizza box. I pointed to the right, toward the kitchen. Seth paused, looking around the apartment. I looked around, too. The old oriental rug glowed against the painted, white-wooden floors, a claw-and-ball-foot table sat next to my grandmother's rocker. The down-stuffed couch was comfy. Paintings, one by Carol and the rest treasured finds, warmed the walls.

"I like it," Seth said. "It looks like you. Full of personality."

"Thanks." I followed him into the kitchen. He put the pizza box and wine on the table. He turned, pulling me into his arms and giving me a kiss so incredible that I felt like a lone ice cube under the Saharan sun. He broke the kiss and stared into my eyes, the ones without any eye shadow or mascara. Personally, without makeup I thought my eyelids looked like fish eyelids, if fish had eyelids. It was not the way I wanted Massachusetts's most eligible, Victoria's-Secret-model-dating bachelor to see me.

Seth pulled out a chair for me. I hesitated.

"I can leave you the pizza and wine if that's what you want. But that kiss didn't seem to say that's what you wanted."

What was that song? Something about lips don't lie? Stupid lips. I sat in the chair and realized the song was about hips, not lips—not that it really mattered. I gestured for Seth to sit. Instead of sitting across from me, he moved the other chair next to mine and took my hand as he sat down.

"No one can see us here," he said. "We've spent the past six months meeting at hole-in-the-wall restaurants in towns that feel like they're farther away from Ellington than the northern tip of Maine. Are you ashamed to be seen with me?"

"No. That's ridiculous." No one would be ashamed to be seen with Seth. He looked like he could be a model—high cheekbones, wavy, dark hair with some silver woven in, broad, thick shoulders. The only thing keeping him from actually being a model was his nose, which was a bit broad, not aquiline—and that made him all the more sexy because he looked like a real man, not some photo-shopped, starved version of a human male.

"You date models. Not regular women who look like this." I air-circled around my face.

"I see a beautiful, vibrant woman who eats actual food instead of surviving on liquids and carrots. One who doesn't pretend to like pizza and the Red Sox because I do. One who isn't interested in me because of my last name." He kissed me again. "You're still afraid that CJ will find out you're seeing me, that someone will spot me sneaking out of your apartment at dawn." He grinned, but I could see his feelings were hurt.

"You'll be leaving after we're done eating. Not sneaking out at dawn." I got up and grabbed a corkscrew. "I've told CJ we need to see other people. But I haven't told him who I am seeing. It's none of his business." I didn't want to hurt CJ, and he would be hurt if he found out I was dating Seth. "It's awkward that you two have to work together." Seth was the district attorney of Middlesex County, and since CJ was Ellington's chief of police, they worked cases together on the rare occasion when a crime of significance occurred in Ellington.

"I agree. I don't like it."

I opened the bottle of Merlot and poured us both a glass.

"A woman with the strength to open a bottle of wine." Seth sighed and batted his eyelashes at me. "You're amazing."

"Oh, stop," I said as I handed him his glass and sat back down.

"CJ's a good guy, but I'm better for you."

I glanced at him out of the corner of my eye.

Seth leaned forward in his chair. "I wouldn't have let you slip away in the first place."

"Oh." His statement bounced around in me like a ball in a pinball machine, touching this emotion and that until it settled in a spot so tender, so hurt that I'd kept it locked away for months so I didn't have to feel anything.

I leaped up. "We need plates." The door on the cupboard stuck, as it tended to do. I yanked, and it opened with a screech. After setting the plates on the table, I sat back down.

Seth opened the pizza box and stared. "I ordered a meat lovers. There's no meat on this pizza."

The pizza was a *bianca* (white) pizza with tomatoes and garlic. My favorite. CJ knew that. "Did you mention me while you were at DiNapoli's?" I asked.

"No, but while I waited to order I looked to see if your light was on and your car was home."

"Angelo and Rosalie know this is my favorite pizza. So either they're psychic or you were really obvious."

"I'm a skilled trial attorney. There's nothing obvious about me." He grinned.

I grinned back at him. We both knew he stood out in any crowd. Seth put slices of pizza on our plates, muttering something about any decent pizza needing meat.

After my third piece, I pushed back from the table, glad for my yoga pants but embarrassed when I realized I still wasn't wearing a bra. "Excuse me." I hurried into my bedroom and threw on a bra and a Red Sox T-shirt. While a pair of jeans would have looked better, the thought of fastening anything over my full belly dismayed me. Yoga pants it was.

"I liked the other outfit better," Seth said when I returned.

"Why'd you come here tonight?" I asked.

"I saw that you made a statement about the murder this morning. I wanted to make sure you were okay. Are you?"

I gritted my teeth and tried to shut out the picture of the victim sprawled on the floor. "I'm fine." I pushed my chair back and refilled our wineglasses. "Do they have any suspects?" Maybe since CJ had yet to return my calls, Seth would know something.

Now Seth was the one to look down. "They're looking at a lot of angles." He grabbed another piece of pizza and bit into it—a sure sign he knew something he didn't want to tell me. I thought about what it could be as I sipped my wine. "Is it Carol?" I asked. A hint of color going up Mr. Trial

Lawyer's not obvious face told me I was right. "How can she be a suspect? She didn't know the guy."

"I can't talk about it."

For once, I decided to let it go. Maybe if I kept up some casual chatter, something would slip out.

An hour later, we stood at my door after Seth had cleverly dodged all my attempts to talk about the murder. He'd never even mentioned the victim's name. Darn him and his skilled trial lawyer ways. Seth kissed me, garlic breath and all, at the door after trying to convince me he should stay. The jury was still out on that one. We'd slept together exactly once, the first night we'd met, and I'd put the brakes on that whole issue. It surprised me that he still came around.

"Out," I said, pushing gently on his chest until he stood outside my apartment.

He snagged my wrist and kissed it, right where my pulse beat madly. I almost reconsidered but found some last bit of willpower and closed the door.

A couple of minutes later, I heard another knock on my door. I frowned. If it was Seth coming back for another try, the only piece of me he was going to get was my mind. If it was CJ, he would have seen Seth leaving. I eased open the door, debating which scenario was worse. Carol stood there. My first thought was, What has gone wrong now? We'd already covered burglary and homicide. Arson, vehicular manslaughter, mail fraud?

"Are you going to let me in?" Carol asked.

"Of course." I felt more than a little guilty for having such thoughts and chalked it up to being tired. Carol had put up with me ending up on her doorstep a number of times when CJ and I were divorcing. I even called her store Paint and Whine because I'd been over there so much grousing about my life. She'd been my cheerleader and confidant. I needed to do whatever I could for her.

"Who was that guy I saw leaving your building?" Carol asked.

I hadn't told her anything about Seth. I shrugged. "Maybe someone Stella's seeing." Another thing to feel guilty about. Carol was my "tell everything to" friend. As the words came out of my mouth, I realized the air still smelled of Seth's delicious aftershave. And—worse—in the kitchen, the two chairs were pulled close together, and two wineglasses were on the table next to the pizza box with only one piece of pizza left. Carol knew I loved pizza, but she also knew I couldn't eat a large DiNapoli's on my own.

Carol pursed her lips as she took in the scene in the kitchen. "Can I have a glass of wine? It looks like there's a little left in the bottle."

If Carol wasn't going to question me about who had been here, something must be really wrong. I scooted into the kitchen, poured her a glass, and was back in a flash. Carol sat on the couch with her head leaned back and her eyes closed.

"What's going on?" I asked. I put the glass of wine on the vintage trunk I used as a coffee table. Carol didn't even reach for it, but she did finally open her eyes. This time I noticed they were red and puffy from crying. Maybe she'd found out she was a suspect in the murder. I picked up the wineglass and handed it to her.

She took a sip. "After I left you this morning, I told Brad about the body. And then the missing painting."

"How'd he take all of that?"

"After he got done yelling?"

"It probably scared him." I refrained from adding that it could have been her dead on the floor.

"Brad's furious with me."

"Why?" I was stunned. Brad usually indulged Carol's every whim.

Tears rolled down Carol's cheeks. She sat up and grabbed the wine but didn't drink any. "Because I copied *Battled*."

"He knows you've copied famous paintings before."

"I've copied a few paintings for family and friends. But I usually sell originals only to people I don't know." Her tears increased. "And I've never been paid this much for a painting, original or copy."

"How much are you being paid?" I wondered

if she'd answer since she'd been so evasive about it the first time we talked when the painting disappeared.

"If I get the fee and the bonus, nine thousand, nine hundred, ninety-nine dollars."

I sucked in a breath. I'd worked part-time for a financial planning company a long time ago. I knew that amount was one dollar under what triggered alarm bells with banks and the government. And from the look on Carol's face, she knew it, too.

"Brad pointed out that was five times more than I'd ever made for a painting," Carol said after a couple of minutes and a couple of sips of her wine.

"That's a lot of money. Not that I don't think you're worth it."

"They raised my rent, and I thought I'd be further along by my third year than I am. The shop hasn't made as much money as fast as I thought it would when I wrote the business plan and convinced Brad it was a good idea."

"So the infusion of cash seemed like a good idea."

"It still is," Carol said.

"Someone must have seen the painting and wanted it—maybe one of your customers or one of the tourists who were here over the weekend. Have you reviewed your security tapes?"

"The cops took them. It's not that sophisticated a system. I only have one camera, and it points into the front of the shop. My studio and the back door aren't covered. I didn't think a bunch of paints were that valuable. And no one goes back there but me, Olivia, and occasionally you or Brad."

"The police will probably check any cameras near the store to see if they caught anything," I said.

"That'll take time. And it's Ellington. It's not like the town is plastered with security cameras. On top of that the state police showed up and interviewed me too."

I thought for a moment. What could I do to help her? Seeing Carol cry hurt my heart. "Maybe we can figure out who took the painting. And get it back."

"You'd do that for me?"

"Of course. We'll start with your client list."

"You think it's one of my clients?"

"It's a possibility. We'll start with people who came in on Saturday. We can question the ones who aren't familiar to us."

"When can we start?" Carol asked.

"When they let you reopen."

"Did you hear any more about Terry McQueen? Who he is or why he was in my store? Assuming we have the name right," Carol said. "What did CJ say?"

"CJ hasn't called me back," I said. "I found out a Terry McQueen worked on base."

"I wonder if he knew Brad," Carol said it more to herself than me.

"I'm not sure where he worked." But that was

something for me to find out. "Laura told me that Terry and Bubbles had started a financial planning company together, and some people weren't very happy about that."

"Who is Bubbles?"

"Dave Jackson. An old friend of mine. Do you know him? He's in the air force, too. Do you have any money invested with him?"

"I don't know him. All our extra money is invested in the shop right now." Carol shook her head. "I'd better get home." Carol hugged me as she left. At least she'd quit crying, and her shoulders weren't slumped as she trotted down the steps. She didn't seem to know she might be a suspect in the murder. Maybe that was for the best. I realized I'd do whatever it took to clear her name.

CHAPTER 8

I washed the wineglasses and plates and put them away. I wrapped up the last piece of pizza in aluminum foil and stuck it in the fridge. After tossing the pizza box in the recycling bin, I set the chairs back at opposite sides of the table. Carol had been so worried about her problems that she hadn't grilled me about Seth. It was only 8:30, but it felt much later. As I cleaned, I thought about my promise to help question Carol's clients whom neither of us knew. What had I been thinking? There were probably lots of people on the list. Knocking on their doors and asking them if they'd swiped a painting didn't seem practical.

Another knock on my door interrupted my thought process. I usually didn't have more than one person stop by my apartment in a given week, and that person was usually Stella. Maybe Carol had decided to come back and grill me about Seth, after all. I opened the door to one very tired-looking CJ. I hoped the apartment didn't still smell like Seth.

CJ trudged by me and over to the couch. He flopped onto it, making no attempt to kiss me in the process. I was grateful since only an hour ago I'd been kissing Seth. I may need to rethink trying to date more than one guy at a time. I'd done it in high school, but the older, wiser me understood the consequences, especially when one of the guys was CJ, although we weren't really dating. I blew out a huge breath.

"What was that for?" CJ asked.

Trust him to notice the breath. "I guess I'm surprised to see you."

"You left me multiple messages. I thought you might have information for me."

"Carol's a suspect," I said.

CJ narrowed his eyes. "How do you know that? Have you been talking to one of my guys? The ones who all promised they wouldn't discuss this case even with their own families?"

Rats. I couldn't very well tell him Seth had been over. And sadly, his reaction confirmed my fears. "You know your guys don't like me, so why would they talk to me?"

"Then how?"

"I was over at DiNapoli's." I had a pizza box in the recycling bin that would corroborate my story. "It's just gossip in town. Toss the newcomer under the bus." Even though Carol's business had been open three years, in an area where people traced their families to the Mayflower if not the Vikings, Carol was a newcomer. Just as I was.

"You sounded more certain. You made a statement instead of asking a question."

And that is why CJ was such a good cop. Sometimes I wondered if he was wasting his talents being a chief of police instead of a detective. "I was married to you, a cop, for twenty years. There was a dead body in Carol's store. I assumed she was a suspect. I guess I was hoping you'd deny it. And don't give me any of that 'I can't confirm or deny' crap."

CJ managed a grin.

I continued, "Beyond the fact the dead guy was in her store, I bet her fingerprints are all over that frame because she bought it at Ellington's yard sale."

"Hanging around with cops might lead you to think you know more about investigating than you do."

"I never said I knew anything about investigating."

"It also might lead you to conclusions that may or may not be true."

"There's a piece of pizza left if you want it." Feeding CJ a piece of Seth's pizza seemed awkward, but he looked like he could use some food.

"Only one?"

Arrgh. "Carol was over." Another verifiable statement as long as the subject of pizza didn't come up. I suspected that, if it did, Carol would cover for me and then grill me about what was going on.

I went into the kitchen and heated the pizza in the microwave. I rustled up a salad. CJ wasn't a big fan of salad, but he needed more to eat than one piece of pizza. "Do you want a Sam Adams Summer Brew?" I asked. I had one six-pack left. Octoberfest was the seasonal beer, but I liked the Summer Brew better.

"Sure."

I poured the beer into one of the special Sam Adams glasses I'd bought at the brewery. According to them, it was the perfect beer-drinking glass because of the shape, the thickness, and the laser etching on the bottom. I put it all on a tray and placed it on the trunk in front of CJ.

"Bianca. Your favorite," CJ said.

Another thing to be grateful for and feel uncomfortable about. CJ would have been shocked if I'd brought out a slice of meat lovers pizza. It's probably the last on my list of kinds of pizza I'd order. Not that I wouldn't eat one if someone else ordered. I turned on the Red Sox game but hit mute in case CJ wanted to talk about the case. I flipped through a magazine while he ate. It felt comfortable, not that different than any night we'd spent together during our marriage.

When CJ finished, he carried the tray into the kitchen and rinsed everything off, leaving the dishes in the sink. I heard Stella singing in her apartment. Stella was a former opera singer and a voice teacher at Berklee College of Music in Boston. She also taught private lessons in her apartment. I listened and realized she was singing an aria from *Pagliacci*, an opera that ends with the husband killing his cheating wife and her lover. She'd taught me a thing or two about opera since I'd moved in.

CJ came back into the living room, and I turned up the volume on the TV.

"Does her singing bother you?" he asked.

"Not usually." Tonight might be the exception, though. "How's the investigation going?" Sometimes CJ talked cases over with me.

"Slowly."

But I guessed he wasn't going to talk this one over with me. I couldn't blame him. He didn't know where we stood anymore. I was still surprised he even stopped by. We watched as the Yankees tied the game at the top of the ninth. The Red Sox left two men on base, sending it into extra innings. I got CJ another beer, then sat back down. "Carol swears she doesn't know McQueen."

CJ jerked up. "Where'd you hear that name?"

"I overheard it after you left Carol's shop this morning. Am I right that Terry McQueen is the victim?"

CJ stared at the TV, but I don't think he saw the game. A relief pitcher struck all three Yankees out.

CJ finally looked over at me. "The next of kin

were notified this afternoon, so I guess it doesn't matter that you know. His wife identified the body. It will probably be on the news tonight and in the paper tomorrow morning."

I couldn't imagine how sad Terry's wife must be. "Is there an official cause of death?"

"No."

"Unofficial?" I asked. "Was he strangled?"

"Where'd you hear that?" CJ almost shot out of his seat.

"I didn't hear it. I deduced it from looking at the scene."

"I don't know if that makes me feel better or worse," CJ said as he sank back onto the couch.

"I heard he was in business with Bubbles. Have you talked to him?"

CJ hesitated. "He's really shaken up. But doesn't think it has anything to do with the business. We're looking at other angles, too."

That was almost the exact wording Seth had used. I was going to ask about the other angles, but a bat cracked loudly from the TV. The Red Sox's new, young phenom hit a home run with the bases loaded and won the game.

CJ finished his beer. "That new hotshot DA brought the staties here."

Seth. As prosecutor, he would turn the case over to the state troopers. "Isn't that typical?" I asked.

"Yes. But it doesn't mean I like it or that I'm going to sit back and not do anything."

My hand shook a little as I turned the TV off. Footsteps pounded up the stairs. Since the apartment next door was empty, I assumed it was someone coming here. I opened the door. Bubbles stood there, with Stella behind him. His usually cheerful face looked pale and set. He held a white piece of paper in his hand.

"Look what I found on my windshield."

CHAPTER 9

CJ took the piece of paper as Bubbles and Stella came in. We all huddled around it. "You're next" was written in sprawling letters. I looked at CJ. His eyes narrowed as he studied the note. Who would threaten Bubbles? He had to be terrified, considering his partner was dead.

"When did you find this?" CJ asked.

Bubbles clutched Stella's hand. Her wide-open green eyes looked at me, asking a question I didn't understand.

"Just now. I said good-bye to Stella, went out to my truck, and found this tucked under my windshield wiper. I figured it was just some flyer until I read it."

"Let's take a look at your truck," CJ said to Bubbles.

Stella and I followed the two men down the stairs and out to the truck. The night was cool; stars popped in the sky. There wasn't much traffic on Great Road. No one lurked in the dark shadows cast by the church.

"Did you see anyone near your truck?"

"Not at all. I saw your SUV parked out here, so I came up."

CJ had driven his official police vehicle over instead of his personal car, meaning he was going back to work after he left here. Which made me wonder why the heck he'd come over. Even though the truck sat under the streetlight, CJ grabbed a gigantic flashlight from the car and used it as he moved around the truck. I followed him. I couldn't see anything different than when it had been parked out front yesterday.

"How long were you at Stella's?" CJ asked as we went back up to my apartment.

"A couple of hours."

"What were you doing? Did you hear anything?"

Bubbles and Stella looked at each other. Stella turned a shade of bright red usually only seen in dyed carnations. Bubbles's face relaxed momentarily into a grin.

"I didn't hear anything, except for Stella's amazing voice," Bubbles said. "She's getting ready for a faculty recital."

He sounded proud. They must really like each other.

"Do you recognize the handwriting?" I asked. CJ shot me an "I'll ask the questions" look, but I knew this was an important question. The paper was plain white copy paper, eight and a half by eleven, pristine and probably untraceable because it was sold in reams everywhere.

Bubbles took the paper back from CJ. We all stared at it again. Bubbles shook his head. "I don't. Do any of you?"

I reached for it, but CJ snatched it from me. "Who else has touched this, Bubbles?"

"Just me. And Stella."

"Hold it up to the light and see if it has any special watermarks," I said.

CJ did, but there weren't any watermarks on it that would differentiate it from millions of other pieces of computer paper.

"Let's take it down to the station. I'll get an official statement," CJ said to Bubbles. He headed to the door. "Thanks for the pizza," CJ called as he hurried out. Again no attempt to kiss me. I still didn't know what to make of that.

Bubbles brushed a quick kiss across Stella's lips and rested his forehead against hers for a few seconds before leaving.

Stella turned to me. "Have any wine? Or should I run down and get my scotch?"

"I have wine." I wasn't a big fan of scotch. "Cabernet okay?"

We settled on the sofa with our glasses, tapping them in a silent cheers.

"What do you think about that note?" Stella asked.

Maybe because I'd been married to a cop she

thought I had some kind of special investigative skills, which couldn't be further from the truth. "A piece of plain white paper that's available everywhere isn't going to help narrow a search for who wrote on it. The writing looked unremarkable. Maybe they'll get some prints from it."

Stella brightened a bit at that thought.

"They might need a set of prints from you," I told her.

"If they use any national database, I'm sure mine will pop up." Stella had some troubles in her youth.

"Bubbles must have been terrified," I said.

"I've never seen him look like that. We haven't known each other that long, but his face was drained of color. And his gorgeous brown eyes just looked blank, like he was shell-shocked. I've always heard that term, but that was the first time I'd ever seen someone actually look it. We were both relieved CJ was here."

"Did you hear that he was in business with the guy who was murdered at Carol's shop?"

"He called me earlier today and told me. I asked him to come over so he wouldn't be alone."

"You wanted to distract him?"

A smiled flashed across Stella's face. "Yes. But then this happened. It scares me that someone tracked him to my house."

"CJ will have realized that. I'm sure we'll have increased patrols." I hoped so. I hadn't thought yet about the killer coming by here. I shook my head. "I can't believe what's happened over the last few days. A murder. Threatening notes. And Carol's painting disappearing."

"What happened to Carol's painting?" Stella asked.

I was surprised it wasn't on the town grapevine. I filled her in. "Please don't mention it to anyone. She's already started another copy." I picked up my wine. "So you're singing an aria from *Pagliacci* for a recital?"

"Nedda's. Maria Callas made it famous in the midfifties. I find love triangles fascinating, don't you?"

I drank some wine, feeling heat creep up my face. I hoped Stella thought the color was from the wine and not my embarrassment.

"Who was that hottie I saw trotting down the steps from your apartment?"

Rats, I'd finally been caught. "Insurance salesman. Did he stop by your place? He had some good rates on term policies. Never buy a whole life policy. They're a rip off. Too expensive. Most people stop paying for them before they have full coverage." Stop babbling, I told myself.

"I thought we were way beyond lying to each other at this stage of our friendship. And, trust me, I recognize Massachusetts's most eligible bachelor when I see him."

"It's a long story." And maybe one I needed to quit hiding.

"I'm all ears," Stella said.

I filled her in on our relationship.

"You like him," Stella said.

"I do. But what if he's just that rebound guy you always hear about?"

"He must be more than that to put up with your shenanigans."

"Did Bubbles see him?" Not that Bubbles would know who Seth was, but he might tell CJ he saw someone leaving my apartment. I didn't want CJ to know I was dating Seth, but I wouldn't lie about it, either.

"No. I was taking out the recycling. Dave was inside. Seth looked awfully happy."

"Not for any reason you might be thinking." I sat up. "What about McQueen? Could he be in a love triangle? His wife or a pissed-off girlfriend?" One who liked to paint, maybe? "Had you met him?"

"I've known Terry for years. He grew up here, although he's a bit older than me. I think my Aunt Gennie knew him pretty well."

"When's the last time you saw him?" I asked.

"Dave and I ran into him at the Colonial Inn when we were having lunch a couple of weeks ago."

"And?"

"And what? I'm starting to feel like I'm being interrogated."

"I'm sorry. It's just . . . I saw him dead this morning. I'm trying to understand why."

"I'm guessing you're worried your friend Carol is going to be in trouble since Terry was in her store."

"Yes. I'll shut up."

"It's okay. Everyone needs a friend she can count on in a crisis."

"What was Terry like?"

"Polite. He asked how Aunt Gennie was doing. He knew she was getting ready to retire. We only talked for a few minutes."

"Have you met his wife?"

"No. She's not from around here. Why?"

"Maybe she had something to do with his murder." Maybe that was one of the other angles CJ and Seth had referred to.

CHAPTER 10

On Monday morning, I sat across from Nancy in her office at the town hall. The town had spared every expense on the utilitarian furnishings. Nancy had brought in a rug with thick swirls of bright color to soften the room. It didn't help. A pipe angled across one corner but was painted the same shade of off-green as the wall to try to disguise it. The joints had rusted, and there was a damp spot where it disappeared into the ceiling. No one could accuse the town of wasting funds here.

"We could have compared calendars over the phone," Nancy said. She had stacks of paperwork on her desk. Behind her was her wall of fame. Photos of her with John Kerry, Patrick Duval, and Tom Menino when they were senator, governor, and Boston mayor. There was a picture of her throwing out a first pitch at a Red Sox game and plaques from various organizations. "And we didn't need to do it today."

I knew we didn't need to do it today, but it wasn't why I was here. I wondered how informed she was about the McQueen murder, and what I could find out. "I thought if we were going to go to two days, we'd better plan early. We don't want to be on the same weekend as Bedford Days, and you probably have other events that I wouldn't even think about."

Nancy nodded with an "of course I do" nod. She opened a computer file, and I tapped open the calendar on my phone. We coordinated a couple of potential weekends. Nancy would take it to the selectmen and town council for their input.

Nancy closed her calendar and folded her ringless hands on the table. "Anything else?"

"I was worried about you. Because of the murder, right after the fires and yard sale—it all must feel a bit overwhelming." I still wondered where she'd disappeared to in the middle of the yard sale. Maybe I could worm that out of her.

Nancy's eyes popped wide open, and then her expression softened. It seemed as though she wasn't used to people asking how she was doing. A Yankee through and through, she gave off a definite, brusque "leave me alone" attitude. Up until now I had bought it. "I'm an administrator not an investigator."

"But I know how much you love this town. I'm guessing that when things go wrong it affects you."

Nancy shuffled some papers on her desk. "You're right, it does."

"Stella told me Terry's from Ellington. And that he and Gennie were friends." It wasn't exactly what she'd said, but getting Nancy to open up was harder than prying a clam open with a toothpick.

Nancy snorted. "Friends is a stretch. He was a counselor when Gennie was at camp one summer. The summer she learned to fight." Nancy shook her head and obviously didn't approve of something, but what I couldn't tell, the fighting, the camp, the counseling. She clasped her hands on her desk until her knuckles turned white.

I opened my mouth to ask another question, but a knock on the door interrupted us. CJ stood there. He didn't look happy to see me. I stood. "Let me know which weekend works best for next year's yard sale," I said to Nancy. I slid by CJ with a nod and wondered whether, if I lingered outside the door, I'd hear anything useful. CJ took one look at me and closed the door.

After leaving Nancy's office, I headed over to Gennie's house to start photographing the items I didn't think I could price myself.

"If you don't mind, I'll start putting tags on items I can price as I go through each room," I said when Gennie let me in.

"Why would I mind?" Gennie asked. She was dressed in shorts and a tank top again.

"It's not going to look very good when Nancy comes over. She'll wonder what's going on."

Gennie pondered that, then sighed. "She's going to find out sooner or later—although I'd rather it be later. But I also need to get this place ready to go on the market. I can always tell her I'm downsizing and let her think it's to somewhere close by."

I started with the Victorian room. First, I took pictures of the whole room from several different angles. Then I started the laborious process of taking individual photographs. Where I could, I photographed the name of the artisan who made the piece, which would help establish its value. I opened drawers and snapped pictures of how the pieces were put together. Some had joints that were dovetailed, using interlocking pieces of wood instead of nails. That told me the piece was older or handmade, and that made a difference in its pricing. When I downloaded the pictures to my computer at home, I could zoom in and start an inventory list. This wasn't going to be any ordinary garage sale.

After I worked for an hour, tagging and photographing, Gennie came in. She'd changed into jeans and a black top. "Ready for a break?"

I was lying on the floor, taking photos of the underside of a settee where a bit of the original horsehair stuffing was coming out. I snapped a couple of pictures showing the way it was pegged together before standing up. I stretched my back. The piece didn't have any manufacturer's markings, but that didn't mean an expert wouldn't know who made it. "I'd love a glass of water."

"Me too. I went to a yoga class at the community center this morning and just finished my at-home workout," Gennie said.

We settled in her kitchen. It looked like it had barely been used. Either that or Gennie was inordinately tidy.

"Yoga?"

"Mixed martial arts requires more than brute strength. You should come watch me. I only have one match left. I'll get you good seats where you can see the blood, sweat, and, in the case of my opponents, tears."

I'm not sure I wanted to be that close. "It would be an experience," I said.

"And you should think of a career as a diplomat with that kind of answer. Anyway, there was a lot of talk about the murder at Paint and Wine."

Of course there was. Maybe Gennie had found out something interesting. "What were they saying?"

"It went from the wild—that Carol's a madam running prostitutes out of the shop—to the more sane—that she had some kind of relationship with Terry. One woman swore she saw them having dinner together in Concord." Gennie stared down at her glass of water while she talked. A frown made her look troubled. But she'd known Terry for a long time. I'd look troubled too if it were one of my friends.

"Carol told me she didn't know him. I can't believe she'd be out with him. I hope this doesn't hurt her business."

"People in Ellington don't take to dead bodies in shops."

"It's not like Carol wanted it there. She's a wonderful person." I paused. "Maybe you should come paint with me some night."

"I can't draw a straight line." Gennie shrugged.

"How well did you know Terry?"

Gennie tapped her strong hands on the island. "Everyone in Ellington knows Terry. And his family."

That wasn't much of an answer. "But you went to school with him."

"He was a couple of years ahead of me." Gennie shifted in her seat several times as though she wanted to get comfortable but couldn't.

"And a counselor at the camp you went to?"

Gennie gave a short nod and shifted again.

"He was Dave's partner in the financial planning company."

"Son of a . . ." Gennie swiveled to stare at me, veins popped in her muscled neck. "Where'd you hear that?" She took a couple of long breaths, drawing them in deep, then slowly letting them out. It was a good thing she did yoga because for a moment I thought she was about ready to have a coronary.

"From several people. They said he's good with numbers."

"He always was." Gennie looked at her over-sized kitchen clock. "I have to meet a contractor in Dorchestah. Just close the door when you're finished. No need to lock it. I don't expect you to have everything done right away. It's a lot."

I stared after Gennie as she scurried out. A couple of seconds later, the front door slammed. Everyone in Ellington might know Terry McQueen, but I got the impression that at least two people didn't like him—Nancy and Gennie Elder.

After I'd worked for several more hours, I eventually opened a closet in the hallway. It was stuffed full of coats for every season. I pushed them aside and spotted several large canvases. I pulled them out into the hall and took them to the Victorian room, where the lighting was better. They were beautiful, with vivid colors and broad brushstrokes. They reminded me of Carol's paintings. I examined them more closely. The stickers on the back were from Paint and Wine. I flipped the paintings over and saw Gennie's signature. But these paintings didn't look like the stock paintings people copied from. These were all unique, a large bowl of mixed flowers, a cityscape of Boston, and a woman reading a newspaper with an oversized cup of coffee by her hand. And they were larger than the ones people normally painted at Paint and Wine.

Gennie had said she couldn't draw a straight line when I asked if she'd like to come with me to Carol's shop. I realized she hadn't answered my question. While there weren't any straight lines in these paintings, judging from these examples she was very talented, so why lie? I put the paintings back where I'd found them. I'd have to find Carol and ask her about Gennie.

As I left Gennie's house, I pulled the door closed behind me, a little uncomfortable with leaving it unlocked. But maybe if you're a professional mixed martial arts fighter you aren't afraid of intruders because you could knock them senseless. Still, there was a murderer at large. As the door clicked into place, a thought clicked in my mind. If you were the murderer, you wouldn't worry about unlocked doors, either.

CHAPTER 11

I'd found out very little, certainly nothing that would help Carol. In fact, I'm not sure I'd found out anything at all. Maybe Nancy and Gennie didn't dislike Terry and I was just misinterpreting their nonverbal cues. I decided to go see CJ and headed down Great Road to the police station.

As I sat in the lobby of the Ellington Police Station, I tried to hear snippets of conversation but failed miserably. The lobby was a unit unto itself; a person sat on the other side of a wall, with only a small glass window to talk through. There was no receptionist at a desk, which might have allowed one to snoop if one were so inclined. I was beyond motivated when it came to snooping right now. I wanted to know if they were building a case against Carol. But I couldn't just walk through one of the two doors leading off the lobby. I had to be buzzed through.

Only a few officers had wandered through

the lobby while I was there. One glanced at me curiously but moved on quickly. I sat there twiddling my thumbs, something I'd seen my father do many times. Did CJ know I was out here, or was someone annoyed with me because of all the work the yard sale had created? Or maybe I was just paranoid; after all, six months ago the whole department seemed to be mad at me, though after I'd knocked out a murderer, things had changed. I hadn't been pulled over for speeding, accused of loitering, or ticketed for jaywalking since. But that honeymoon phase between the department and me may have just ended.

After sitting in the lobby of the police station for twenty minutes, I was buzzed through. CJ sat behind his desk, which was covered with paperwork. It was unusual for CJ not to have everything tucked away in folders and filed.

He smiled, but it was brief.

"I sat in the lobby for over twenty minutes. When you show up at my place unannounced I don't make you wait." I settled on the edge of the chair across from him.

"What do you need?" CJ asked.

Whoa, I wasn't expecting that. CJ could be direct when necessary, but it usually was accompanied by some Southern boy charm or manners. I tried to think if I came in here too often needing something. The last time I remembered was when CJ was being held on a murder charge. That was six months ago.

"I wondered how the investigation was going." I decided to be direct. Beating around the bush with Nancy and Gennie hadn't yielded much information. "And how you were doing."

"You wondered if I was going to give you inside information about an ongoing investigation, not how I was doing."

"That's a bit harsh."

"I'm not going to give you any information. And if you really cared how I was doing, I'd be sleeping next to you every night."

There was a bitter note in his voice I'd never heard before. "Are you going to twist everything back to that?" I asked. I stood as someone knocked on the door. Pellner came in.

"They found a fourth incendiary device at the chicken coops. The fire marshal says it matches the ones from here." He trailed off when he spotted me. "Sorry, Chuck, er, Chief. I didn't realize you were busy."

"No worries, Pellner. I'm leaving." My voice came out low and mean. I darted out. I didn't slow down until I climbed into my Suburban across the street from the station. Not that anyone came after me.

Kids played in the tot lot. Moms sat on benches, gossiping. I pounded on the steering wheel and accidentally hit the horn. All the moms jumped and turned to stare. Heat crept up my face, and

I sketched an "I'm sorry" wave as I started my car and left. Somehow I ended up at Bedford Farms Ice Cream. New England was dotted with ice cream stands, places that typically made their own offerings on site. Bedford Farms was my favorite. I ordered a small cup of Almond Joy ice cream. Someone here had a sense of humor, calling this serving small, because it contained two softball-sized scoops, but I wasn't going to complain.

What CJ had said about the inside information was true. He was dead wrong about the caring part, though. The easy thing to do would be to have him back in my life without first making sure where our relationship had taken a wrong turn. If I didn't care about him and myself, he'd be back already, although I wasn't going to convince him of that anytime soon.

Then again, when I'd asked for a divorce, CJ had acquiesced. He didn't fight it or try to convince me to stay. I stopped with my spoonful of ice cream raised halfway to my mouth, wondering why I'd never thought of that earlier. Seth had said something about not letting me go in the first place. Why had CJ done that?

After parking at my apartment, I walked across the town common to Carol's shop. I could tell from a distance that the crime scene tape was down. But the CLOSED sign hung on the door. That surprised me. If Carol was having financial troubles with the shop, I'd have thought she'd be open. I banged on the door, anyway. Carol finally answered.

"Why are you closed?" I asked as I walked in. Carol's usually animated face looked shadowed and drawn. Maybe she really had given up sleeping, or maybe she knew she was a suspect in Terry's murder. Clouds had covered the bright autumn sky, so I flipped on a few lights. It was too depressing with them off.

"First, I had to clean the store and my studio. Then two groups canceled this afternoon. I left the OPEN sign up for a while, but not a soul wandered in. So I just shut things down, and I've been working on my client's painting."

"The mystery client?"

Carol shot me a steely glare. I guess she didn't find me amusing.

"Have you given any thought to who it might be? How many people have asked you to paint for them in the last couple of months?" I asked.

"The number of people who asked went up after that article in the newspaper about me. Remember? They featured me leading up to Ellington's Art Walk in June. But the number of people who hire me is small when they hear my prices."

"Do you think it could be any of the people who called after the article was in the newspaper? Did you keep a record of their names?" That might be really helpful. Carol could call them back and see if they sounded like the mysterious client. A little leap of hope bound through me.

"I didn't keep a list. There didn't seem to be any point at the time." Carol studied her ceiling. She shook her head. "I just don't remember the voice sounding similar. Come on back and take a look at what I've done so far."

"You're braver than I am—working back here where you found the body," I said as we walked into her studio.

"The light's good. I don't have much choice." Even though it was a back room, Carol had installed special fixtures that produced lighting that was similar to actual daylight. So on cloudy days, when the skylights didn't provide much light, she could still work. Without a dead body back here it looked cheery.

A new oriental rug covered the floor where Terry's body had been. "Isn't that going to get ruined as you paint?" I asked.

"It's from HomeGoods, and I got a great deal, so I don't really care what happens to it."

"When did you go to HomeGoods? And why didn't you call me?" The closest HomeGoods was in Bedford.

"I went on the spur of the moment this morning after Brad's mom arrived."

"Brad's mom is here?" Brad's mom and Carol didn't have the best relationship. No wonder she looked even more drawn.

"Brad suggested it so she could take care of the

kids while I painted. Suddenly, he's all on board with me getting this painting done and collecting the money."

"That's great. He should be supporting you." Unlike CJ. Even the ice cream hadn't erased the sour taste left in my mouth after our encounter. "Why don't you paint? I'll flip the sign to OPEN and stay out front. Maybe someone will come by. Or a group of people."

"Okay." Carol didn't sound enthused.

"While I'm out there, I'm going to go through your records. To see if there's any connection between you and Terry. Maybe he came in and you just don't remember him." I'd also look for any signs of Gennie being here. But I'd keep that to myself for now.

"That'd be good. The sooner the murder gets cleared up, the better for business."

"I'll call and confirm appointments, too."

"Thanks. I set up my backup computer out front. It should be all ready to go. Olivia was supposed to come in this afternoon, but she hasn't shown up yet."

"Maybe she saw the CLOSED sign."

Carol shrugged and grabbed a paintbrush, turning to the almost empty canvas. I headed to the front of the shop, pulling the studio door mostly closed behind me, and fired up the computer. I called the three people who had a group class scheduled for tomorrow. One canceled; one wanted to, but I cajoled the woman into coming.

The third person I talked to seemed a little too excited about painting in a "haunted" store. As long as the group showed up, I figured it wasn't my problem, although I probably needed to warn Carol.

I ran Terry's name through Carol's computer. Nothing popped up. I wasn't surprised Terry's name didn't show up. I assumed the police had searched the computer, and if his name had been in there she'd probably have been questioned at the station. Next, I tried Gennie's name. Zero results. But I'd seen the paintings at Gennie's house. Her name should have shown up. It didn't seem possible that Carol took cash from clients and didn't report it to avoid taxes. I'd known her for years. It was out of character. But so was the drawn face and the mystery client.

I started doing Google searches linking Terry's name to Carol's list of clients. A few connections popped up, but they were tenuous at best. Things like two of them running in Ellington's 10K harvest race and several people who'd gotten awards for service to the base. Nothing that screamed so-and-so had a reason to kill Terry.

I remembered I'd promised to question Carol's clients about the missing painting. It had been stupid, but maybe Google could help me out here, too. I ran her client list against phrases like "art collector" and "art theft." Again, nothing leaped out as sinister or a motive for art theft or murder.

Raindrops splatting against the window jarred me out of my Google trance. It was dark. I checked my phone. I'd missed dinnertime. I stood and stretched. "Carol?" No answer. I hurried to the back room, trying to remember the last time I'd heard any noise back there. It had been a while ago. She'd talked to one of her kids about scoring a soccer goal, how she wished she'd been there and how excited Grandma must have been.

My heart rate increased as I pushed open the partially closed door and looked into the room. Carol was slumped over her desk, head facedown on her blotter, motionless.

I glanced around the room, which looked empty, although someone could be behind the curtains that led to the storage area. Part of my brain screamed "Run!" but I listened to the calmer part.

"Carol?" My voice sounded loud in the still studio. She didn't react. I ran to her and put my fingers on her neck to check for a pulse. She jerked up and slapped at my hand.

"What are you doing? You scared the crap out of me," Carol said. "Did you put ice on my neck?"

I snatched my hand back and held it to my heart. "No. Just my fingers." I clasped my hands together. My fingers were icy. "You were so still. I thought you were . . ."

"You thought I was dead?" Carol shook her head. "Just call my name next time. I'm a light sleeper."

I had called her name, twice. If that was a light sleeper, I'd hate to see a heavy one. My stomach rumbled just then, breaking the silence and making us laugh.

Carol stood and stretched. "I have sandwiches in the fridge. You want to eat here with me?"

I really wanted to go home and take a long bath, but one look at Carol's face changed my mind. "Sure, that sounds good. Do you have any wine, or do you want me to run to the packy for something?" I asked.

"Packy? Are you going all native on me now?"

"Packy" was short for package store, the state-run liquor store. "When in Rome," I said.

"I know for a fact you've been to Rome and don't speak a word of Italian," Carol said. "But no worries. There's a reason this place is called Paint *and* Wine." She went to a closet and came back holding a tray with a bottle of Cabernet, two wineglasses, a corkscrew, and sandwiches. She popped the cork with way more grace than I ever managed and poured two glasses, hers only a quarter full. "I can't drink too much when I paint."

"There's not enough alcohol in the world to make me able to paint," I said.

Carol rolled her eyes. We'd had this conversation before. She had more confidence in my ability than I did.

"Did you find anything on my computer that would shed some light on who took my painting?"

THE LONGEST YARD SALE   115

"Nothing." I took a drink of my wine. "Did I tell you about my latest garage sale job?" I asked, knowing full well I hadn't. "I'm sorting through Gennie 'the Jawbreaker' Elder's house. She's a world-renowned mixed martial arts fighter. Do you know her?"

Carol was suddenly very interested in unwrapping the sandwiches. "I've heard of her," she said. "It sounds like an interesting career choice. I can't imagine getting beaten on on a regular basis." She handed me one. "Lobster rolls from West Concord Seafoods."

It was my favorite local place to get lobster rolls. They were on hamburger buns instead of the traditional New England–style hot dog bun. Each roll overflowed with big pieces of lobster and mayo—no fillers like celery or lettuce. I bit in. We munched in silence, both holding on to secrets.

"I know I said I'd call your clients and ask about the missing painting, but I think I'd end up alienating a lot of people."

Carol nodded.

"So I ran your client list through Google, matching names against phrases like 'art collector' and 'art theft.'"

"Did you find anything?"

Carol sounded so hopeful I hated to tell her the truth. "No. Nothing that looked incriminating. No Facebook pages with your painting as the header."

Carol had eaten only a few bites of her sandwich. She wrapped it back up as I finished mine. "I'll come back tomorrow and try again," I said.

"Thanks. Go on home. I'll get back to painting."

CHAPTER 12

The drive-through at Dunkin' Donuts had a long line on Tuesday morning. I saw Bubbles's truck in the parking lot and decided to go in. Bubbles sat at a table, his laptop open in front of him. A man dressed in BDUs—battle dress uniform, or camouflage—sat across from him. The eagles sewn on the shoulders of his uniform told me the guy was a colonel. Bubbles didn't look too happy.

By the time I got my coffee, the colonel had left, so I went over. Bubbles didn't notice me as he typed away on his computer.

"Bubbles?"

He jerked his head up, hands still on the keyboard. "Sarah." Bubbles smiled and stood, giving me a quick hug. "Join me?"

I slipped into the chair across from him. Bubbles closed the computer. "How are you doing?" I asked.

"It's hard concentrating on the business with Terry gone. His murderer's out there. I've been trying to figure out what that frame around his face meant." Bubbles's voice cracked. "Then with the note I got on top of that . . ." He shook his head and looked down.

I drank some of my coffee to give him a minute to gather himself.

"Did CJ find anything out about the note?"

Bubbles shook his head. "He said chances were slim they'd find anything useful."

"Did anyone threaten Terry?" I asked.

Bubbles's slight hesitation before he said no spoke volumes. Terry must have been threatened, too. But CJ had told Bubbles not to tell anyone. I didn't want to push him. He looked stressed enough.

"I heard Terry had lived here all of his life," I said.

"A lot of his life, but not all of it. He just moved back about a year ago. We met one morning when we were both out for a run on base."

"Why'd he move away?" It seemed to me that New Englanders liked to stay put; an hour's move was a long distance to them. Some had even questioned why I didn't move back to California to be close to my family.

"He had some kind of falling out with his dad. Terry wanted to be his own man. I guess his father wasn't happy about that." Bubbles drained his coffee and stood. "I've got to go. Great seeing you." He bent and kissed me on the cheek.

"Take care of yourself, Bubbles." I watched him walk out to his truck. He looked over his shoulder several times and walked around the truck once before he got in and took off. He must have been more worried than he let on.

After spending the rest of the morning organizing and sorting at another client's house, at one-thirty I headed over to Gennie's. The afternoon had turned cold. Wind tugged at the brightly colored leaves as though it wanted to finish with fall and start on an early winter. I, on the other hand, wanted winter to hold off for as long as possible. When winter set in, garage sale season would end. I didn't know what I'd do for a job then.

By three, Gennie was still roaming around the house, checking in with me periodically. I'd hoped she'd leave me alone, as she had yesterday. I wanted to dig through the closet again, but not necessarily with her here. Instead, I worked in the Art Deco room. The room she'd re-created amazed me. It included sleek leather chairs, lots of bronze statuary, and Erté posters on the walls. I snapped a bunch of pictures. Later I'd check to see what such things were selling for on eBay and consult with a professional as needed.

Occasionally I heard music blasting from the

basement where Gennie worked out. "Eye of the Tiger" seemed to be a favorite. I decided to get a glass of water from the kitchen; on my way, I'd check out the closet. I opened the door and whirled around when I felt someone behind me. Gennie stood there. She moved like a cat without any noisy collar tags.

"There's nothing in there for the sale," she said.

I looked anyway. All the coats still hung in their places, and a smattering of boots covered the floor where the paintings had been. I wished I'd snapped a couple of pictures of the paintings yesterday.

"Great. I forgot to check when I was here the other day. I'm going to get some water, if that's okay?" I headed to the kitchen, pondering the empty closet.

Gennie followed me. I grabbed glasses while she got a pitcher from the refrigerator, which she pronounced "refrigeratah." We chatted about how her place in Dorchester was coming along.

"I was over at Paint and Wine last night," I said, watching for any reaction. I'm not even sure why I cared if Carol and Gennie knew each other but weren't willing to admit it. I guess with the murder and the threat to Bubbles, everything seemed colored with a different light.

Gennie turned away and put the water pitcher back in the refrigerator. "I have to get to my Pilates class. Why don't you come back tomorrow?"

Yesterday she was fine with me staying here by myself, and today she wanted me to leave. I finished my water and followed her out.

After parking my car in front of my apartment, I glanced over at Carol's store. The CLOSED sign hung in the window again. I knew she had a group coming in thirty minutes because I'd confirmed the appointments. I hefted my purse up on my shoulder and trotted across the common to her store. The lights were off. I knocked, but no one answered.

I stood there for a moment, hands on hips, and then decided to see if Carol's car was parked in the alley. I hurried down the street and around the corner, worried, yet again, about Carol's well-being. The alley was broad and sunny, not the scary, dark kind women in slasher flicks entered. The back door to DiNapoli's was open. The clatter of dishes being washed rang through the old wooden screen door.

I spotted Carol's car, not knowing if that made me feel better or worse. I knocked on the back door. While I waited for Carol to answer, I shaded my eyes with my hand and scanned the alley. On one side were garages, backyards, and the backs of rambling houses. I spotted a few flower and vegetable gardens, but nothing sinister, although I noted that the yards would provide a good escape route for anyone fleeing from a crime.

The other side was a block of businesses and then houses that faced the town common. I studied the backs of this side of the alley: a drugstore, DiNapoli's, an optometrist, Carol's shop, and the headquarters of the Fitch Historical Society. Maybe the crime had happened in the wrong store. Genius. But each of the stores had signs clearly marking the business name in bold letters. So much for me being a genius.

I looked again at the houses across the way. Maybe I should knock on doors and ask if anyone saw someone fleeing from Carol's shop the night of the murder. A yellow sports car roared up and screeched to a halt beside me. Carol's assistant, Olivia, locked lips with the driver. I pounded on the back door. As Carol opened it, her assistant broke the kiss and hopped out of the car. The driver watched with interest as Olivia tugged down her minuscule black skirt. He caught my look and sketched a quick salute before tearing off, kicking up gravel and anything else that happened to be in the alley. At the end of the alley, he careened left, seemingly without stopping to look for oncoming traffic.

"Jett's got to stop tearing off like that, Olivia," Carol said as we entered the store. "Mr. DiNapoli's after me as it is. If Jett wasn't his godson, I'd really be in the doghouse."

Olivia started to say something, but Carol waved her off. "I know you're in love with him. I don't care. You're late again."

"Class was held over." Olivia shrugged her thin shoulders. She quickly headed to the front of the store, slipping a Paint and Wine apron over her short, purple hair as she did. She tied the apron around her waist as she disappeared into the shop.

"If I had a hundred bucks for every time I heard that I wouldn't be worried about finishing this painting," Carol muttered before looking at me. "What are you doing here?"

"I just got home from Gennie's house and saw the store was closed. I knew a group was coming in thirty minutes."

Carol smiled. "And you were worried. Again."

I shrugged. "You caught me."

"I got lost in my painting. Come look."

Most of the background was done. Rolling hills with open fields, separated by low stone walls, filled the canvas. While that was impressive, I knew the hardest part would be adding in all the detailed soldiers, some wounded and anguished. Then she'd have to add the smoke hanging in the air, as it did in the original. I had no clue how she'd manage that.

"Wow. I'm impressed." I paused, thinking again about the alley.

Olivia walked past us to the storage area. "I have to grab more paints."

I waited until she slipped through the curtains. "What time did you leave the shop the night before McQueen was murdered?"

Carol continued to paint. "It was around nine-thirty. Why?"

"Did the police ask you that?"

"Of course they did. Why are you asking?"

"I was standing in the alley wondering if someone across the way saw anyone back there."

Carol straightened up. "You think I'm a suspect, don't you? You know how these things work. It's why you've been hovering."

I swore silently. I'd been a bull in a house made of glass lately. "You must have known you'd at least be considered. Your store, your frame, your fingerprints." I watched for any signs Carol was going to crack. Nothing. Maybe that was more worrisome.

"I suppose on some level I did know. But I didn't want to think about it. I wonder if that's why Brad's mother showed up."

"They're looking into other angles. It's not just you."

Carol's face lit up. "What other angles?"

"I don't know. But I'm trying to find out."

We heard the group of women as they streamed into the shop, chattering and laughing.

Carol looked at me. "Thanks for your help. I've got to go."

I slipped back through the curtains to the storage area. Olivia was on her cell phone.

"The group is here," I told her.

"I'll see you later then."

For a moment I thought she was talking to me, but it was to the person on the other end of her phone call. She made a kissy noise as she hung up.

I went back out into the alley and turned in a slow, full circle, thinking maybe I'd missed something the first time I was out here. I decided to walk the length of the alley, up one side and down the other. This could be how the murderer went in and out of Carol's shop. Whoever killed Terry might have left some evidence that CJ's team had missed—if they'd even looked back here. I walked along, looking in corners and kicking away papers that had blown into corners. I didn't see a thing that didn't seem to belong in the alley.

I kicked at a bit of debris behind Carol's store. A mouse scurried off, and I managed to swallow a scream. That was the last thing Carol needed to hear—that there were mice in the alley. I shaded my eyes and studied the two houses with the best view of Carol's back door. The one to my right had all of the shades and drapes drawn. The one to my left had most of them opened. It looked like one of the closed curtains on the second floor twitched. Maybe a nosy person lived there, one who might have been up in the middle of the night—a night owl or new mother, or a baker getting ready for work early in the morning. Someone who might have seen something.

I took a step toward the house as tires squealed. A siren sounded. I turned as a police car rounded the corner of the alley from the right. It stopped a few feet from me. I twisted frantically, trying to spot what the cop was looking at or for. Then, as the window curtain twitched again, I realized. He was looking for me.

CHAPTER 13

A male voice boomed out of the car's loud-speakers. "Down on your knees. Hands behind your head."

I dropped to my knees because I knew better than to mess with people who carried guns even when they were wrong—terribly, embarrassingly wrong. I slapped my hands to the back of my head. I heard more sirens. Another police car raced down the alley from the left. It screeched to a halt, and Pellner climbed out.

"I should have known it would be you," Pellner said. He helped me up and trotted over to the other police car as I brushed bits of gravel and dirt off my knees. The dishwashers from DiNapoli's gathered by the screen door, watching. After Pellner talked to the other officer, he reversed his patrol car down the alley and took off with a squeal.

A man clumped out from the house with the twitchy curtain and moved across the alley with the help of a cane. He pointed an arthritic finger at me. "That's her. Cuff her."

I'd been right about a nosy person living in the house. The man stood as straight as he could with the cane. His trim body and crew cut screamed military or law enforcement.

"That's the perp I called about. She was casing the joint," he said. "I'm not sure which joint because she's been up and down the alley staring at all the businesses and houses." He shook his head. "Obviously up to no good. It's a sad day when you aren't safe in your own home in Ellington."

"Get in the car," Pellner said to me.

"My car's over by my apartment," I said.

"The police car," Pellner said, pointing at his patrol car.

"Aren't you going to cuff her?" the old man asked.

"I'm not going to cuff her, Herb. I can handle her," Pellner said. He jerked his head toward the car.

"Why in the world would I get in your car?" I asked.

The old man studied me. "You're right. She doesn't look like she could hurt a flea."

I found that a bit insulting. I was plenty strong.

"But you shouldn't let your guard down, young man," Herb said to Pellner.

I started to protest.

Pellner turned toward me. "Please, I'm begging

you. Just get in the car." He turned back to the old man. "Thanks for your help. I'll take her down to the station and question her."

The old man lifted his chin in acknowledgment but didn't move. "I'll wait till you get her in there, just in case."

I headed to Pellner's patrol car. I started to open the front passenger-side door.

"The back," Pellner called out.

I started to protest, but Pellner looked so stressed that I complied and climbed in the back. The car smelled of disinfectant and defiance—the second being the emotion I felt. A partition between the back and the front would keep Pellner safe from me attacking him. And at this point the thought of doing just that tempted me.

After a few more words with Herb, Pellner slid into the front and started the car. The old man stayed in the alley, watching, as we drove away.

"Who is that?" I asked.

"Herb Fitch. He used to be on the force. Years ago. It's just easier to humor him."

"Fitch? As in the air force base Fitch family?" Fitch Air Force Base was named after one of the founding fathers of Ellington. Their family was instrumental in the opening Revolutionary War battle on April 19, 1775.

"Yes, that Fitch family."

I glanced back over my shoulder. Herb Fitch stood there watching as we turned the corner.

"What was that all about?" I asked when we were out of sight.

"I could ask you the same question. What were you doing back there?"

"I was looking for Carol's car."

"And then?" Pellner's eyes met mine in the rearview mirror.

"I took a walk." He didn't need to know what I was doing back there and wouldn't approve if he did. "I wasn't casing anything."

Pellner shook his head and turned left onto Great Road.

"Are you really taking me to the station?" I asked.

"I should," he said, but he took another left onto Oak Street and stopped in front of my apartment.

"Did you find anything useful back there?" Pellner asked.

"No. Are you going to let me out of here or not?"

Pellner came around and opened the door for me. He even extended his hand to help me out. I chose not to use it. I glanced over at the common, relieved to find no crowd gathering to see me climbing out of a police car. I expected a lecture about interfering and yada yada. Instead, Pellner went back around the car and opened the driver's-side door. He leaned against the patrol car, arms on the roof. "Are you okay? You looked pretty upset when you left the station yesterday."

"Did CJ notice?" I asked.

"It's not like he said anything, but from the thundercloud that followed him for the rest of the day, I'm guessing he noticed."

I wanted to smack my hand to my forehead but refrained. "I don't want him feeling sorry for me."

"I get that." Pellner shoved off the car. "Thanks for getting in the back. It made my day a lot easier."

I trudged up the steps to the house. Stella came out of her apartment, forehead wrinkled in worry.

"What were you doing in the back of a police car?" she asked.

"Humoring Pellner," I said.

"That's a first. Come in. I'm between lessons."

I followed Stella into her apartment. She had a big, inviting couch and a couple of matching chairs. I'd found some art for her at a tag sale, a cityscape of Boston and one of a lighthouse. They looked great in her living room. It made me think of Gennie's paintings.

"Hot chocolate or something stronger?" Stella asked, heading to her kitchen.

"Hot chocolate sounds good. Anything stronger and I'll fall asleep."

Stella came back in a few minutes with two steaming mugs. "I just made this for my last student, a ten-year-old girl whose mom insists she take lessons." She handed me one of the mugs. "The girl has the voice of an . . ."

"Angel?"

"No. More like the noise a garbage disposal makes when it has a piece of metal in it." Stella shook her head. "I'm not sure who hates the lessons more, me or her."

I laughed and sipped my drink. The chocolate was rich and dark, not instant. I let its deliciousness roll around in my mouth for a moment before swallowing. "Did you know I'm doing a sale for Gennie?" I asked.

Stella's eyes widened, and she shook her head. "Why?"

"She wants to downsize. Gennie doesn't look that much older than you."

"She's not. My mom's twenty years older than her. And Aunt Nancy is fifteen years older."

"Interesting choice of career."

"Grandma says she came out fighting and never gave up. Grandpa died not too long after Gennie was born, and Aunt Nancy spent a lot of years trying to raise Gennie while Grandma worked."

"They seem close."

"Now they are, but I guess back in the day it was a whole different story. Aunt Nancy wanted Gennie to wear pink, frilly clothes. Gennie wanted to be a tomboy and raise hell."

"How'd she get into cage fighting?"

"After one of her escapades, she went to some kind of camp for troubled kids. It's where she learned to channel her energy into boxing and martial arts. Aunt Nancy almost had a coronary. But after that the police never dragged her home."

So Terry was a counselor for troubled kids, another angle to think about. Maybe something had happened at the camp or with one of the kids. One of them could still be in trouble. "Where'd she learn to paint?"

Stella set down her hot chocolate. "I don't think she knows how to paint. She never could sit still for long enough." She narrowed her eyes. "Why'd you ask?"

If I tried to lie, Stella would see right through me. She always did. "I came across some beautiful paintings stuck in a closet. They were signed by her and also had a Paint and Wine sticker on the back."

"So you thought she might have something to do with Carol's missing painting?" Stella asked.

"The thought entered my mind."

"And then you realized she'd be strong enough to strangle someone," Stella said, her voice tight with tension. She walked over to a minibar she kept in a corner by the kitchen and returned with a bottle of peppermint schnapps.

"Terry was strangled? Where'd you hear that?"

I took a drink of my hot chocolate. It wasn't exactly shocking news, but I wondered how she'd heard.

"It's all over town," Stella said. She poured a splash of the schnapps into each of our mugs. "People are arguing about whether Carol was strong enough to do it or not."

I almost spit out my drink, which caused me to choke.

"Are you okay?"

I nodded.

"Most people think she looks too scrawny," Stella said.

Gennie wouldn't be too scrawny. But Terry hadn't been *that* big of a guy. I wondered if this was one of the other angles CJ and Seth had mentioned. They'd certainly know about Gennie's past since she'd lived here all her life.

"Why would Carol do it?" I asked Stella.

Stella lifted a shoulder in a "how should I know?" motion. "What I do know is that my Aunt Gennie is only violent in the ring." She raised her chin and looked down her nose at me in a way that would make any Boston Brahmin, the elite of the city's society, proud.

I hoped Stella was right. I drained my hot chocolate, briefly forgetting about the peppermint schnapps. Warmth flooded my body, and weariness settled over me. After a quick goodbye, I went up to my apartment to take a nap. I stretched out on my couch, and as I drowsed, I thought about how furious Gennie had been when she'd found out Terry was part of Bubbles's company. She also somehow knew Carol. Although I didn't have any idea why Terry was murdered in Carol's shop, I realized I might have stumbled on an important connection.

CHAPTER 14

Laura walked into the Dunkin' Donuts on Great Road. The morning sun slanted in from the east, almost blinding me. I changed tables to escape the glare while Laura ordered her coffee. She'd sent me a text last night saying we needed to talk and to please meet her at nine this morning. Now she sat down with a glare that equaled the sun's, but I couldn't escape hers by changing tables.

"You knew Terry McQueen was dead when you came to see me," Laura said. "I can't believe you didn't tell me."

I was just pissing off friends left and right. "I really couldn't say anything."

"Are you letting CJ boss you around all of a sudden?"

"No. It's a murder investigation. Not whose turn is it to cook dinner."

"I'm still mad at you," Laura said, sitting on the

edge of her seat with posture that would have impressed the queen of England.

"If I buy you a coconut donut will you forgive me?" I knew Laura liked coconut donuts as much as I did.

"Maybe," she said, relaxing into her seat as much as one could here.

A few minutes later, after navigating the long line, I came back to the table with two coconut donuts. "Do you know Terry's wife?"

"Yes," Laura said.

Darn her. She was still mad at me if she wasn't going to volunteer any further information. "I don't think I've ever met her. What's her name?"

"Anna." Laura picked up her donut and took a big bite.

I thought for a moment. "It doesn't ring a bell."

We munched on our donuts. "Does she participate in any base activities?" I asked.

"She's around occasionally. But she's quiet and studious."

"What's she studying?"

"She's getting ready to take the exam to become a CPA. She seems really smart."

"What's she look like?"

"Tall, thin. I think they both were runners," Laura said.

"I just can't place her. Did she ever volunteer at the thrift shop?"

"I don't think so. Not everyone loves the place like you do."

"You love it, too," I said, sweeping coconut crumbs into a little pile on my napkin.

"Yes, but we're a special breed."

"Or shoppers who want to see the stuff as it comes in."

Laura laughed. "Are you calling me a control freak?"

"As my momma used to say, 'If the shoe fits.'"

"I've never heard you refer to your mother as 'momma' or anything but 'mother.'"

"Okay, my mother never said that, but she could have. Have you talked to Anna? Since Terry died?"

"I took over a casserole. We chatted for a few minutes. I felt like she only talked to me because of Mike's position on base. Personally, I think she would have preferred to slam the door in my face."

As the wife of the wing commander, Laura had a certain status on base—and a three-page-long list of duties that included everything from serving as an adviser to the Spouses' Club to helping families separated by deployments. The list started with a regulation stating that none of the listed duties were required. But there were few commanders' wives who took heed of that, and most, like Laura, enjoyed their duties, even though they made up a more than full-time job.

"Where does she live?" I asked.

"On base."

"She lives on base?" When there was extra housing available, bases would allow civilians working for the government, like Terry, or military retirees to rent houses.

"Yes. Why do you sound so surprised?"

"Terry's from Ellington. You'd think they'd want to live in town instead of on base."

"You know how expensive it is to live off base."

I did indeed. I'd been lucky that I needed only a small place and that I'd found Stella's rental before anyone else did. "Maybe I should take a casserole over, too." That would give me a chance to size Anna up for myself."

"Really?"

My lack of cooking skills was well known. "I can cook," I said. "Or I could get something from DiNapoli's."

"Get something from DiNapoli's, please."

"Do they have kids?"

"No." Laura glanced at her watch and scooped up her empty coffee cup. "I have to get back to base."

"Will you sponsor me on later so I can take something over for Anna?"

"If you think that's the right thing to do."

"I found her husband's body." Well, Carol had, but I was there soon after. "It seems like the only thing to do."

"What if she wants details?"

I stood and grabbed my trash. "I can be discreet."

Laura gave me a quick hug. I was about to follow her out when I saw Olivia's boyfriend, Jett, pull into the parking lot. I arranged myself so I could get in line right in front of him when he walked in. There were several people ahead of us, and thankfully he was alone. He stood behind me jiggling a handful of change. I took the opportunity to accidentally bump into him. The change fell on the floor and rolled away.

"I'm so sorry," I said as I busied myself collecting coins from various cracks and crevices. When I'd found as much as I could, I straightened up and handed the coins to him. "Oh, hi. You're Olivia's friend."

He cocked his head and looked me over before a slow grin spread across his face. "That I am. I'm Jett. And you are?" He puffed his chest out a bit so his already tight white T-shirt stretched to almost the breaking point.

Oh, Lord. He was an "I can charm the pants off anyone" kind of guy. But in the long run that might work to my advantage. I grinned back and batted my eyelashes. He had to be fifteen years younger than me. While that might be acceptable in Hollywood, I didn't think it would play well in Ellington, Massachusetts. I took a quick glance around and didn't spot anyone I knew.

"I'm Sarah. Winston." I added the last reluctantly, not really wanting to give him my full name for some reason. "Olivia works for my good friend Carol over at Paint and Wine."

"Of course. I remember seeing you there. How you doin'?"

I managed not to roll my eyes. I was pretty sure he didn't remember seeing me at all. "Did you hear someone was murdered at Paint and Wine?"

Jett shifted his weight from one foot to the other and back again. "I did. Olivia's pretty shook up about it. She didn't want to go back. I told her lightning doesn't strike twice, ya know?"

"Did you know the guy who died?" I asked.

Jett turned his head to the side and cracked his neck. "Naw, he wasn't from town. He lived on Fitch."

Hmmm, he said he didn't know the guy, but he did know he lived on Fitch. Everyone else in Ellington seemed to know McQueen, but he was a lot older than Jett. However, in Ellington news blew through town faster than a nor'easter in February. The line moved forward, and it was my turn to order. I probably didn't need any additional caffeine, and I absolutely didn't need another donut. I settled on a latte, and Jett ordered the same. We both headed out, Jett holding the door for me.

"I'm sorry about knocking the change out of your hand."

Jett grabbed my hand that wasn't holding the coffee and brushed his lips across it. "If it meant meeting you, it was worth it."

"Sarah."

I turned to find CJ striding toward us.

Jett winked at me, dropped my hand, and hustled over to some kind of fancy red car. How many cars did this kid have? By the time CJ arrived at my side, Jett was pulling out of the parking lot at a sedate pace—a drastic contrast to how he had been driving yesterday.

"What were you doing with that thug?"

"I wasn't doing anything with anyone. Thug or not." CJ's attitude bugged me. "Is he a thug?" At first, I thought CJ wasn't going to answer.

"He's a regular. Lots of weekends eating McDonald's at the jail."

"Why weekends?"

"After noon on Friday the court's closed. So you have to wait until Monday to be arraigned."

"Why McDonald's?"

"We're too small a department to pay for a cook."

"So you offer free lodging and a healthy dose of salt and cholesterol?"

CJ's frown indicated he didn't find me amusing. "You didn't answer my question. What were you doing with Jett?"

"Nothing. Our orders came out at the same time. We walked out together." I couldn't tell if CJ was jealous or concerned.

"He's bad news. Stay away from him."

"I can't believe you think I'd want to be around him." I couldn't believe we were having this conversation out in public. "He dates Carol's assistant."

CJ jerked his head back like he did when something surprised him.

"What?" I asked.

"Nothing. I need some coffee." CJ brushed past me and went into Dunkin's.

I headed to my car thinking about CJ's reaction to the information about Jett's dating life.

CJ must be worried about a known criminal hanging out at the scene where a murder had been committed. I wondered what kind of crimes Jett had been involved in to get CJ so worked up. Then I realized I could kill two birds with one stone easily enough.

I knew that by ten someone would be over at DiNapoli's prepping for their eleven o'clock lunch opening. I hoped that someone would be Angelo. Even though the CLOSED sign hung on the door, I rapped on the glass. Angelo spotted me from the back of the kitchen and waved me in.

"What do you need?" Angelo asked. Although it came out like "whadda ya need." "I hope you aren't looking for breakfast. We don't do breakfast."

I knew full and well they didn't do breakfast, but Angelo continued. "Why does anyone need someone to cook them breakfast? It's eggs or cereal. You need someone to make you cereal?"

I shook my head no, knowing better than to interrupt when Angelo was on a roll.

"You can't fix yourself an egg or pour a bowl of cereal, you go to Dunks and get yourself a donut. Who can't do that?"

I kept nodding and shaking my head as necessary while Angelo talked. I, myself, liked waffles or pancakes on occasion. When I tried to cook them on my own, they were burned or runny, not fluffy like they were at Helen's in Concord, my favorite breakfast place.

Angelo took a breath. He looked at me. "What do you need?"

This time I knew he wasn't talking about breakfast. Now that I was here, it wasn't as easy to bring up Angelo's errant godson as I thought it would be. "I want to order a small pan of ziti to pick up this afternoon."

"What time?"

"Say three?"

"Sounds good." He didn't write anything down. I didn't think I should suggest he should. "What else besides the ziti did you come in for, kid?"

Angelo had taken to calling me "kid" in the not too distant past. It seemed like a term of endearment. I hoped he wasn't calling me a goat. But at thirty-eight it seemed a little odd to be called "kid."

"Come with me," Angelo said. "You talk. I'll work." I followed him to the big six-burner range. He pointed to a stool, and I sat as he started making a marinara sauce. He heated a pan, poured in a generous amount of olive oil and began chopping onions. He tossed the onions into the olive oil and crushed garlic with the broadside of what a native would call a wicked big knife. "I'm working. You're supposed to be talking." He added the garlic to the pan.

I took a deep breath. "I was wondering about your godson, Jett."

"Why?" Angelo said as he chopped tomatoes at a breathtaking speed.

I didn't want to throw CJ under the bus or have Angelo think that CJ was blabbing things when he shouldn't be. "He's dating Carol's assistant. I want to make sure he's good for her."

Angelo turned for a second, giving me a look I couldn't decipher before turning back to the sauce.

"I heard he's been in some trouble," I added. "I wondered what kind."

Angelo shook his head. "The kid's middle name should be trouble. Nah, his first name should be trouble. He just needs someone to take a firm hand to him. And don't get riled up. I don't mean beat him. I mean tell him no."

Angelo waved his knife in the air. "It started with a little shoplifting, some minor vandalism. He moved on to drag racing, robbed someone at knifepoint. I'm guessing your ex knows him pretty well. Instead of getting punished, he gets a sports car." Angelo dropped some tomato paste in the pan, sautéing it with the onions and garlic. Even though I was full from the donut and two coffees, the sauce smelled amazing.

"I've seen him in a couple of different sports cars. How many does he have?"

Angelo frowned. "He wrecked the one his dad gave him. I thought he was driving an old clunker. If you can consider a ten-year-old Mercedes a clunker."

From my perch on the stool, I saw Rosalie

hurry by the large front window. She flung the door open, and it banged shut behind her. "Did you hear?" she asked.

Angelo added the tomatoes to the pan and turned down the heat before turning to Rosalie. "Hear what?"

"I was just over at Giovani's getting my hair cut."

"It looks gorgeous, Rose. Like the day we met," Angelo said, kissing her cheek.

Rosalie blushed a little. I sighed inwardly as I silently reflected "How sweet," which wasn't something people normally thought about Angelo.

"Someone stole *Battled* from the library," Rosalie said. "And replaced the original with a forgery."

CHAPTER 15

I leaped up off the stool, sending it careening into the cabinet behind me. "What?" I said as I straightened the stool. "Someone stole *Battled*? And it was replaced with a forgery?" I hoped it wasn't Carol's painting. "When?"

"They don't know. The copy is so good it could have been there for a while," Rosalie said.

"I've got to go. I've got to talk to Carol."

"I'm calling her a lawyer," Angelo said. "My cousin, Jett's dad. He might not be much of a father, but he's an ace defense attorney. Trust me. He's kept Jett out of jail."

Angelo must have heard about Carol's missing painting if he thought she needed a lawyer. "Why would you do that?" I didn't want to spell out that it was common knowledge he didn't like Carol.

Angelo made a shooing motion. "You go talk to your friend and don't worry about why. Vincenzo's office is in Bedford. If he's not in court, I'll make sure he comes right over."

"Thanks. I'll be back at three for the ziti," I said as I headed out the door.

I heard Angelo telling Rosalie as I left, "She thinks I'm going to forget her ziti because I didn't write it down."

I ran over to Carol's shop. "We've got a problem," I yelled as I ran in. Thankfully, no one but Carol was in the store. She sat in her studio in front of her easel, paintbrush in hand. I blurted out what I'd just heard at DiNapoli's.

"Why do you think I need a lawyer?" Carol asked.

That stopped me. "I just assumed it was yours because of the timing and the quality." Carol's face paled, and she dropped her paintbrush.

"Angelo said he'd send his cousin, who is some big-name defense attorney. He's kept his son, Jett—you know, Olivia's boyfriend—out of jail."

"Jail? You think I'm going to jail?"

I put my hands out and shook my head. I hoped I was wrong. "No. But better to have a lawyer."

"Why?" Carol straightened herself up. "First, we don't even know that it's my painting over there. Second, it was stolen from here—that's been documented. And third . . ." Carol slumped a little. "I don't have a third. But I can't afford a fancy-schmancy lawyer. Which is why I painted *Battled* in the first place."

"You're right. Maybe it isn't your painting." I

wished I could buy into that, but I didn't. How many copies of *Battled* could there be in one little town?

Carol stood and went to a closet at the back of the studio. She whipped out a purple wrap dress, Jimmy Choo heels, and a makeup kit.

"What are you doing?" I asked.

"I keep everything I might need here just in case."

"Just in case you need to meet with a lawyer?"

"In case an important client comes in at the last minute. I can't meet people in paint-spattered clothes."

I didn't see a speck of paint on her jeans or sweater. Carol disappeared into the tiny bathroom.

Carol's nonchalant attitude puzzled me. I slumped onto the stool in front of the painting she was working on and waited. Twenty minutes later I heard the front door of the shop open. I went to the bathroom door and knocked. "Carol, someone's here."

"Go see who it is. Please?" Carol called through the door.

"Okay." I walked into the shop. A man stood there; he was tall and broad, looked to be in his fifties. His suit fit like it had been sewn on him, probably with pure wool or silk thread. He was an older version of Jett.

"Carol Carson?" A deep voice rumbled out of the man. As he reached out to shake my hand, I noted the Rolex and the gold pinky ring with what looked like a large embedded ruby.

"I'm her friend, Sarah Winston." I shook the large, cool hand; mine felt swallowed up but safe in his grasp.

"I'm Vincenzo DiNapoli."

He somehow managed to check me out as thoroughly as Jett had earlier, but Vincenzo's technique was much subtler than Jett's eyes sweeping over my body.

"Is Carol here?" Strands of his silver hair shimmered in the lights as he looked around the shop. Not a strand moved, nor could it, with the amount of gel he'd used.

"I'll get her." Where was she, anyway? I'd thought she'd be out here by now.

I hurried to the back room. Carol was applying lipstick. She'd done something to her hair, and she'd changed into the purple wrap dress and Jimmy Choo heels.

"Do you know anything about Angelo's cousin?" she asked.

"Not much. He's a Mob lawyer. Last spring Angelo told me he got Mike 'the Big Cheese' Titone cleared of multiple charges." I hoped Vincenzo was a lawyer for the Mob and not actually in the Mob. I also hoped to hell Angelo knew what he was doing.

Carol adjusted the front of her dress until just a touch of cleavage showed. "Great. Then he should be able to help little old me." She swept out of the room, looking as glamorous and confident as any movie star. I felt underdressed in the jeans and black sweater I'd thrown on to meet Laura. Then I understood Carol's wardrobe change: the clothes gave her the confidence she needed to get through this. I hurried after her, not wanting to miss the upcoming show.

Carol flirted. Vincenzo preened. They agreed that if Carol needed representation she'd do some paintings for him as payment.

"I need to freshen my office," Vincenzo said as they negotiated the exchange of paintings for services.

"If you need any unique furnishings, you need to talk to Sarah. She's brilliant at finding interesting pieces."

Vincenzo tore his eyes away from Carol's cleavage and glanced at me. "I'll keep that in mind," he said in a voice that indicated he'd forget as soon as he walked out the door, which he headed toward as he spoke.

CJ walked in. He glanced at Vincenzo, registered who he was, and dismissed him as no threat in a matter of seconds. I doubt anyone but me could tell he'd done that.

"Carol, I need you to come with me," CJ said. "Please," he added with a quick glance at Vincenzo.

Carol's flirtatious attitude disappeared. Vincenzo stepped between her and CJ. "Where do you need her to go?" Vincenzo asked.

CJ sidestepped Vincenzo so that he was speaking directly to Carol. "I need you to come to the library to look at a painting and see if it's yours. I assume, since he's here"—CJ flicked a glance at Vincenzo—"that you've already heard that *Battled* has been stolen and replaced with a forgery." He looked at Vincenzo briefly and then back at Carol. "It could be the painting you reported missing."

Carol took a step forward, but Vincenzo put a hand out. "You're under no obligation," he told her.

"I'd like to go see it. To see if it's mine," Carol said.

Vincenzo turned to CJ. "We'll meet you there in fifteen minutes."

CJ opened his mouth, then shut it. He gave a quick nod and left.

Carol slumped onto a stool. "Are they going to arrest me?" she asked Vincenzo.

"Certainly not."

I hoped he was as confident as he sounded.

"Can Sarah come, too?" Carol asked, grabbing my hand.

Vincenzo nodded. "Of course."

CJ, Vincenzo, Pellner, Carol, and I looked at the fabulous, fake *Battled*. The colonials had the British on the run, smoke hung in the air, and bloody men lay on the ground, while others ran for their lives, dropping their heavy muskets as they tried to escape. Vincenzo moved up closer to study the painting.

"How'd they discover this wasn't the original?" I asked.

Pellner opened his mouth, but CJ shot him a look. Vincenzo turned to see why no one was answering.

No one said anything. My best shot at finding out would be when I picked up my ziti.

"Vincenzo, please, let me take a closer look," Carol said. "It must be mine. Who else would have copied it?"

"Many people," Vincenzo said. "My uncle, Stefano, tried to buy *Battled*. He was bitterly disappointed when the town refused. I believe he had a copy made."

I couldn't believe Vincenzo had just thrown his uncle under the bus for Carol.

"There was also a competition back in the late seventies, at Middlesex Community College, to see who could make the best copy," Vincenzo said. "There's probably fifty or sixty copies from that event alone."

Carol started to speak, but Vincenzo cut her off to address CJ. "You and your department have your work cut out for you finding whose painting this is and what became of the original. I'm guessing the people of Ellington aren't going to be happy that their beloved painting, sitting right across from the police station, was taken."

Wow, knife in and twisted. I turned away to keep my smile hidden and silently thanked Angelo for the gift of Vincenzo. Vincenzo grabbed Carol and me by the elbows and rather forcibly escorted us out before we had a chance to say anything.

"I'm sure that's my painting," Carol said as we settled into the tan leather seats of Vincenzo's Lincoln Town Car. He was the only person I knew who had a driver. "Whoever stole it must have added the signature."

Vincenzo leaned toward her. "We shouldn't discuss this in front of Sarah. We have client-attorney privilege, but Sarah's a third party and isn't privileged."

"I'm not worried about what Sarah hears. I didn't do anything wrong," Carol said. "Why didn't you let me tell CJ that was my painting?" Carol asked.

"I did it to buy you time. If you'd said it was yours you'd have had officers showing up at your business and home with search warrants within a matter of hours. This allows you some time in case you have any tidying up you need to do."

"You think I have the original *Battled*?" It came out so loud I wondered if people out on the street heard.

"I don't care if you have it. But let me again stress the importance of not discussing the case here."

"But CJ knows my painting was stolen. I told him."

"You didn't report it immediately. Who besides you saw it?"

"My assistant, Olivia."

"Ah, yes. The young woman who dates my son

and has a rap sheet equally as long as his, if not longer."

Carol and I exchanged surprised looks. I'd assumed she'd checked out Olivia's background, but this was obviously news to her.

"What does any of this matter, anyway?" I asked. "Carol's admitted to making a copy. She has pictures of it in progress on her computer. She showed them to me."

"She has pictures of someone's painting in progress on her computer," Vincenzo said smoothly.

I was confused. Then it dawned on me. That's what Vincenzo did. He confused juries so he could get his clients off. I smiled at him, and he gave me a slight nod.

We pulled up in front of Carol's shop. The driver opened the door for us and helped us out.

Carol looked a bit dazed. She looked over at the common and at her shop as if she didn't quite recognize them.

Vincenzo leaned out of the backseat. "Don't speak to anyone about this without me present. Go do what you need to do. And be prepared for a search of your home and business in the near future," Vincenzo instructed Carol.

He handed us his business cards. I stuffed mine in my purse.

"I want either of you to call me at the first sign of a police officer. I don't care if it's for jaywalking. The Ellington police have a bit of a reputation for harassment." Then he got back in his car, and it pulled away from the curb.

"They certainly harassed you last spring," Carol said.

I had had my share of tickets last spring, but in the end much of it was just a show of loyalty to the department's new chief, CJ. "There's a fine line between harassment and good police work."

Carol shook her head. "Why do you think Angelo called Vincenzo for me? I thought Angelo hated me."

"I guess he doesn't. All I know is that if I had to go through something like this, I'd want to go through it with Vincenzo."

"I have to go tell Brad. That will be another great conversation to get through. His mother will be reminding him he should have married his high school sweetheart and not me."

"He'd have been bored stiff with the high school honey. He loves you. Try not to worry."

At three I zipped into DiNapoli's. Rosalie met me at the counter.

"You look a little frazzled, Sarah."

I ran a hand over my hair, hoping to smooth down any flyaway pieces.

"Do you want some iced tea? Angelo is finishing up your ziti."

Angelo waved from over by the oven.

"Tea would be great."

Rosalie filled two large plastic glasses and stuck in two straws, the bendy kind that always made me feel like a kid again. We sat off to the side at one of the vacant tables. A number of high school kids filled the others, eating mozzarella sticks and drinking sodas.

I leaned forward and spoke softly. "Do you know how they figured out the painting was a fake? I saw the one hanging in the library, and it looked real to me." I looked around to make sure no one was listening. The kids were wrapped up in their phones and each other.

"Why are we talking so quietly? The whole town knows."

I leaned back. "Oh. From the way CJ acted, it was classified."

"Marge was bragging about the discovery at Giovanni's when she got her perm this morning."

"Who's Marge?" I asked.

"The head librarian. CJ asked Marge to keep it quiet. But to her that meant telling only her closest friends, who told their closest friends."

"In other words, the whole town knows how she discovered the forgery."

Rosalie nodded.

"But I still don't."

"Marge was dusting the frame. She knew there was a small nick on the bottom left-hand corner. The duster would get caught every time. She dusted this morning. It didn't catch. She looked to see if it had been repaired and realized it hadn't." Rosalie stopped and took a drink of her tea. "Then she took a good look at the painting.

The signature looked wrong. A little too shiny."
Rosalie leaned in. "Her assistant said Marge was
so upset she called 4-1-1 instead of 9-1-1. Marge's
version of the story made her sound like Super-
woman."

"I wonder why CJ was so secretive. It doesn't
seem like that big a deal." Then again he was
probably worrying about evidence and building
a case when and if the perpetrator was caught.

Rosalie lifted her shoulders. "Who knows?"

I paid for my ziti and headed out to pay my
respects to Anna McQueen.

CHAPTER 16

I pulled up in front of Anna McQueen's house on the base. Sometimes base life felt like a throwback to the fifties, with lots of stay-at-home moms hosting coffee klatches and volunteering for every organization imaginable. I missed being part of that.

Anna lived in the oldest section of housing, in a gray town house with a small front lawn. Blinds covered all the windows, making the place look like it was asleep. I climbed out anyway and knocked on the door while balancing the still-hot aluminum pan of ziti. The door opened to an expressionless woman. Everything about her sagged—the bags surrounding her very red eyes, the clothes hanging loosely on her thin frame; even her dull, red hair seemed to slump.

I felt bad about intruding. I thrust the ziti at her. "I'm very sorry for your loss." She looked as though she didn't want to take it, but she straightened herself. "Thank you."

"I'm Sarah Winston."

She started to close the door, but some bit of recognition widened her eyes. She held the door wider, "Come in. Are you hungry? I've got every kind of casserole imaginable. An assortment of pies, and now"—she peeled the aluminum off the corner of my casserole—"ziti. It smells good."

"It's from DiNapoli's. You wouldn't want mine."

"Let's sit in the kitchen. Coffee? I just was getting ready for a cup."

"Sure." I followed her through her house. The living room, instead of being furnished with couch, chairs and end tables, had been turned into a game room. A dartboard hung on the wall, a poker table was dead center, and various pin-ball and other arcade games filled the corners. A large-screen TV took up most of one wall, with a gaming system underneath. Anna noticed me noticing.

"Some guys never grow up. Terry loved games. I don't know what I'm going to do with all of that now."

The rest of the house was sparsely decorated with barely any furniture. A desk and chair sat in what should have been the dining room. Only the blinds provided by housing covered her windows. She hadn't added her own drapes. Few pictures hung on the walls.

A picture of Anna and a man—I assumed it was Terry even though he was tanned and healthy-looking instead of blue—hung in the hall. What had to be the Tetons, were in the background.

They both smiled at the camera, heavy-looking backpacks at their feet. Terry looked like a runner, lean and muscled. Bubbles had mentioned they'd met when they were both out for a run. So why didn't Terry run that night at Carol's store? Maybe that meant he knew his attacker and hadn't realized he was in danger.

Anna's kitchen counters were full of various kinds of desserts. She opened the fridge to get some half and half and gestured to its overflowing contents. "What could I possibly do with all of this? It's just me now. Not that Terry and I together could have polished all this off." Her eyes reddened, and she busied herself getting out mugs and pouring coffee.

"That's a lot. I could take some of it to the homeless shelter in Ellington for you."

"Would you? I don't want it to go to waste." I followed her to the small kitchen table. She pushed aside a stack of finance books with her elbow and set the coffee cups down. "I heard you were there when Terry was found. What can you tell me?"

I wondered why she'd asked me in. Now I wished she hadn't. Laura warned me this might happen. "I don't know much."

"I saw him at the morgue," Anna said. "I know what he looked like. I just wondered if you knew anything else. Something to help catch the bastard who did this." Her voice caught midway through the sentence. Her eyes started filling with tears, which she blinked back.

"My friend Carol found him in her store. There was a frame around his face."

"I heard that too. It doesn't make sense. Terry was quiet but well liked."

"Did he know Carol? Had he mentioned her before?" I took a sip of my coffee. It was more like colored water than coffee, which I was actually grateful for because I'd had my fill of caffeine today. I hated to think this, but even though Brad was retired, Carol still had a dependent ID that allowed her to get on base whenever she wanted. So maybe they'd met someplace and Carol wasn't admitting it. She hadn't fessed up to knowing Gennie, either.

"Not that I know of." She ran her hands through her hair.

"Were either of you interested in paintings or learning to paint?"

"Not really."

Most of the walls in the house that I'd passed or could see were bare. I guess I could cross art collector off the list.

"Maybe he was going to see if she was interested in investing," Anna said. "I know that Dave and Terry were aggressively growing their business. They've been very successful."

Aggressive. Interesting term. I'd felt like killing more than one salesman in the moment.

"I don't mean aggressive as in an obnoxious, hard sale. I mean that they worked hard on their business plan and ways they could grow the company."

This is why I didn't play poker. Even when I thought I'd maintained a neutral expression I obviously hadn't.

"They understood the needs of active-duty military and veterans," Anna said.

"Bubbles is smart and charming," I said. "One of those 'could sell sand in the Sahara' salesman types."

"And both Terry and Bubbles are good with numbers. But over this last month . . ." Anna shook her head.

"What happened over the last month?" I wondered about market performance during the past several weeks.

"Terry got some threatening notes."

My eyes widened. "You told the police?"

"Of course. And base security, the OSI. Anyone who would listen."

OSI was the Office of Special Investigations, a branch of the air force that looked into serious crimes. "What kind of notes?"

"They were stupid. Terry wanted to toss them, but I kept them. Just in case." Anna drew in a ragged breath. "I didn't think 'just in case' would ever really happen."

"Do you have them?"

"The police took them."

I was disappointed, but it wasn't really any of my business.

"But I kept copies. Let me get them."

I wasn't sure why she was willing to share them with me. Maybe she just needed someone to unload on and I happened to be available.

Anna spread the five notes out on the table. They did seem childish. Things like "I'll make you pay," "Watch out," and "You're wrong." From what I remembered, the writing seemed similar to the one Bubbles received. CJ sure hadn't let on that Terry had gotten notes, too.

"Where did Terry find them?" I asked.

"On the windshield, in the door. Places like that." Anna shrugged.

"On base or off base?"

"Both. Do you think that's important?"

"I don't know. Could I take photographs of the notes?"

Anna hesitated before nodding.

I took two shots of each note with my phone. "Where did Terry work?" I took another sip of my tepid coffee. Maybe Brad was the one who knew Terry, and not Carol.

"In the vaults on base. I don't know what he did."

The vaults meant Terry was involved in some kind of top-secret program. Brad had worked as an administrator at the clinic. So their paths wouldn't have crossed based on work. But working in the vaults meant Terry knew a lot of secrets— another area CJ and Seth might be looking into.

I'd never find out anything about that, and they might not be able to, either.

"Did you or Terry have any idea why someone would threaten him?"

Anna shook her head. "We wracked our brains trying to figure it out. Terry reviewed the company figures. They haven't had a loss worth mentioning with any of their accounts." Anna stood, so I did too. "I'll help you load the food in your car."

The threats must have been directed at Terry. Or maybe Anna was the target and Terry had gotten in the way.

My car was a ten-year-old Suburban that I babied as much as possible. It was the perfect vehicle for hauling stuff to and from garage sales. I had to curtail my garage sale habit since I lived in a one-bedroom apartment. Throwing yard sales for other people kept me busy on most weekends, anyway, and thus out of trouble.

After I dropped the food off at the homeless shelter, I drove home and cleaned up. I headed up to New Hampshire to visit a couple of thrift shops I'd heard about near Nashua, in search of some furniture for a friend. After I'd finished at the thrift shops, I was meeting Seth for dinner, so I felt a bit giddy. I tried to analyze that feeling as I drove. What was it about Seth that made me smile? I hoped it wasn't the whole rich and handsome thing, but if I was that shallow, I wouldn't be holding back. He was smart and funny, and he liked me. Nothing not to like there.

I pulled up to the first thrift shop and walked in. It was filled with clothes, baby items, and assorted glassware—not what I was on the hunt for this afternoon. But I took a quick turn around the place just in case something was tucked in a corner. No luck.

As I listened to the directions my phone gave me to the next place, I wished there was something along those lines to guide the heart. Detour around this guy, exit before that one, take the express lane to another—he's the one. But unfortunately, I had to figure out the whole Seth/CJ thing on my own.

A white wicker furniture set consisting of a love seat, two chairs, and a table sat out in front of the next shop. That could be just the thing. I parked and tried not to scamper over. Be cool, I told myself. The closer I got, the more beat-up the set looked. I hoped it just needed a fresh coat of paint. But after walking around it and turning it over, I realized the wicker was broken in too many places to repair.

I went into the shop and poked around. An hour later I came out with a small oil painting of a vase of roses and nothing else. But the owner had been lovely. She'd attended New England's Largest Yard Sale and thought it was fabulous.

Next year she wanted to have a booth. I promised to send her details as soon as I had them.

As I drove down a winding lane lined with low stone walls and towering trees, I spotted a pile of stuff set near someone's driveway. There was a FREE—TAKE ME sign hung on an old stereo console. I pulled over and hopped out, tempted by a jumble of old chairs, a spindled, rocking cradle with no bottom, and some old iron pieces and flowerpots.

I couldn't resist two of the chairs. One was a square-back with a ripped and stained seat. The other had a delicate carving of a shell and a broken cane bottom. I thought both were probably American-made, based on their simplicity. English and European chairs were generally fancier and more decorative. I loved chairs, but they aren't a very practical thing to collect when you live in a small space.

I picked up the cradle. It was pegged together and would come apart easily. The various pieces would look fabulous in someone's garden, where flowers could climb the spindles. But there wasn't any place to garden at Stella's, so I turned my back on it. The two chairs fit easily into the back of the Suburban. As I got behind the wheel, I wondered how much it would cost to fix up my "free" chairs. I took one last look at the cradle and climbed back out. If I didn't end up selling it myself, I'd take it to Carol for her garden in the spring.

* * *

I'd arranged to meet Seth at a little diner on the outskirts of Nashua. Lots of people from Massachusetts shopped up here because New Hampshire didn't have a state sales tax. There'd been a few scandals when Massachusetts officials were caught coming out of liquor stores or other shops with merchandise. There were laws about buying things here and reporting it in Massachusetts, but I'm fairly certain most people ignored them.

I'd taken some time getting ready for our dinner before I'd left. After all, Seth was used to dining with Victoria's Secret models. My hair shone, my makeup was as flawless as I could achieve on my own, and my eye shadow was smoky. I waited, studying the menu and the clientele, hoping I wouldn't run in to anyone I knew. But since I didn't know a lot of truckers, I felt fairly safe.

Seth slid into the booth across from me. "How many more greasy spoons are you going to make us eat at?" he asked. He held up his spoon, which was indeed greasy.

This didn't seem to be a good start to the evening. He smiled to soften his words or me— one of the two. "You look awfully nice for someone who was up here, what did you call it, junking?"

Yep, that had been my excuse to meet him up here—that I was already going to be out on a buying expedition for a friend who wanted help furnishing her new home. "Just because I was junking doesn't mean I have to look like junk."

He grabbed one of my hands, so I had to stop shredding the paper that recently covered my straw. "You never look like junk to me."

His dark, long-lashed eyes looked sincere. The cook slapped some burgers on the griddle. They sizzled and popped. Seth's look had me sizzling, too. What was wrong with me that I kept him at a distance? And what was wrong with him that he let me?

"Thank you," I said, biting my tongue to keep from joking off the compliment. The waitress arrived, and we ordered. When Seth asked for clean silverware she snapped to, obviously wanting to please him, even though she was probably old enough to be his grandmother.

I poked at my salad of iceberg lettuce that was on the verge of being spoiled. Seth powered through country-fried chicken, mashed potatoes, and gravy, sharing bites with me in the process, asking why anyone would order salad at a diner. He ordered chocolate cream pie with a graham-cracker crust for us to share. When the towering piece of pie arrived, he left his seat and moved over to sit beside me.

"Bench sharing?" I asked. "Isn't there a Seinfeld episode about this?"

"There's a Seinfeld episode about everything."

I dug my fork into the pie and wrapped my mouth around it. Seth leaned in to wipe a bit of the cream off the corner of my mouth before he took a bite.

"I didn't realize you decorated houses for people," Seth said.

"It's not really decorating. I find pieces I think they'd like and help them arrange what they have to go with it. Just for a few friends." I took another bite.

"I'm your friend, right?" Seth said.

I almost choked on the pie, thinking I'd just walked into something. I swallowed. "Of course."

"Great. I just bought a house in Bedford. I need help finding some things for it."

Bedford? One town over from me. He'd been living in an apartment in Lowell, a more comfortable twenty-five minutes away.

"I love your apartment," Seth said. "It feels homey. I'd like something similar."

"But you can afford any decorator in Boston."

"I don't want some overly decorated apartment that's been 'done' as a showcase. I want a home," Seth said, flashing his smile. "Please?"

Working closely with Seth to set up his house seemed about as smart as running across the base shooting range in front of the targets. The risk of getting hurt seemed enormous. "I'll think about it."

"One more favor?" Seth asked. "A ride home?"

I looked at him suspiciously. "Where's your car? How'd you get here?"

"I was in Nashua for a meeting with other DAs from around New England. A bunch of us carpooled up here. You don't want to strand me here, do you?"

"What did you tell them you were doing?" I asked.

"The truth. Meeting a friend for dinner."

I didn't like it, but I was kind of stuck. I couldn't just leave him here. "Okay, let's go." I sighed inwardly. What could go wrong?

CHAPTER 17

Thirty minutes later we pulled up in front of his apartment complex.

"Come up?" Seth asked. Before I could say no, he added, "In a strictly professional capacity. To assess my current furnishings and see what you'll be able to use."

"I guess. Since I'm here."

"You sound reluctant. I've never made a pass at any of the people who work for me."

I wasn't sure if that made me feel better or worse. "Without seeing where you're moving to, it's going to be hard to tell what's usable and what isn't."

After a quick jog up two flights of stairs, Seth unlocked the door and gestured for me to go in first. I only had the vaguest of memories of the place. I'd been here once and was drunk when I'd arrived. The following morning I'd scooted out as fast as possible.

The furnishings were sleek, modern, and soulless. The shades of gray felt lifeless; I was actually a fan of gray, just not these grays. A large modern painting of splashes of gray hung on one wall.

"How do you stand it in here?" I asked. "It's so cold and depressing."

"I'm usually just passing through. And it's why I asked you for help."

We walked from the living room to the small eating area. The table was a tall, wrought-iron-and-glass combo with three low-backed stools around it—one of those pieces that looked cool but wasn't comfortable to use. The table was covered with a couple of computers and lots of papers. Seth added his briefcase to the mess. The tiny kitchen opened to the rest of the room. "Do you want some coffee?" Seth pointed to an espresso machine that looked well used.

"No thanks." I didn't plan to stay that long. A few memories started flashing in my head, and heat warmed my face. "Let's look at the rest of the place."

Seth seemed to be fighting a grin. He grabbed my hand and led me down a hall. One of the rooms was an office full of Red Sox memorabilia and a beautiful, large walnut desk. Its smooth top was clear of clutter and polished to a mirror-like shine. Oh, no. Had we . . . ? In here?

I pulled my hand from his. "We can use the desk. For your office. In your new place," I added hastily, my face growing even warmer. "And all your Red Sox things. They'd be perfect in a man cave, if you plan on having one in your new home."

"My last decorator wanted to me to toss everything in here, even after I explained the desk was my great-grandfather's."

I shook my head. "The desk is amazing," I said, turning to him. His eyes smoldered, and I rushed out of the room.

I peeked in his bedroom. It held a large antique sleigh bed. That I remembered all too well. I hustled back to the living room and opened the front door. "The bed will work, too. Depending on the size of your bedroom."

"Sarah, wait. Don't rush off."

"I have to," I said over my shoulder as I slammed the door behind me. I zipped down to my car. I sat in the Suburban and fanned myself. I was having very X-rated thoughts on what was supposed to be a G-rated night.

At seven the next morning, the sound of car doors slamming blew in through my bedroom window, along with a chilly breeze. I tossed the covers aside to see what had caused the racket. I flung open my curtains. Carol stood outside her store across the town common. Its door was wide open. Two police cars were parked out front, and police officers strolled in. Vincenzo's black Town Car slid to the curb. He exited and headed to Carol's side.

The police must be executing the search warrants Vincenzo warned Carol would be coming. I spotted Seth walking up the street toward Vincenzo and Carol, carrying his briefcase. CJ walked down the sidewalk from the other direction, also heading toward Carol and Vincenzo. I watched in horror as they arrived and shook hands, first with each other, and then with Vincenzo and Carol.

This town was just too small. They all turned and looked over in my direction. I ducked back in what I hoped was the nick of time, whatever the nick of time actually is. I took a hasty shower, threw on a long-sleeved top, jeans, and boots. After spending a few minutes on my hair and makeup, I was ready—for what I wasn't sure—but a knock on the door proved my instinct was right. Please, don't let it be all four of them. My heart couldn't take it.

I took a deep breath and opened the door. Stella stood there. I stuck my head out and looked around.

"Expecting someone else?" Stella asked as she followed me into my apartment. "You look awfully nice. You must have been expecting a man."

"Can't I look nice anytime?"

"Sure, but this early in the morning?" Stella was in yoga pants and a sweatshirt but still looked cute. "I need to go on base and wondered if you'd go with me."

"Why are you going on base?"

"Dave's out of town for a few days, and he

wanted me to check on his cat. I don't want to go on base by myself."

"Why not?"

Stella let out a breath of air. "I don't know—guilty conscience, fear of wandering into a secure area. Maybe it's just the guards, fences, and razor wire. And I haven't been on Fitch since my senior year of high school for a swim meet."

"You were a competitive swimmer?"

"No. But I liked one."

It might be good to get out of here while CJ and Seth were both in such close proximity. I'd check in with Carol when I got back. "As long as we swing through Dunkin' Donuts on the way," I said. "I'll drive."

Twenty minutes later we drove onto the base. We'd already gone to the visitors center to get a pass. That was the easy part because Dave had left instructions allowing Stella to get on base.

Stella looked around as we drove. "Is the bowling alley still here?" she asked.

"It is."

"I spent a lot of time there my junior year."

"Let me guess: you liked a guy."

"No. I was on a team. Back then there wasn't any razor wire, gates, or guards. Anyone could come on. Then after 9/11 they beefed up all the security."

I took a right, and we passed the youth center, a place for kids to hang out, then the elementary and middle schools, and the base swimming pool. We drove up Luke Road. Bubbles lived in one of the older two-bedroom town houses near the top of the hill. It was an end unit that was connected to three others.

Stella looked up at the two story-building as we parked. "These look old."

"They are," I said. I was so used to the rows of white buildings that I didn't pay much attention to them. Some were right on the street; others sat back on U-shaped courtyards. All the garages were behind the units.

"Wonder why he doesn't live in one of those?" Stella mused as I parked, pointing across the street to the cute, brick Cape-style houses.

We walked up the short sidewalk to his door. "I'm guessing he could have. It's all based on rank and number of dependents."

Stella unlocked the front door and went in. I picked up a base newspaper that was on the minuscule front porch before following her. A scrawny black-and-white cat met us and wove through our legs, purring its contentment.

"This is Tux," Stella said. "Dave rescued him a couple of years ago."

"You're a sweet baby," I told Tux, patting him on the top of his head. We busied ourselves with feeding Tux and putting out fresh water. When we finished, I picked up Tux and cuddled him to my chest. "I'd take you home with me, but my mean landlady doesn't allow pets." Tux licked my cheek with his little rough tongue.

"I thought you said you're allergic," Stella said.

"I am. Tux doesn't understand that."

"But he understands I'm the mean landlady?"

"I didn't say *you* were my landlady." Tux squirmed in my arms, so I put him down. I went to the bathroom and washed my hands thoroughly. "Are we done?" I asked.

"I forgot the litter box. It's upstairs. I'll be right back," Stella said as she trotted up the stairs.

I picked up the base paper, and some ads fell out, along with a piece of paper. I stared down at it. "Stella, we have a problem," I yelled.

CHAPTER 18

Stella and I stared down at the note. "Beware" was scrawled across the plain white sheet of paper. Stella bent to pick it up.

"Don't touch it." I said it so loud that Stella jumped back. I took out my cell phone and snapped a couple of close-ups. Later I'd compare this one to the ones I'd taken at Anna's house. Stella watched me but didn't ask why I was taking the pictures. "I have to call the base security force." I dialed the nonemergency number and gave a brief explanation of what had happened.

"Who's doing this to him?" Stella asked.

I tapped my hand against my thigh. "I don't know. Is there a room we can put Tux in? We don't want him to slip out, and I have a feeling a lot of people are going to be in and out of here in a few minutes."

Stella picked up Tux and carried him to the upstairs bathroom. She murmured to him as she did.

James, one of my favorites on the security force, showed up first. As we explained the note and its possible connection to McQueen, I studied James. His dark brown hair was shorter than he normally wore it, and his cheekbones were more pronounced. He'd been deployed and looked tougher than he had before going overseas. James was now the epitome of a lean, clean, fighting machine. He did a quick walk-through of the house, and then the party really started as the house filled with more security personnel and other base officials.

Thirty minutes later, Scott Pellner and another guy in a suit, whom I recognized as one of the detectives from the EPD, pulled up and joined the already large crowd of security forces personnel milling around. The base had a memorandum of agreement with Ellington, so Ellington helped with some crimes on base. Since this might have something to do with Terry's death, it made sense that Pellner and the detective were here.

Stella and I had been questioned and told to wait in a corner of the living room. I hadn't mentioned I'd snapped a couple of pictures of the note. Neither did Stella. Pellner's eyes widened when he spotted me, and he said something to the detective, who then glanced at us. But they ignored us and went over to talk to James. I could see through the large living room window that a crowd of moms and kids stood out on the sidewalk talking as they tried to figure out what was going on. This time last year I would have been out there with them.

Bubbles's living room doubled as an office. A closed laptop sat on a desk next to some pictures of Bubbles with two kids who looked to be college-age. I wondered if they were his. A shelf above the desk held books about investing and war. Across from the desk was an overstuffed black leather couch. A large flat-screen TV filled a corner. Pictures of different places Bubbles had been stationed hung on the wall above the couch.

Stella's dark green eyes were large as she observed the goings-on. "This is why I don't like to come on base alone."

"This doesn't usually happen," I said.

James came over to us. "How've you been, Sarah?"

"Good. I heard you were off on a four-month deployment."

"I just got back a couple weeks ago."

Things had been a bit awkward between James and me. After my divorce, he'd come around a few times, at first I thought as a friend, but I think he was interested, and CJ hadn't liked it one bit.

"You two can head out. We've got your contact information. I'll walk you through the gauntlet out there so you don't have to answer any questions," James said.

I waved at a couple of women I knew who stood off to one side. They'd been my neighbors before the divorce. One of them, Michelle Murphy, had a teenage daughter who always used to drop by when I still lived on base. I wondered how Lindsay was doing. James opened my car door for me.

"Thanks, James. Take care," I said. My phone was ringing before I'd pulled away from the curb, but I ignored it.

Back at my apartment, I transferred the photos from my phone to my laptop. I studied each one. The white paper the notes were written on looked the same in each photo. But that wasn't helpful since that kind of paper was available anywhere. Some were more smudged than others. The handwriting looked the same. Each note had different wording, but they did contain some of the same letters. I'm sure an expert could look at pressure points and loops to be more precise.

But my uneducated eye told me the same person had written all of them. And from what I remembered of the note Bubbles had showed us the other night, the same person had written that one, too. Now, how to figure out who that person was.

I assumed whoever it was had disguised their handwriting. The words leaned a bit to the left, but not a lot. After studying the pictures a while longer, I realized no answer was going to magically appear. I hoped Anna didn't tell anyone I'd asked about them or taken pictures of them. CJ wouldn't be happy to know I was snooping around, and neither would anyone else. But I was fairly certain that Carol was in more trouble than anyone was saying.

I plopped a bag with two sandwiches from Ken's Deli in Bedford on CJ's desk a little after noon. I always felt like I was cheating on Angelo when I went to other restaurants, but Ken's offered a mean chicken on pita that I knew CJ liked.

CJ opened the bag and spotted the two sandwiches and bag of chips to share, like we'd always done. He looked weary or wary. It was hard to tell which.

"Another attempt to get information out of me," CJ said as he passed me one of the sandwiches. I sat across from him. His desk was back to its ordinary neat state. It made it darn hard to snoop.

"No. An attempt to get you to eat because I know what happens when you have a lot going on. And you have a lot going on." CJ would forget to eat for hours when he was busy. I'd always been the one to make sure he ate.

"Do I?"

"A dead man, mysterious fires, and an art theft. Oh, and Bubbles being threatened. It sounds like a lot to me."

"I heard you found another note," CJ said, as he bit into his sandwich.

I nodded. "Bubbles is out of town, and Stella asked me to go with her to feed the cat."

"Maybe Bubbles should stay out of town for a while."

"I thought the same thing." CJ and I were so often on the same wavelength it frightened me sometimes.

"But Bubbles isn't one to run from trouble, so he'll probably be back," CJ said.

We munched on our lunch for a few minutes. Until recently, everything had been so easy when it came to CJ that it made me question myself. We got along fine—better than fine. For months, CJ had wooed me with flowers, dinners, and day trips. He'd even surprised me last month by whisking me off to the fabulous flea market in Brimfield. He hated going to flea markets and garage sales. The last one he'd been to was on our honeymoon nineteen years ago. Now that I thought about it, our trip to Brimfield was the last time he'd taken me out. I'd been so busy with the community yard sale, I hadn't even noticed.

"What?" CJ asked. "You sighed."

"Life's complicated."

"It doesn't have to be," CJ said.

I wished I'd kept my big mouth shut. I saw a lot more shades of gray than CJ did. He followed rules of law and thought rules like those applied to everyday life.

An officer stuck her head in the door. "Excuse me, Chief, but could you come down the hall for a sec?" She gave me the stink eye. I recognized her as the woman CJ had dog-sat for last spring.

CJ glanced around his office as though he

wanted to make sure nothing important was out for me to see. I guess I wasn't the only one with trust issues. "I'll be right back."

Another officer came in and laid a stack of files on his desk. After he left, I scooted closer, wondering what I could see upside down.

Chanting "I won't look, I won't look," I picked up the trash from our lunch. I walked around the desk to toss the trash in the wastebasket CJ kept in the kneehole under his desk. CJ's computer chirped, announcing that a new e-mail had arrived. This place was a minefield of temptation. I swear I accidentally bumped the mouse, which lit up the screen. Clicking on it was a whole different story, and I chastised myself as I opened the message. It was a timeline of when they thought *Battled* had been stolen. The report surmised the crime had occurred during New England's Largest Yard Sale. At that time, the police force was spread thin with traffic and crowd control and, worse, helping with the fires. The station had all but emptied to battle the blaze at the football field just down from the station.

The report said a silent alarm had been triggered from the library, but by the time anyone had been able to respond, everything had seemed okay. It was written off as a system problem.

I hurriedly clicked the file closed, marked it as unread, and returned to my side of the desk. So someone must have used the fires as a distraction to steal the painting. It made sense that the police would help save the new AstroTurf field.

A lot of the guys had kids on the football team and had put in hours raising the money for the field. The fires created a perfect opportunity for a crime. And now that I thought about it, the library had had a big outdoor book sale that day, so it was probably understaffed indoors. How dare someone use my event to steal *Battled*? It made me even more determined to figure out what was going on. I stood up to leave as CJ came back in. His eyes went from the folders to me.

"I didn't touch them." At least I could say that honestly. "I have to go. Take care of yourself." I considered giving him a peck on the cheek, but he moved around to the back of his desk. Thankfully, the computer screen was dark again.

"Thanks for lunch," CJ said as he sat behind his desk.

The timeline kept circling through my head as I walked to my car. And then I remembered that Nancy had disappeared from the yard sale about the time the fires were burning. My sandwich rolled a little in my stomach.

CHAPTER 19

At home, I sat on my couch, opened my laptop, and started searching for more information about Terry McQueen and his family. His dad had owned a sports agency for thirty years and represented a lot of Boston Celtics, Patriots, Bruins, and Red Sox players. He'd even worked with some of the Revolution pro soccer players before selling the business five years ago.

Terry had run the Boston Marathon more than once and finished with pretty good times. There was an occasional mention of him at charitable events, so even though he'd moved away, he'd stayed a part of the community to some small degree. But there wasn't any mention of him as a camp counselor or anything about the camp. Then I thought of someone who might know something.

* * *

Fifteen minutes later I knocked on Herb Fitch's bright red door. When it opened, I said, "They let me out."

"Yeah, I know," he said through the old wooden screen door. "I followed up. You're Chief Hooker's ex-wife." He stepped out onto the porch, wincing when he moved his left leg.

"Sarah Winston." We shook hands. I was gentle with his arthritic one.

Herb motioned to a couple of Adirondack chairs on the left side of the broad covered porch. He might have jumped the gun by calling the cops on me, but he was sharp enough not to let a stranger into his house.

"I wondered if you saw anything the night McQueen was murdered," I said.

"It was one of the few nights my arthritis medicine actually worked, and I slept well. More's the pity," he said.

It was worth a shot, but not my primary reason for coming. "I heard there used to be a camp for troubled kids in Ellington and that Terry McQueen was a counselor there."

Herb squinted up at the porch ceiling. "I started the program. Tried to keep kids on the straight and narrow. You thinkin' that might have something to do with the murder?"

"It was a thought. That's all."

"It's a pretty good thought. Some of those kids didn't turn out so well. Wonder if anyone over at the Ellington PD thought of it. You tell 'em?"

"Not yet. Nothing really to go on at this point."

"Terry spent a week there himself after his junior year of high school."

"Why?" I asked.

"Record's sealed," Herb said. "He was a juvenile."

I guess that was Herb's way of saying none of my business. "And then he got to be a camp counselor?"

"After he straightened up. He only worked there for a couple of summers while he was in college. I thought at the time it might show those kids you can turn your life around."

"Sounds smart."

"Then he started working for his dad."

"I heard he and his dad had a falling out."

"Yep."

I waited. It took me a minute to realize Herb wasn't going to add anything additional on that topic. "Gennie 'the Jawbreaker' Elder went through there, too."

"Another success story," Herb said. "Too bad the program got swept up into a county program. It was more successful on a local level." Herb pushed himself up out of his chair, so I stood, too. "Might be better for me to mention this theory of yours to the Ellington police."

I nodded. Anything that might take suspicion away from Carol was fine with me. "Thanks for your time."

* * *

I stopped over to see Carol after I left Herb. A class was just finishing up, so I had to wait a few minutes. Carol smiled and joked with the students in the class. After they left, she leaned against the door and shook her head.

"You managed a class after having the place searched."

"I have to keep the business going," she snapped.

"I meant it as a compliment. That couldn't have been easy."

"Oh." Carol pushed herself off the door and started cleaning up. I helped.

"What did they take during the search?"

"Some of my painting supplies. Paint thinners. Turpentine. A couple of tubes of paint. They already had the computer. Not much else around here to take."

I thought about it for a minute. "Everything they took was flammable."

"I thought the same thing."

That didn't sound good. None of what they took seemed like it had anything to do with the murder or the missing painting. I thought about the fires and the incendiary devices. Did they think Carol had some connection to those? For once I didn't say it out loud.

As I got back to the apartment, Stella pulled up.

"You look dejected," she said, climbing out of her car. Her arms were full of bags from a local crafts store. "Come in. I bought some frames for the sheet music I got at the yard sale last weekend. Want to help me?"

"Sure." We set up at Stella's kitchen table and got to work. I took the frames apart and cleaned the glass while Stella assembled the sheet music and put the frames back together.

"What is it with this town?" I asked her after we'd worked for a while. "Either you hear everything or everyone acts like they're guarding matters of national security." Which in actuality, if they worked on the base, they could be.

"What are you trying to find out?"

"McQueen was in trouble in high school and got sent to a camp for troubled teens. He straightened himself out and became a counselor there during the summer while he was in college. During one of those summers, your Aunt Gennie was at that camp with McQueen. After college McQueen worked for his father's sports agency. They had a falling out, Terry moved, and started working for the government." It seemed that plenty of sources of trouble had circled around Terry. His own problems as a juvenile, his work with at-risk kids, and then some kind of conflict with his father.

"And?"

"And . . . I don't know. Maybe it has something to do with why he was murdered."

"Want me to call my mom? Maybe she remembers something."

"I'd be grateful." I hesitated. "Do you remember any of this?"

Stella finished framing the last piece of sheet

music. She pursed her lips as she worked. "Not really," she finally said. "I'm enough younger than Aunt Gennie that we didn't hang out with the same people. My mom wasn't that close to Aunt Nancy or Aunt Gennie. I think it's one of the reasons she moved to Florida." Stella picked up her phone and dialed her mom.

After exchanging pleasantries, Stella put the phone on speaker and filled her in on McQueen's murder. "Didn't Aunt Gennie know Terry?" she asked.

"Know him? She loved that boy. They met at a, uh, summer camp."

"Mom, I know Aunt Gennie got sent there because she was in trouble. She's still trying to protect me from the 'bad' things in life."

"They were an item," Stella's mom said. "Then when Gennie went pro, Terry was her agent. But that didn't last long. Things ended on a bad note. People should listen to that old adage: don't mix business with pleasure."

"What kind of bad note?"

"Let me think," her mom said. "I can't remember. Ask your Aunt Nancy; she'd know." Stella and her mom talked for a few more minutes while I mulled over the fact that Gennie and Terry had more than a business relationship, that he'd been Gennie's agent, and that things ended badly. Was whatever happened between them bad enough that years later it was a motive for murder?

CHAPTER 20

Back in my apartment, I made a salad for
dinner. I grabbed my laptop and searched for
Gennie "the Jawbreaker" Elder. Wikipedia had a
full biography. It mentioned that she'd signed
with the McQueen agency briefly but left them
shortly after her first fight. It had a full list of her
fights and the people she'd beaten. Her first fight
was against a woman named Missy "the Meat"
Tucker. I kept digging and found some dirt.

There were allegations that Gennie threw that
first fight. Missy Tucker vehemently denied it, as
did Gennie. I thought about what Gennie had
said about that photo of her from her first fight.
She never wanted to feel like that again. Maybe
she hadn't been just talking about getting knocked
out. If she'd thrown it, maybe Terry had pres-
sured her into doing so. And maybe his dad
had found out and that's why Terry had left the
agency and Ellington. Unfortunately, all I had
were a lot of maybes and no answers.

I did another search, this time for Missy Tucker. She lived in Concord, and her phone number and address were listed. I called and left a message, saying I'd like to interview her about her career as a fighter. I hoped she'd call back.

I spent most of Friday putting the finishing touches on a garage sale that was going to be held on Saturday. Vicki O'Malley was the second cousin of Nancy and Gennie Elder by marriage. She'd been following my column in the newspaper and had been an enthusiastic supporter of New England's Largest Yard Sale. Vicki hired me to organize and price the items for her sale. While she loved going to garage sales, she knew throwing one was a whole different skill set and a lot of work. She didn't need me on Saturday because she was from a large family who'd come over and help.

Vicki met me in her oversized, two-car garage. "I'm not sure how to price these clothes," Vicki said.

"I usually go ten to twenty-five percent of the original cost, depending on the condition. Thirty to forty if it's a name brand."

"This jacket hasn't ever been worn," she said. She held up a classic black wool blazer from Talbots. The ticket was still on it.

"Do half of the ticket price on that one. It leaves room to haggle but still gets you a good price."

"What are you going to do once the snow sets in and you can't throw garage sales?"

"I'm not sure." It had been on my mind. I couldn't just sit around all winter and do nothing, even with the nice nest egg I'd built up over the summer doing garage sales and with the money the city had paid me. I'd been out of the job market so long as a military wife that my skill set was rusty. And the financial world relied so heavily on technology now that I'd have to take classes to get back up to speed.

"What about estate sales?" she asked.

"That's a whole different field. You have to know a lot more about antiques and jewelry than I do."

"I guess you could learn," she said. "New England's Largest Yard Sale was certainly a boon for the town, although the way Nancy's acting you'd think she thought of it and did all the work herself. But don't worry; everyone in town knows it was all you."

"Thanks. How is Nancy?"

Vicki paused and looked away. "I haven't seen her since the morning of the sale."

Interesting. I'm pretty sure she wasn't telling the truth but couldn't figure out why she'd lie. "She disappeared for a few hours in the middle of it."

"She's a busy lady," Vicki said.

We finished up a few hours later. All Vicki had to do on Saturday morning was throw open the garage and drag one table out.

"Have fun tomorrow," I told her as she paid me. "Tell Nancy I said hi."

Vicki nodded but didn't make eye contact as I left.

Instead of heading home, I decided to take a walk on the Rails to Trails path. I was curious about the fires and wondered if there was anything to see. The parking lot at the start of the path was crowded, but I managed to snag a spot. This must be the after-work rush. An old train caboose, parked in the lot, now served as a snack shack. Across the street, a strategically located bike shop sold gear and bikes, and helped people with flat tires and bent rims.

Old oak and maple trees lined this section of the asphalt path. I remembered that Nancy said the fire had been started near the beginning of the path. But I walked about a half mile, dodging bikers and joggers, before I noticed the burned area off to the right side. Singed grass stretched out in front of me for about twenty feet. Some of the trees beside the path were scorched. An acrid odor still hung in the air.

I looked back down the path. It turned just enough that I couldn't see the parking lot from here. What I did notice was a lot of litter, but that would be taken care of in a couple of days. I snapped some pictures and walked all around the edges of the burned area. I turned into the woods to see if anything was back there. Even with all the people on the path, it was a little creepy with all the overgrowth. After getting scratched by a couple of thorns, I popped back out on the path.

"What are you doing?" Seth called out, startling me.

He jogged up to my side, glistening with sweat. His T-shirt was plastered against the hard muscles of his chest. I tried not to stare or drool.

"Taking a walk."

"In the brambles?"

Darn. I guess he'd seen me leaving the woods. "I was curious about how far back the damage went from the fire. But after getting tangled up with a couple of bushes, I decided I didn't care that much."

"Can you stop by my house this evening? I've moved most of my stuff over to Bedford today. I could really use your help."

I studied him, hoping he really did want my help and not just me. "Okay. I'll come by at seven."

"Great. I'll text you my address." Seth jogged off with a wave.

At seven, I knocked on the door of Seth's little bungalow in Bedford. I was surprised it wasn't grander, considering his family. I pictured him in Revolutionary Ridge in a large house built for entertaining and sporting a three-car garage. This house had a one-car garage, two dormers, and a green front door that stood out from the

white siding and matched the trim. It's the kind
of house I'd want to live in. I looked over the yard
as I waited. It needed a white picket fence, a
puppy, and a couple of Adirondack chairs.

"Like it?" Seth asked from behind me.

I'd been so lost in my daydream, I hadn't
heard the door open.

Seth looked me over. I'd dressed in a black
pantsuit with a silk shirt underneath. My hair sat
in a low bun. I thought if I looked professional, it
would be easier to keep things professional. The
little flips my heart did told me I wasn't immune
to Seth at all. My outfit hadn't helped one bit.

Seth led me into the small living room. His
sleek couch looked out of place in a room with
built-in shelves, alcoves, and a charming brick
fireplace. I whipped out my cell phone and
started making notes. I murmured more to myself
than Seth, "Couch, end tables, lamps, art." Then
I went through the living room, kitchen (updated), and dining room, oohing and ahing over
its built-ins, adding to my list of what needed to
be purchased. I headed to the basement to avoid
the bedrooms.

"This can be your man cave. We'll put up your
Red Sox memorabilia. The couch upstairs will
be perfect down here. The tall table from your
old place can go over in that corner. It's going
to look great." I turned to see why Seth hadn't
said anything. Maybe he didn't like my ideas
and was regretting his decision not to hire a professional decorator.

He smiled at me. "You're cute when you're enthused, tapping out notes and waving your hands around. Thank you."

I tried to squelch back the glow from his compliment but smiled back at him. We went back upstairs. "Ready to see the bedrooms?" Seth asked.

I nodded. I had to get it over with sometime. The desk was already in one of the bedrooms. Seth had it pushed up against the wall.

"Let's reposition this. Do you want to look out the window or toward the door?" I asked.

"It's probably better with my back to the window so I don't get distracted."

I ran out to my Suburban and grabbed some pads to place under the legs of the desk. That way we could glide it across the wooden floor without scratching it or having to lift the desk.

We pushed the desk into position and moved the chair. The office didn't need much else. The other bedroom contained a double bed and a tiny dresser. Not much else would fit.

"Where's your sleigh bed?"

"Up here."

I followed Seth up a narrow flight of stairs that opened into a large master suite. The sleigh bed sat at the far end, and an oak tall boy stood against one wall. "Be professional," I muttered.

"The bathroom's over here," Seth said.

Someone had done a beautiful job updating the bath. A large, glassed-in shower had multiple shower heads. A free-standing soaking tub sat next to a window. I took a deep breath and tried to stop envisioning all the wonderful, fun things that could happen up here. "It's great." I scampered back down the steps as though I was a squirrel and a fox was chasing me.

"Do you have any paper?" I asked Seth when he came down.

"Hang on. There's some in the office." He came back with a plain white sheet of paper. It reminded me of the notes Bubbles had gotten. I shook myself. Everyone had this kind of computer paper. I took the sheet over to the counter in the kitchen and started sketching.

"You could do a great little reading nook in the space opposite your bed. A couple of great chairs, shelves full of books, a bench by the window." I sighed, picturing it in my head. "Oh, and a couple of great rugs. Old and soft. What do you think?" I handed Seth my sketch.

He shook his head. I should have known. He'd want something more sophisticated. I felt foolish.

"It's amazing," he said. "You got it just right." He ducked behind me, trailing a finger across my lower back. He opened the refrigerator and pulled out a bottle of champagne.

"I have to go," I said, listening to my head and ignoring my heart yet again. I kept turning down Seth's overtures but didn't completely understand why. Maybe it was because of the way our relationship had started—as a one-night stand.

I so wasn't that person. I wanted to be sure Seth knew it, but I guess he must by now.

"It's my first night here. Just one drink to celebrate our partnership?"

Part of me wanted to run screaming. "Be professional." I muttered to myself, again.

"What?" Seth asked.

I blushed and gave in. "Nothing. Just one drink."

CHAPTER 21

I woke up early the next morning, in my own bed, alone and happy I'd indulged in only one glass of champagne and one heart-stopping kiss. There were many temptations when it came to Seth and his sleigh bed. I grabbed my computer and downloaded the pictures I'd taken by the Rails to Trails path. As I blew them up, I noticed a scrap of fabric clinging to one of the bushes. I zoomed in. It looked like a piece of camouflage from a BDU.

It didn't mean someone from the military had started the fires, although it was true that someone from the military might have the skills to make an incendiary device. This bit of fabric didn't look like the latest iteration of a BDU. The military constantly updated the pattern and material to make troops as safe as possible. Anyone shopping at the base thrift shop or a military surplus store could own this. It also didn't rule out someone in the military because lots of people could easily have clothing made of this fabric. I'd have to show it to CJ just in case he didn't know. However, it was unlikely he'd be at the station at 5:30 on a Saturday morning.

I popped out of bed, showered, ate a couple of Fig Newtons (invented in and named for the town of Newton, Massachusetts). I was nothing if not loyal to the products of my adopted home state of Massachusetts, whenever possible. That philosophy gave me an excuse to eat fluffernutter sandwiches, Boston cream pie, Parker House rolls, and chocolate chip cookies without guilt. Patronizing Dunkin' Donuts also fell under that same category since the first one had opened in Massachusetts.

Even though I'd grown up in California, something about New England just felt like home. My parents wanted me to move back after my divorce, but I just couldn't do that. My mother had recently discovered her ancestors had landed in Hingham, Massachusetts, in the 1630s. Maybe that was why New England felt like home to me: the place was in my genes.

I trotted down the stairs and grabbed a newspaper off the front porch. I took it back up, grabbed my computer, and searched "garage sales." I studied the listings in both to find the ones that sounded the best. It was the first Saturday I hadn't had to run one in a very long time. The thrill of the hunt got my heart zinging with anticipation. Even better, I was spending Seth's money and not mine. This was almost my perfect scenario. Perfect would be my own money and the space to fill it with whatever I found.

I charted a route that wended its way through Ellington, Bedford, and Concord. It was always hard to decide which sale to hit first. Fortunately, this morning a lot of them had different starting times. Many sales listed antiques, but that term was thrown around a lot when stuff was actually only vintage or old, or when someone decided to call a fifteen-year-old Beanie Baby an antique. In the trade, anything over one hundred years old was an antique, fifty to one hundred was vintage, and everything else was just old. Some people used the word *vintage* to refer to things that came from a specific era.

I hit an ATM to get cash before I headed over to Bedford, my first stop. Even though the person throwing the garage sale should have plenty of change, I wanted to have my own in case someone didn't. At a garage sale, cash was required. Often, estate sales or auctions were set up so people could use credit cards, but I'd yet to see a garage sale that was. At 6:55, I pulled up to a house with the most promising ad. People already milled about as the owners pulled stuff out of their garage onto the drive. I joined the throng.

A carved oak end table caught my eye. It had two shelves, and the top was about a twelve-inch square. The scale was perfect for Seth's living room. It looked handmade. I turned it over to check for markings but didn't find any. That didn't bother me. I didn't care if things were labeled or signed; tramp art often wasn't and yet could be valuable, although finding pieces by Stickley or Hitchcock was always a thrill.

I carried the table with me to another piece I spotted: a comfy-looking chair that would fit perfectly next to Seth's fireplace. The chair would have to be reupholstered—I didn't think Seth would like the pink cabbage roses on the fabric—but if the price was right, the size was perfect. I plopped down in the chair, and it was as comfortable as it looked. I tried to get the attention of one of the people working the sale; the chair was too large for me to carry, and I didn't want to lose out by leaving it to another avid shopper.

I couldn't find a price on either piece, which worried me. It meant one of two things: either they wanted too much and I'd have to walk away when I really didn't want to, or they didn't know the value, which would work in my favor.

A woman came over and we began to haggle. She tossed out a price of $75 for the table and $150 for the chair. We went back and forth; I pointed out that the table wasn't signed, and she pointed out that the chair was stuffed with down. We finally agreed on $25 for the table and $75 for the chair. I felt good about the table and so-so about the chair. In the end, both pieces were worth more than I paid for them, so overall I was happy.

The woman's son, a teenage grumpy Gus, grudgingly helped me carry the chair and shove it into the back of the Suburban. Later today, I'd drop it off at an upholstery shop I liked in Ellington. I loaded the table, thanked the kid, and took off. The next two sales were a bust; either I was too late or their idea of antiques consisted of some old, plastic dinnerware and clothes from the eighties.

I had a heck of a time finding the next place on my list. It was on the far outskirts of Concord, and I passed the hidden driveway three times before I saw it and turned in. They needed balloons by the entrance and bright signs far enough from the turn so people could find it without zooming past and having to circle back around. No one else was even at the sale. Their loss was my gain, I hoped.

I headed to the furniture first because it was what Seth needed most. The owner had two large walnut wardrobes, both in excellent condition but too big for Seth's place. I ran my hand across the smooth walnut with a sigh. Too big for my place, too. I checked out a mahogany dresser. The veneer on the top curled up, which I could fix, but even from a distance the piece smelled musty, so much so that I didn't think putting charcoal in the drawers would clear up the odor.

I drifted over to the tables loaded with smaller

items. I enjoyed digging through a box full of
artwork, turning over the odd, lone spoon to see
if it was silver, and sorting through a box of
paperbacks to see if there was a book for me.
Before long, I'd purchased three old framed
maps, two lamps, and a dining room table that
folded to a size small enough to work behind a
sofa and that expanded to seat ten. It came with
four chairs, enough for now. I was tempted to
keep it for myself.

As I shut the back of the Suburban, I turned to
the homeowner. "You really need some signs out
on the side of the road. And some balloons on
your mailbox. I drove by three times before I
found the drive."

"Kids," the woman yelled, "get your poster
board and markers. Thanks," she said. "I wondered why things were so slow. My friend told me
all I had to do was put an ad on Craigslist and
I'd be swamped."

The back of the Suburban was pretty full, but I
decided to make one more stop at a house in
Concord since I was already out here. This sale
was well marked and crowded. I sorted through
a rack full of clothing, which wouldn't do anything for Seth but might do something for me.
All of the pieces were clean, fairly new, and, best
of all, cheap.

"I can't believe Terry McQueen's dead," a
woman said.

At first, I thought she was talking to me, but she looked at a woman beside her.

"I'm worried he was the brains in the investment business he owned with Dave Jackson."

My ears perked up faster than a dog's who heard a whistle.

"That's not what I heard. My husband says Dave's the genius and Terry just crunched numbers." Her friend carried a large decorative mirror in her arms. "Did you hear that Anna McQueen has already moved off base?"

"So soon? Did they kick her off?"

"No. She could have stayed for a year. I wonder why she left and where she went."

I wondered the same thing. The two drifted off to look at a Little Tykes playhouse. Maybe Anna's house was so bare because she was packing. But I hadn't seen any moving boxes. I'd have to get hold of Laura and see what she knew. I started to leave but spotted a rug rolled up off to one side of the garage.

I went over to where it leaned against a wall. I could only see the very end, but the colors were variations of navy and red. I pressed my nose to it to see if it smelled.

"It's from a smoke-free, pet-free home," a man said.

"Will you help me unroll it?" I asked. "How big is it?"

"Eight by eleven." He set it on the ground, and we unrolled it. There was a small hole in one corner, but the pattern was lovely. We flipped it over so I could look at the backing. He said it came from a pet-free home, but I wanted to make sure there weren't any stains on the back. Trust but verify.

It looked good to me.

"Its sister rug is in the garage. Same colors, slightly different pattern, slightly smaller."

We dragged that one out, too, and negotiated the price for both. One would work in Seth's living room and one in the dining room. They'd look good together but wouldn't be too much of a match.

"What about that love seat in the garage?" I asked. "Are you getting rid of that too?" A neutral cream with a tufted back, it was just the right size for Seth's living room and would go well with the cabbage-rose chair once it was reupholstered.

The man nodded and gave me a good price. With all of that stuffed in the back of my Suburban, I headed over to Seth's. He'd given me a key last night—not a "you can move in key," but one that I could use for unloading things as I found them. I knew I'd need help with all of this and hoped I'd catch him at home.

A brand-new, black, sporty-looking convertible was parked at the curb. I thought about going on by but really didn't want to haul this stuff all over town. And who knows, maybe the car wasn't even at his house. I rang the bell, not wanting to use the key unless I had to. A woman opened the door. Good heavens, she was stunning—all high cheekbones, round sapphire eyes, and long lashes that must not be real. I couldn't take my eyes off her.

I realized she was the Victoria's Secret model who'd been hanging on Seth in the picture from the newspaper. She was so thin her leggings were baggy. Her oversized sweater made her look like a waif in borrowed clothes.

"Can I help you?" she asked. Her glossed lips were so full it looked like they might burst at any moment.

Her voice was kind of high and squeaky. It ruined the whole effect, so I managed to close my mouth. I'd been expecting some husky "will you go to bed with me" voice. Well, this felt awkward, another woman asking *me* if I needed help at Seth's house. I could ask the same of her.

"Is Seth here?" I didn't know Seth all that well. Maybe he handed out keys to every woman he knew.

She looked me over and dismissed me with her eyes. I didn't look that bad, did I? I glanced down and noticed some dirt on my pink, scooped-neck top and a bit on my jeans, too. Garage sales weren't necessarily the cleanest places in the world, especially when I was always sticking my nose in drawers, and on rugs and upholstery to make sure they didn't smell. I wiped my hands on my jeans.

"I'm Sarah. I have some furniture for Seth."

She glanced over at my Suburban and grimaced. "I'll get him." She closed the door in my face.

CHAPTER 22

I stared at the door, trying to decide what to do next. Part of me wanted to hightail it out of there, clean up, and come back the best version of myself. But another part wanted to let her know I wasn't that easily dismissed. I got out the key Seth had given me. I was about to unlock the door when Seth swung it open.

"Sarah," Seth said. "Come in. This is Barbie."

Of course, I'd heard of her before. Her last name was Doll; her mom had named her Barbie. If names were destinies, hers certainly worked.

Barbie spotted the key in my hand and attached herself to Seth, clinging like a grape to a vine. Wow, this was uncomfortable. Seth detached her.

"Sarah's a friend of mine," he said to Barbie. "She's decorating the place." He didn't seem uncomfortable at all. "I was hooking up the TV downstairs when Barbie showed up."

It seemed like an explanation and apology all

at once. From the pout on Barbie's face, she picked up on it, too, or maybe her lips were going to blow. I took a step back.

"I have to go," Barbie said. She tried to kiss Seth on the mouth, but he turned, and all she got was a bit of cheek. Barbie flounced out, glancing back once before taking off in her convertible.

Seth turned to look at me. "Sorry about that. I didn't expect Barbie to show up. I didn't think she'd ever leave Boston to come out to what she considers the country."

"No apologies necessary. It's not like I think I'm your only friend." Maybe I put a little too much emphasis on the word *friend*, and maybe I was more jealous than I realized.

"I'd be happy if you were my only friend," Seth said.

I wasn't fishing, was I? I pointed to Seth's cheek. "You have a bit of gunk on your cheek." Pink gloss was smeared across his cheek where Barbie's lips had landed.

He swiped the back of his hand across it. "Did I get it?"

I nodded. Seth ran his finger down the length of my nose, creating a shiver through my body. "You have a bit of something left over from your shopping expedition today." He held up his finger, and there was dust on it.

Disturbed by his touch, all I could do was change the subject. "Let's unload my Suburban and see if you like what I found."

An hour later, the rugs were down and the dining room set arranged, and we'd hung the old maps in his office. The living room looked bare with only the love seat, oak table, and rug, but I envisioned what it would eventually look like and smiled.

"I saw another chair in the back of your Suburban. Is that for me?" Seth asked. He tried to sound casual but sounded worried.

"Yes. I thought the pink cabbage roses would really add a pop of color to the room. Let's go haul it in."

Seth paled. "O-k-a-y." He drew the word out to four syllables.

I laughed. "It is for you, but I'll get it reupholstered. Unless you really like the roses."

Seth looked so relieved I laughed again as I headed out.

"Scaring your client with cabbage roses isn't funny. What goes around . . ." Seth leaned against the doorjamb.

"Never threaten your decorator," I called over my shoulder as I climbed into my car.

When I made it home, I ate a quick sandwich for lunch. Even though it was only eleven, I felt like it was much later. That happened to me every time I got up at 5:30. I called Laura to ask about Anna.

"I heard Anna McQueen moved. Where'd she go?" I asked.

"She *moved?*"

I don't know which of us was more astonished—me that I knew something before Laura for the second time in a week, or Laura because something interesting had happened on base and she'd didn't know.

"I was at a garage sale in Concord and overheard two women talking about it. Did she have to move?"

"No. She could have stayed on base."

"Do you know where she's from?"

"No. But I don't think she'd move far because of the CPA exam. Did you ever make it over to her house?"

"I did. She wasn't into decorating from the looks of things."

"I guess that's because she was packing up to move."

"Let me know if you hear anything about where she went," I said. "I'd like to check on her again." Anna's house didn't look like it was in the middle of a move to me. It just looked empty. Puzzling.

"What are you doing this morning?" Laura asked.

I'd been thinking of that long bath I'd been planning to take for several days. "Nothing important."

"Why don't you come over to the thrift shop with me for a while? We're short of help, and you can meet Beverly, the new manager."

I agreed and met Laura at the thrift shop thirty minutes later.

Beverly was working in the office when we entered. Jewelry was spread out all over her desk. Some of it looked expensive. She was a plump, affable-looking woman. Her gray hair floated around her ears like a cumulus cloud.

"Nice to finally meet you," Beverly said as she shook my hand. "I've heard a lot about you."

I hoped it wasn't all the affair and divorce stuff but let it go. "Do you want me to work in the sorting room?" I asked. Even though you came across some disgusting stuff while sorting, I still enjoyed doing it. You never knew what you'd find next to some old, stained T-shirt.

"Follow me," Beverly said.

"Do you need to lock the office?" I asked as we went out, gesturing to the jewelry.

"It's just costume pieces. I'm sorting what's good enough to put out."

Laura went off to run the register as I followed Beverly to the sorting room.

"Ta-da," Beverly said, beaming.

I turned in amazement. "There's nothing to sort," I said. I remembered Laura telling me the sorting room was no longer a death trap, but this was astonishing. Clothes hung on hangers in neat rows by size. A shelf held an assortment of higher-end purses, or pocketbooks, as they called them in Massachusetts. There was a red Michael Kors purse that caught my eye. I had a thing for red purses. A set of Wedgewood china and Waterford crystal sat above it on the higher shelves. On the floor, several Longaberger baskets were stacked next to a pile of clothes with the tags still on them.

"Wow. That's a nice haul," I said. This was a far cry from the jumbled mess the sorting room used to be. Laura had done well when she'd hired Beverly.

"A retired general's wife is downsizing and brought us half her household."

"Do you want me to put it out?" I asked.

Beverly shook her head. "I sell the high-end stuff on eBay. I get a better price. More profits for the shop. I've already photographed all of this and will put it up on the site as soon as I have time."

It was a good idea and would reach a broader audience than just the people who had access to the base. "Do you want me to empty the shed?" There was a shed outside that was always packed with stuff people dropped off when the shop was closed.

Beverly flashed her broad smile. "It's empty. Would you mind dusting the glassware?"

Ugh. I hated cleaning. But I gamely grabbed a dust cloth.

"You forgot your blue apron," Beverly reminded me as I headed from the sorting room to the shop. "We want to make sure our shoppers know who our workers are."

I went to the hall tree all the bib aprons hung on and grabbed one. The name tag said Josie. It had always been a joke to wear an apron with someone else's name on it.

"We don't do that anymore," Beverly said when she saw my apron. "I didn't think it was honest."

Apparently Beverly had amazing organizing skills but no sense of humor. I put Josie's apron back and found one without a name tag. Beverly nodded her approval and left.

I stopped by the register. "What's with all the rules?" I asked Laura.

"I know. She's a bit of a stickler, but look at this place."

Stick-in-the-mud seemed more appropriate. The store looked great, although there was less stock than there'd been in the past. I dusted and polished for an hour until the glassware sparkled as brightly as it would at any fancy department store.

Beverly came out and told Laura she was leaving.

"Thanks for your help today," she said to me.

"You're welcome." After she left, I turned to Laura. "Why's she leaving early?" The shop wouldn't close for another hour.

"It's in our agreement. She lives out in Groton and has to pick her kids up from some activity. Then she heads to a second job running some other shop." Laura glanced around. "I think her husband's a schmuck. She hasn't said a lot, but it sounds like he finds it hard to keep a job or pick up the kids."

I stayed until closing, chatting with people who came in and helping them find things.

"Do you have any Longaberger baskets?" one woman asked.

"We do, but Beverly, the new manager, is going to put them up on eBay. You can watch the thrift shop page. I'm sure she'll have it up in the next couple of days."

"Great, thanks," she said before moving on.

After closing, Laura and I lingered beside our cars for a few minutes. The sun peeked out between the clouds that were flying across the sky.

"Beverly's a whiz," I said. "The shop looks great."

"It does. But part of me misses the old shop. The chaos seemed to be half the fun."

"Oh, thank heaven. I thought the same thing."

Laura left. I checked my phone for messages. Nothing—not that I was expecting any. As I pulled out, I glanced over at the shed. Someone had left a couple of boxes and two black garbage bags outside next to it. I put my car back in park and headed over.

I opened the shed to put the bags in. It was stuffed to the gills. I was sure Beverly had said it was empty. I guess she was some kind of control freak and had to do it all herself. At least that's what I wanted to believe, but a little voice in my head wondered if that was true. I shook myself. Yeesh, I was starting to see a conspiracy wherever I went. After shoving the boxes and bags in the shed, I climbed back into my Suburban.

Back in Ellington, I stopped at the upholstery

shop and dropped off the chair I'd found for Seth. After looking through fabric swaths, I picked a buttery, brown leather to have it recovered in. It was sturdy and wouldn't show much wear. Then I headed to the grocery store before heading home. I hoped I'd finally have a long soak in the tub. After stashing my groceries, I filled my tub with water. It was one of those elaborate, deep, claw-foot tubs—an original. It's probably what sold me on taking the apartment—that and the cheap rent.

After luxuriating in the bath so long my skin went pruney, I ate a light supper. By nine-thirty, I sat in my robe on my couch. Seth had a work thing tonight. He'd invited me, but as usual I'd said no. Now I wondered why. Saturday nights felt lonely. I flipped on the TV and found the Red Sox game. But instead of sitting around moping, I decided to get back to work, pricing things from Gennie's house.

I started with eBay, typing in descriptions. Some things I found prices for, and some items I'd have to explore further. I came across a couple of virtual garage sale sites that piqued my interest. There weren't any in the Ellington area. This kind of site was different from eBay because all the trades were done locally, without shipping or postage. Someone would post a picture of an item they wanted to sell. Another member of the group would say they wanted it. They'd arrange a place to meet to make the exchange. I wondered if I could set one up for this area and, if I did, how I could turn it into a money-making business for the winter months.

I decided to find the thrift shop's eBay store and check the price of the red Michael Kors purse. Maybe it was in my meager price range. Beverly had a lot of stuff up, and I paged through it, passing the Wedgewood china set and the Waterford. I didn't find the Michael Kors purse but did see some of the other handbags. Darn, she must not have posted it yet, because an auction for it wouldn't be over so soon. I'd have to come back later. After working on Gennie's stuff for another hour, I was tuckered out and decided to go to bed. I did one more check of the thrift shop's eBay page, but no red purse.

CHAPTER 23

On Sunday morning, I bounded down the stairs and knocked on Stella's door. She opened it, and we looked at each other's outfits. Yoga pants, zip-up hoodies, and T-shirts.

"I can drive," I said.

"I hope you don't mind, but Dave is coming to pick us up. When I told him we were helping with a cleanup of the Rails to Trails path, he wanted to come along."

"He's back in town?"

"I guess CJ wanted him to stay away after the last note, but Dave said he had work to do here."

"I don't want to be a third wheel. I can meet you over there."

"You won't be. Ride with us."

Stella and I went outside. It was cool, and gray clouds moved across the sky as though they were on a mission. This had turned into one windy week. I fished in my pocket for an elastic band and put my hair in a ponytail. A few minutes later, Bubbles chugged around the corner in his truck. He'd finally washed it, but it wasn't much of an improvement.

"Thanks for letting me tag along," he said, after giving Stella a quick kiss. "I've been working so many hours now that Terry's gone, I could use the fresh air."

"How's the business going now that you're on your own?" I asked.

"I'm getting behind."

"Sarah used to work at a financial-planning company. Maybe she could help," Stella said.

"You did?" Bubbles asked. "Are you licensed? I could really use someone right now."

"I only had licenses to sell insurance and mutual funds, but I let them lapse years ago. I used to enter trades and answer the phones for the most part."

"I need someone who's licensed. Any chance you want to retake the tests?"

"Heavens no. It was bad enough the first time." I shook my head. "I like doing the garage sales."

"What will you do over the winter when it's too cold?" Stella asked.

"I'm not sure yet." Thinking about it gave me the jitters. "Have you gotten any more notes, Bubbles?"

Bubbles glanced nervously at us. "No. But someone left a voice mail on my home phone. It wasn't pleasant."

"Oh, no. What did CJ say?"

"He said he'd try to run a trace on it, but with

all the burner phones out there, he didn't have much hope of finding a solid lead."

I hoped the call would help the investigation.

We parked at the bike shop by the start of the path. A good crowd had turned out, even with the cool weather. Our assigned section was down the path, near where it met the town of Bedford's part of the trail. Bubbles slowed when we got to the burned area.

"I heard about these fires," he said, shaking his head.

"Nancy was so freaked out over the whole thing, she wanted to hold me responsible if the football field was damaged because it happened during the community yard sale."

"That's crazy," Bubbles said. Then he looked at Stella. "I know she's your aunt, but that isn't right."

"My aunt can be a pain," Stella said.

"She disappeared in the middle of the day during the yard sale," I said. "Any idea where she'd go?" Nancy and Stella were so different, I often forgot they were related.

"Not a clue," she said. "Is it important?"

"Probably not," I answered.

We arrived at the section we were supposed to clean. I took one side of the path, while Bubbles and Stella took the other. It wasn't hard work, but the amount of stuff people left behind astounded me. I picked up everything from cigarette butts to Band-Aids to water bottles. As we neared the end of our portion of the path, I spotted Seth walking toward us with a bag slung over his shoulder. Oh, no. I didn't want to introduce him to Stella and Bubbles. He hadn't spotted me yet. I turned, trying to decide whether to dodge into the woods or not.

Stella looked at me in alarm when she noticed my panic. I jerked my head toward Seth. Stella shook her head at me like I'd lost my mind. Seth looked up and smiled. It was too late to run.

I introduced Seth to Bubbles and Stella, hoping Bubbles didn't catch on to my discomfort. After everyone shook hands, I said to Seth, "It looks like you finished up your section. We aren't quite done. Nice seeing you."

"We're done with our side," Stella said. A mischievous look put a sparkle in her green eyes that spelled trouble for me.

"I'll stay and help you finish up," Seth said. He looked around. There wasn't a piece of trash in sight.

"I wanted to go closer to the trees on the way back. Make sure I didn't miss anything. I don't want to hold you up."

"You aren't. I blocked out my morning to help with the cleanup."

Of course you did. Then I smiled. What the heck? I enjoyed Seth's company, and it wasn't like we were doing anything we shouldn't.

"We'll start back," Stella said. Everyone shook hands again and said their nice meeting you's.

"I'll be right behind you," I said before walking over to the trees with another of the garbage bags they'd handed out for the jobs. The ones we'd already filled dotted the path. Someone with a golf cart would pick them up later in the morning.

Seth and I strolled along. I did find more garbage and was relieved that I didn't look like a complete idiot. My phone rang. It was Stella.

"Dave had something come up. Can you catch a ride with Mr. Most Eligible?"

"I'll be right there," I could sprint the couple miles back to the car—in my dreams, anyway.

"Is something the matter?" Seth asked.

"We don't have time to wait," Stella said. She sounded all too satisfied with herself. "Sorry." She disconnected.

I stared at my phone. I didn't realize she'd added matchmaker to her resume.

"What is it?" Seth asked.

"Dave and Stella had to take off. Suddenly."

"Great." Seth glanced at his watch. "It's only ten-thirty. We can go out for breakfast. How about Helen's in Concord?"

Everyone loves breakfast at Helen's. People I knew ate there all the time. They'd see me with Seth. I paused and looked up at Seth. He looked hopeful. Maybe it was time to get over the "hiding Seth" phase of my life.

"Never mind," Seth said, watching my face. "It looked like you were going to say yes, but I'll save that yes for something better than Helen's. I know this great hole-in-the-wall where no one will see us together. And they have exceptional French toast."

Twenty minutes later, Seth pulled into his garage. He shut the garage door with the automatic opener before I got out.

"This isn't exactly a hole-in-the-wall," I said as I climbed out.

"But no one can see you." Seth grinned. "And I have you all to myself."

I read the *Globe* while he cooked. Thirty minutes later, Seth put French toast, strawberries, and mimosas on the table. We ate and chatted.

"Anything new on the McQueen murder?" I asked.

"Nothing to share," he answered.

"You said you were looking at some other angles. Anything interesting?"

"Things are always interesting in a case like this."

"So you aren't looking at my friend Carol anymore?"

"I'm not discussing this anymore."

I sighed. "I give up."

"Good," Seth said. Then he leaned over and kissed me in a way that made me almost forget who I was.

Seth dropped me off an hour later. Bubbles's truck was parked in front of Stella's house. Something came up, my foot, I thought. There was only one thing I could think of that was up that would make them leave in such a hurry. As I climbed the stairs to my apartment, I heard Stella singing. It put a little pep in my step.

After a quick shower, I crawled into the storage area under the eaves and pulled out the square-backed chair I'd found on the curb in New Hampshire. I tugged the cushion off and removed the ripped fabric that covered it. I ducked back into the storage space and dragged out a box that held assorted fabrics. Most of the stash was vintage forties material I'd bought at garage sales. But a forties fabric didn't go with the colonial feel of this chair.

I finally found a piece of blue-and-white toile. Perfect. I laid it over the cushion and cut it to the right size. I folded the fabric and used a staple gun to keep it in place. When I was done, I popped the cushion back into the chair and put the chair in the corner of my bedroom. It went well with my blue-and-white duvet cover, white curtains, and the dresser I'd painted white. As I admired my work, the phone rang.

"This is Missy Tucker."

The woman who'd beaten Gennie in her first fight. I'd begun to think she wasn't going to call me back.

"You wanted to interview me?" she asked. "I'm out of town until late Wednesday night."

I felt a little guilty because she sounded so excited. I'd left her with the impression I worked for the newspaper and wanted to interview her about her career. She probably wouldn't think a column on garage sales would count as working for the paper. We agreed to meet at her home in Concord on Thursday morning at ten.

Sunday night around eight, I checked eBay again for the red Michael Kors purse. It wasn't on the thrift shop eBay page yet. I realized it probably wasn't the only red Michael Kors purse out there. So I typed it into eBay's search engine. "Red Michael Kors purse" had 800 entries. I narrowed it down by typing in "shoulder bag." I flipped through them and clicked on the one that looked like the one at the thrift shop. It had a "see more at my store" link.

I clicked it, and it took me to Groton Goods. There in all of its full-colored glory was the jewelry I'd seen on Beverly's desk at the thrift shop.

CHAPTER 24

I gasped as I studied the jewelry on the page. Although Beverly had told me it was costume, the prices and descriptions said she'd lied. The store had high ratings and reviews. I called Laura and filled her in. I waited while she pulled up the store on eBay and began cursing.

"Also, I told Beverly I'd clean out the shed, but she told me it was empty. As I left, I noticed some stuff outside. I decided to put it in the shed, and it was almost full."

Laura huffed in disbelief. We agreed I'd pick her up and we'd go through the shed together. Twenty-five minutes later, we dragged some of the bags from the storage shed into the sorting room of the thrift shop. The first few bags we opened held an assortment of household goods— all unremarkable, but in good enough condition to sell at the shop. And blessedly clean.

"These are the bags that were left out that I stuffed in the shed before I left yesterday."

The next bags were full of nasty clothes that needed to go to Goodwill, where they could be shredded and recycled. Laura and I exchanged a mystified look.

"Maybe we're wrong," Laura said. "When Beverly told you the shed was empty, she knew it was just this junk."

"I hope so. But I'm sure it was the same Michael Kors purse, and the jewelry looked like what was on her desk."

We opened several more bags of the same.

"I'm going back out to the shed," I said. I hefted a bunch of the bags out the door. I cleared enough space so I could drag out the bottom bags in the very back corners. After hauling the bags in, we unpacked them. I pulled out more old clothes.

"She's just storing the old stained stuff until we can get it to Goodwill," Laura said.

I kept digging through my bag. Halfway down, I pulled out a beautiful quilt, then another and another. "These are hand-stitched," I said to Laura, holding one up so she could see the tiny stitches. They were neat but had too much variation to have been done by a machine. "And to my eye, they're from the thirties or older." I shook one out. "This one is made from old feed bags." Feed bags used to be made of colorful cotton fabric on the front and burlap on the back. During the Depression, when little was wasted, women cut out the usable bits of fabric and sewed them into their quilts.

The next bag was full of old dolls, some china

or bisque, a couple of Shirley Temple dolls in their original boxes. A few of the dolls looked unremarkable but must have some value given that they were in with the others. Another bag was full of designer clothes and purses in excellent condition.

"That witch," Laura said. "When she asked if she could sell the higher-quality items on eBay, I told her only if it never left the store. It's supposed to be boxed and sealed for shipping here. Then we have UPS come pick it up—just to make sure this very thing doesn't happen."

"Beverly told me wearing an apron without my own name tag wasn't honest. She has a very warped sense of morality."

"I can't believe she'd steal from us. She's taking money from the people we donate to for herself. Let's drive out to her house right now and have her arrested."

"Tempting as that idea is, we don't have a lot of proof."

"What about the purse? And the jewelry?" Laura asked. She was as close to stomping her foot as I'd ever seen her. Usually it was hard to ruffle Laura's feathers.

"There's a chance she has another purse like it and I'm wrong about the jewelry."

"So we're just going to let her get away with it?"

"No. We just need to set up a sting."

Laura beamed. "Count me in. But how?"

"We'll call the base security forces and see how they can help us."

I decided to call James, since I knew him best. We met him down at the squadron headquarters. Laura ended up calling her husband. He met us there along with the new commander of the security forces. We came up with a plan to put some wireless security cameras in and around the shed and sorting room and to plant tiny GPS tracking devices on a few of the items from the bags.

Laura and I went back to the shop. James installed the cameras while another guy attached the GPS devices. We inventoried and photographed every single item from the bags. Laura, a couple of the security officers, and I would monitor the Groton Goods store just in case she somehow got these things off the base without us realizing. By the end of the evening, Laura was smiling again and almost rubbing her hands together with glee. I dropped her back at her house.

"And now we wait," Laura said as she climbed out of my car.

I pulled up in front of my apartment after a quick trip to Dunkin's for coffee Monday morning at nine. Across the town common, I saw a police car in front of Carol's store. Oh, no. I hoped nothing else had happened. I raced over and arrived, panting, as Carol came out of the store with Pellner. Both were grim-faced. Carol locked the store before turning to me. Pellner gripped her arm and led her to the police car.

"What's going on?" I asked.

"Nothing you need to worry about," Pellner said.

"They're arresting me for McQueen's murder," Carol said as Pellner gently pushed her into the backseat. "They think I killed Terry and stole *Battled.*"

I tried to wedge myself between Pellner and Carol, but he turned and blocked me.

"I have a group coming in at ten. Call Olivia; maybe the two of you can run the class."

"Of course," I said. "Pellner, this is crazy." He slammed the door, shutting Carol in. "She doesn't even know him."

"Butt out," Pellner told me as he climbed in the car.

Small clumps of people watched from various spots on the town common and sidewalk. "I'll call Vincenzo," I shouted to Carol. "And Brad." She nodded. Tears rolled down her face. As they drove off, I searched in my purse for Vincenzo's number. Fortunately, I still had the card he'd given me. His secretary put me through to him right away.

"I'll be at the station in a few minutes," he assured me.

"Can't you file charges against them? They humiliated her in the middle of town." I glanced at the small crowds stopped on the common and on the sidewalk.

"I'm guessing that might have been better for her than in front of her children."

He was right, of course. It calmed a little of the fire burning through me.

"And they did it early enough in the day that she should still be able to be arraigned. They could have picked her up on a Friday afternoon. Then she'd have sat in jail all weekend before she saw a judge. If indeed they charge her. They might be trying to scare information out of her."

"I'll meet you there," I said.

"There's no need. They have nothing. I'll have her out before you know it."

He said it with such confidence. He'd had tougher cases and defendants than Carol to deal with.

"Let her husband know what's going on. See if he needs anything."

I hung up and dialed Brad. It's not the kind of call you want to make to a friend. It's the kind of call you had to make.

My conversation with Brad was brief. I'd barely gotten the words out when he hung up to head to the EPD. I wondered what had happened to the other angles both Seth and CJ had mentioned. And why they thought there was a connection between Terry and Carol. Next I called Olivia. She agreed to meet me, and we decided that between the two of us we could run the class.

By the time Olivia arrived, I'd set up all the easels and put out the painting supplies. Carol had already set up the picture the group had chosen to paint, a modern-looking tree. Olivia thought she could handle the instructions and even seemed excited about doing so.

"I'm going to go clean up the storage area while we wait," Olivia said. "I promised Carol I'd do it. I really feel bad for her."

"Because you've been in trouble before?" I asked.

"Because I know how it feels to be accused of doing something you didn't do." She wheeled around and hurried to the back.

I followed her even though her body language clearly said "leave me alone."

"How's Jett?"

Olivia sighed and got a dreamy look on her face. "He's my soul mate."

I wanted to laugh or to warn her. It's exactly what I'd thought when I'd met CJ, and I was probably a few years younger than her at the time. I no longer believed in soul mates, but maybe I could at least get her thinking about life. "Why do you think that?" I kept my voice light and friendly.

Olivia moved around Paint and Wine's small back storage space. She shoved the boxes of frames Carol had bought at the yard sale to one side, along with a couple of easels. A smile spread across her face as she started putting tubes of paint away. "He's a great kisser."

CJ had been, too.

"He has a lot of cars. Hot, fast cars," Olivia said. "And he's a real good driver."

CJ had only had one car and a clunker at that—a real one, not a Mercedes. But he'd been a good driver. Not that I'd put that attribute all that high on my list of qualities I wanted in a man. Now that I thought about it, I'd never made a list of qualities. Maybe I should have.

"He sings like an angel."

"He does?"

"It's how we met. On karaoke night at Gill-ganins."

"Do you sing, too?"

"A little," she said.

"How does he afford the cars?" I asked.

"I don't know. I guess his dad. He's loaded." She looked me over. We heard people coming in the front door. "I have to get back to work." She tossed her hair and headed back to the front of the store. Game over.

I thought about the cars. Maybe the DiNapolis would know something about them.

At two forty-five someone knocked on my door. I hoped it was Carol and yanked open the door. Lindsay Murphy, my former neighbor, fell into my arms, crying.

"Miss Sarah," she sobbed. I pulled her in, and we settled on the couch.

"What's going on?" I asked. "Is your dad okay?" Lindsay's father was deployed.

She looked up from a curtain of hair dyed black with blue streaks. "It's my mother. I'm done with her," Lindsay said between gasping breaths. Lindsay had lived down the street from CJ and me when we lived on Fitch. She'd taken to dropping by. I liked to think I was a cool aunt type. I'd listen to her problems without freaking out or being too judgmental, at least not in front of her. Lindsay's mom and I knew each other and had been to some social gatherings together, but we weren't close.

"How did you get here?" I asked.

"I walked here after school instead of taking the bus home."

"Your mom's going to be worried. You need to call her and let her know you're here."

"Nooo," Lindsay wailed. "She'll make me leave. I'm not going back."

"I'll call her then. You can't stay if she's worrying about where you are."

Lindsay crossed her arms and looked down. I called her mom and explained the situation. "Just let her stay here with me for a little while," I said. "Until she's calmed down. Then I'll bring her home." It took some convincing, but Lindsay's mom finally agreed. I turned back to Lindsay.

"What's going on?" Although Lindsay said the problem was with her mom, I suspected her father going on his fourth deployment to Afghanistan played a role. The pace of deployments took a toll on all members of a military family. Way too often, the kids were the ones who suffered. And most of the time, instead of being able to talk it out, they acted out.

Lindsay poured out a torrent of wrongs, which included not getting to use the car when she wanted, having to watch her younger brother all the time, and having to study too much. "I called her this afternoon to ask about going to a party Friday night in Ellington. Mom said no before she heard the details." Lindsay brushed tears from her cheeks. "If my dad was here, she'd be nicer to me."

Most of it was typical teenager complaints. But I knew there was probably more behind this—a dad in danger, a worried mom with more on her plate than she should, and a stigma about getting counseling that still pervaded the military. The Veterans Administration saw dependent children only if it related to the military person's case. I knew counseling was available at school and through Tricare, the military insurance, but kids usually didn't always reach out on their own.

"And now because that McQueen guy got murdered, she's more freaked out than usual. She thinks whoever did it is planning to off me next."

"Your mom might be overreacting." I held up my hand when Lindsay started to say something. "But it's frightening. Too close to home."

"His wife probably did it, anyway, and she's gone."

"Why do you think that?" I sat up.

"My best friend lives near the McQueens. We were sitting outside on her patio two weekends ago. I spent the night. They were having one he . . . heck of a fight. The screaming kind. We even heard glass break."

"Could you hear what they were fighting

about?" I almost couldn't believe I was trying to pump a teenager for information.

"Not really. It ended when some old guy showed up in a Porsche."

"Old guy" made me think of Herb. He was always keeping an eye out but then didn't see anything the night of the murder. "Did anyone else know about the screaming match and the old guy with the Porsche?"

Lindsay studied her hands. "Probably not. It was late."

"If you were out back, how did you see the Porsche?"

"We wanted to hear what they were yelling about. We were tiptoeing over there when the Porsche pulled up. So we went back inside."

"Did you notice anything about the car? Like the color or license plate?"

Lindsay shook her head. "It was a dark color— black or dark blue. It was too far away to see the plate."

I decided I shouldn't press her anymore. "Want some iced tea?"

Lindsay nodded and followed me into the kitchen. I poured two glasses of tea.

"Tell me what it was like to grow up in California," Lindsay said. "I've had friends stationed at LA Air Force Base. They loved living out there."

"Monterey's quite a bit quieter than LA." I shared a few of my milder misadventures as we drank. "Your dad being away is hard on your mom too, Lindsay," I said, when our glasses were almost empty.

She huffed out a big sigh, and her eyes filled up with tears. She swiped at them. "I know. Oh God, now I'm going to have to go home and apologize."

When we got to the base, I went in with Lindsay and busied myself with my phone while she talked to her mother in the dining room. After an hour, everyone seemed calm and able to get back to the daily business of their lives. Lindsay's mom followed me out to my car.

"Thank you. I'm glad she has you to talk to," she said.

"I am too. All the deployments are tough," I said.

"Especially when my husband keeps volunteering for them. He loves the action." She shook her head. "Lindsay doesn't understand that someone from this base was murdered. That the murderer is out there. It's scarier than the deployments. Almost."

"If you ever need a break, I could come stay with the kids for a weekend."

Her face brightened. "Thanks. I'll keep that in mind."

CHAPTER 25

When I was on my way home, Carol called. "I'm out. For now."

"Oh, thank goodness. Where are you?"

"At the shop, painting. It's the only thing that keeps me sane with my mother-in-law at my house. I can only take being glared at a couple of hours a day."

"Is it okay if I stop over?"

"I'd love some company," Carol said. "Come in the back door."

Fifteen minutes later, I parked and trotted across the town common to Carol's shop. If I kept this up, I was going to wear my own personal path across the grass of the common. When I walked down the alley I glanced at Herb's house. No twitch in the curtains today.

"How did it go?" I asked Carol after letting myself in. I leaned against the workbench and watched her paint.

"Vincenzo had me through the system so quickly I hardly had time to process what was going on. So I'm out on bail and deemed not to be a flight risk."

"I'm so sorry."

"That I'm out?" Carol managed a grin. "I have to get this painting done. Even with a bondsman, bail isn't cheap."

"I can't imagine."

"I saw a guy in the back of the courtroom who looked a lot like the man I saw leaving your apartment building the other night."

I stared at the floor but felt that awful betraying blush sweeping from my chest to my neck to my face.

"You look great in red," Carol said. "Come on—spill. I need a good distraction."

So I spilled. Carol forgot to keep painting as I told her about meeting Seth, who he was, that he worked with CJ. "I can't believe Seth is even interested in me."

"Why wouldn't he be?"

I stared down at the floor. "When I thought CJ had slept with Tiffany, I felt like there must be something terribly wrong with me. That if CJ would do that to me, no one would ever want me."

Carol turned to me. "But he didn't do it to you."

"I know, but that feeling still clings to me."

"He wants you back. Why don't you go?"

"I divorced CJ for no reason."

"You thought there was a reason. And he agreed to the divorce." Carol let that hang between us. She pointed her paintbrush at me. "You didn't answer my question."

I blew out a long, slow breath. "I don't trust myself. I slept with Seth the first time I met him. Who does that?"

"Lots of people. Especially someone who's vulnerable and needs to feel valued—even if that's the worst way possible to go about it."

I pondered that. Maybe Carol was right.

"Get a grip. Everyone makes mistakes. I can't believe I'm going to say this, but it's what you do after the mistake that matters. How's that for platitudes?"

I really didn't want to talk about this.

"It sounds like Seth's interested, too. At least you didn't pick up some creep." Carol grinned at me. "You're worth more than you'll ever know." Carol started painting again.

I settled on a stool, watching her. Carol was the one facing a murder charge, and here she was, comforting me. I had to do something to help her.

"Can I look at your phone records?" I asked.

"Why?"

"They must have found some connection between you and Terry. We know he isn't on your computer system. But what if he called your cell phone or the shop?"

"I don't remember ever talking to him."

"Maybe he called when the shop was closed or when Olivia was here."

Carol shrugged and gave me the information to access her phone records. I went out into the shop and planted myself in front of the computer.

It was easy to eliminate some of the numbers on her cell and business phone—me, Brad, her home, Olivia. I made a list of ones I didn't recognize and then took them back to Carol. She crossed out the numbers she recognized.

"What are you going to do about the calls neither of us recognize?" Carol asked.

I thought for a moment. "I'll call them. Let's assume most of them are people who booked appointments. I'll ask them if they had a good experience and tell them about your specials."

"I don't have any specials," Carol said, a little crease forming between her brows.

"You do now. Ten percent off for returning parties."

Carol shook her head but smiled. "Okay. Go for it."

I started making the calls and booked several parties. I hoped Carol would be free and able to do them. When I got tired of calling people and wanted to stop, I reminded myself that Carol's freedom was on the line. So I kept dialing. A couple of times I reached suppliers. I told them I had the wrong number. After an hour, my ear hurt from holding the phone to it, and I was only halfway through the list.

I grabbed some water from Carol's refrigerator. I was tempted by the wine, but I needed a clear head for the calls. I dialed the next few numbers.

One rang so long I was ready to hang up.

"Hey, this is Terry McQueen, I can't take your

call right now, but leave a message. You know the drill."

I hung up so fast I felt like my hand had been burned. I went back over the bill. There were three calls from Terry's number to Carol's shop. The length and times of the calls varied, as did the days. I went through Carol's cell phone records again. One call from Terry to Carol's cell lasted about a minute and a half. It was made the afternoon of the day he was murdered. This must be part of what they had on Carol. They would have gone through the records by now.

But Carol must not know about the calls because she wouldn't have wanted me to go through the records if she did.

I walked back to where Carol painted. She used tiny brushstrokes to make the agony on a wounded soldier's face come to life. I hated to interrupt her with this terrible news.

"Carol. There are phone calls from Terry McQueen to your shop and cell phone."

Carol whipped around so fast she almost knocked over her painting.

"There can't be. I've never talked to him."

"One was to your cell phone. The day Terry died."

"Was murdered." Carol shook her head. "That wouldn't look good."

"Where's your phone?"

Carol pointed to the closet where she kept her clothes. "It's in my purse."

I found the phone and took it to Carol.

"He must have left a voice mail. I usually just call the number back. But I know I never called or talked to Terry McQueen."

We huddled over her phone. It said there were three voice mails. Carol hit speaker phone, then play.

"This is Terry McQueen. It's urgent I talk to you about your painting of *Battled*. I'll stop by your store this evening."

"Oh, no. That's bad," Carol said.

"How does he even know you were copying *Battled*?" I asked.

"I have no idea."

"Does his voice sound familiar? Could he be the mystery client?"

We listened to the message again.

"I don't think it's my client."

"But he must at the very least know your client."

"I guess." Carol twisted her wedding ring around her finger.

"Maybe Olivia talked with Terry when he called the shop," I said. "If we're really lucky, you won't have been here when the calls came in. Let's check to see if she worked the day of the calls. If she did, then we need to track her down and see what she remembers."

We went to the front of the store. Carol opened her computer, and we started looking through the schedule.

"Olivia definitely worked on the days of the calls," I said, as we studied the records.

"But there's nothing to prove I wasn't here." Carol clicked away, bringing up different screens on her computer. She pointed at one. "Look at this. During one of the calls a group was here painting." Her voice had a hopeful note in it.

"What difference does that make?"

"I didn't talk to him. I'd never interrupt a group to take a call," Carol said.

"But there's no way to prove you didn't," I said. "Even if Olivia tells them she's the one who talked to Terry, they might twist that in front of a jury. If she's been in trouble before, any good DA will eat her alive on the stand." I pictured Seth, pacing back and forth in front of a jury, hammering his points into them. "Call Olivia and get her down here."

Olivia unlocked the front door about fifteen minutes later. I didn't realize Carol had given her a key. Jett followed her into the store. We explained the situation and asked her if she remembered talking to Terry.

Olivia bit her lower lip in concentration. "I thought he was that famous director calling. I told him all about my acting experience."

"You mean Steve McQueen?" I tried to keep the incredulousness out of my voice. "Why would *he* call here?"

Olivia shrugged. "I just heard the McQueen

part. I'd be a great actress. I was in all my high school plays and even had speaking roles sometimes. And I lied to my mom all the time. She totally believed everything I told her."

Thus all the trouble with the law, I suspected.

"Then all he wanted to talk about was stupid investing, and I hung up. But he called back another day. I've saved up a couple hundred dollars and asked him what I should do with it. He was a very nice man." Olivia looked back and forth between Carol and me. "Does that help?"

Carol patted Olivia's hand. "Of course it does."

They stood to go. I noticed Jett had a tattoo. In blue ink across his bicep were the words "Semper Fi." That was the Marine Corp motto. Had Jett been in the Marines, or was he just a wannabe?

After they left, I turned to Carol. "You'd better call Vincenzo and tell him about all of this."

Carol made the call. "He can meet me later this evening."

"Let's go get something to eat at DiNapoli's. I'm starving."

When we went in, Carol headed over to the counter to Rosalie. "I need to speak to Angelo." She said it loud enough that Angelo could hear her. He hesitated and then came over to the counter. I went over and stood next to Carol.

"Thank you for calling Vincenzo for me. Things are a mess, but they'd be far worse without him."

Angelo looked uncomfortable. He seemed to squirm a bit, something I'd never seen him do.

"Sarah seems to think you're okay, so that's good enough for me." He turned and headed back to a chopping board, slicing through onions like he meant it.

Rosalie patted Carol's hand. "How about some dinner?"

"I need to go spend some time with my kids. While I can," Carol said. She hugged me and left, straightening her posture and attitude as she did.

"What about you, Sarah?" Rosalie asked after Carol left.

"Sure." I really didn't feel like being alone. I studied the menu. Even though the restaurant is called DiNapoli's Roast Beef and Pizza, I almost always ordered pizza or pasta, but tonight I wanted something different.

"How about I make you the best roast beef sandwich you ever had," Angelo called across the kitchen.

Decision made. "Sure," I said. "That sounds good." Fifteen minutes later Angelo set a sandwich large enough to feed a family of four in front of me—tender roast beef cooked to a perfect medium pink, melted provolone, caramelized onions, and thick, beefy tomatoes. I couldn't even close the roll around the mounds of food. Rosalie set a glass of water and a kid's cup in front of me with a wink. I was thankful for the wine.

I used a fork and knife to eat way more of the sandwich than I should have. During a lull in the dinner rush, Angelo came over and sat with

me. "It is the best roast beef sandwich I ever had,"
I told him. Angelo spread his hands apart, like
what did I expect. If he said it, it was so. I made
it through about a third of it. I made a mental
note to take a long walk tonight to work off some
of the calories.

"Vincenzo said your Uncle Stefano had a copy
of *Battled* made. Know anything about it?" I asked.

"Everyone knows about it," Angelo said. "He
tried to buy *Battled* back in the seventies when
the city was in financial trouble. Offered them
more than it was worth at the time." He frowned
at one of the girls clearing tables, like she wasn't
doing it the way she should. "The whole thing
put the town in a big uproar between those that
thought the money was more important and
those that thought the legacy was more important. Obviously, the legacy folks won. As they
should have."

"Does he still have his copy?" I asked.

"As far as I know." Angelo got a glint in his eye.
"Want to go find out?"

CHAPTER 26

Thirty minutes later, we were driving to Cambridge. At 6:30 the worst of rush hour had passed. Angelo was a true Boston driver; he was impatient, made no eye contact, did lots of honking, used a lot of hand gestures, and called out frequently in a colorful vocabulary, some of it in Italian. Somehow, in the two and a half years I'd lived in Massachusetts, I'd adjusted to this style of driving and rarely took notice of it anymore. But when CJ and I had first moved here, I was terrified to drive down Great Road, let alone on the 95 or the Mass Pike. We pulled up to a large, yellow colonial-style house a couple of blocks off Massachusetts Avenue.

"This isn't the neighborhood I grew up in," Angelo said. "My neighborhood wasn't this nice. We didn't know how to be prejudiced because there was just about every country in the world represented in that little area—like the United Nations, only we got along better."

"Why's he so interested in owning *Battled* if he lives here?"

"He lived in Ellington a long time. He's a true Revolutionary War buff. He was so mad when the city wouldn't sell him the painting, he moved back here."

We headed up the neatly trimmed walk, and Angelo rang the bell. A few minutes later, a tower of a man opened the door and grasped Angelo into his arms, speaking in effusive Italian to him before noticing me. He went through the same routine with me. A slight sloop of his shoulders showed his age.

"She doesn't speak Italian, Uncle," Angelo said as we went into the house. His Italian accent was suddenly stronger. "But she's a good girl. She wanted to see your copy of *Battled*."

Stefano let us into the foyer. There was a staircase to the right and a long hall in front of us. Oil paintings and maps of the Revolutionary War hung on almost every available space as far as I could see down the hall and up the wall by the stairs.

"The police have already been here," Stefano said. "If the town had let me buy it, I'da made sure it was safe and gifted it back." He turned to me. "That was my plan all along."

Behind him, Angelo vigorously shook his head no.

We followed Stefano down the narrow center hall; he flipped on a light in a room to the left, and we all stepped in. His copy of *Battled* hung above a fireplace. Bookshelves crammed with books took up the wall on either side of the fireplace. A couple of chairs and a desk occupied the rest of the space. I roamed around the room. Most of the books seemed to be about the Revolutionary War.

"I spend most of my days in here working and admiring my copy of *Battled*," Stefano said; his voice sounded bitter.

"What do you do?" I asked.

"A little of this, a little of dat," he responded.

Good heavens, maybe this family really was a *family*, in the Mob family kind of way. But behind Stefano, Angelo was once again shaking his head, and this time he smacked his hand against his forehead. He mouthed "real estate" at me. At least, I hoped that's what he'd mouthed, and not "godfather."

We stepped closer to the painting; a little spotlight shone down on it. The colors were more muted than in the original, and the facial expressions weren't as clear. Carol's painting was superior, a more accurate copy by far. The frame was almost an exact duplicate, much like the fake in the library.

"It's lovely," I said.

"You don't have the original stuck in storage somewhere, do you, Uncle?" Angelo asked.

"I got it tucked right next to Jimmy Hoffa," Stefano answered. "Has the heat from cooking all these years gone to your head? You shoulda stuck with the family business. I don't have the painting. It's what I told the cops, and it's what I'm telling you."

Stefano sank into one of the chairs. "I wish I woulda thought of it, though."

"Is he telling the truth?" I asked once we were back in the car heading toward Ellington.

"As far as I know," Angelo said as he cut someone off. A horn blared behind us. "His copy isn't good enough to switch with the one at the library. They'd have noticed the difference in five minutes."

"I thought the same thing. Could he have known about the copy Carol was making?"

Angelo seemed very focused on his driving all of a sudden. He shrugged.

"Did you know about it?" I asked.

"Sure. Jett's girlfriend showed it to him. He told me about it."

"Did you tell Stefano about it?"

"I might have mentioned it to him."

"So that's why you gave Carol Vincenzo's information. You were worried Stefano might have been involved with the switch." It was obvious the picture hanging over Stefano's fireplace wasn't the original, but that didn't mean he hadn't stashed it somewhere else, even though he'd denied it.

Angelo pulled up in front of my apartment. "Maybe."

I slanted my body toward Angelo. "Was Jett in

the Marines? I noticed he had a Semper Fi tattoo."

Angelo tapped his fingers on the steering wheel. "It's one of the reasons he never went to jail. Vincenzo promised the judge Jett would enlist. Jett did his stint and got out."

It might explain the ripped body and maybe even the confident attitude, but not the cars. Not on an enlisted salary. "I've seen him driving a couple of fancy cars lately. Where would he get the money for those?"

"I don't know. Vincenzo told me he cut him off after he gave him that old Mercedes I told you about."

"What'd he do for the Marines?"

"EOD."

Explosive Ordinance Disposal? "Holy crap. That's one dangerous job. Finding and blowing up IEDs is high risk."

"We all thought it would settle him. But it seemed to make him worse. I think he misses the adrenaline rush and the sense of purpose."

"What's he do now?"

"Takes classes at Middlesex in Bedford and works as a handyman for the family business."

There was that family business again. I wondered what the heck a "handyman" did for the Mob.

"Real estate," Angelo said. "Jett fixes things for various properties." He yawned, and I climbed out of the car. "Have a good night, kid. Don't worry about Jett. There's some explanation for the cars."

I nodded and closed the car door. I could think of a couple of explanations. Jett probably knew how to make explosive devices, not just how to blow them up. Maybe he'd sold his services to whoever wanted the fires started so the painting could be taken.

Where was the original of *Battled*?

I woke up with too many things on my mind. But I decided I could check one of them off the list. Finding out where Nancy Elder had disappeared to during New England's Largest Yard Sale was first up. I didn't care how inappropriate, by New England standards, it might be to ask her outright. I needed to know. I showered and got ready. Then I made a fluffernutter sandwich for breakfast and a pot of coffee.

I read the local news online while I ate. Nancy was going to be at a ribbon-cutting ceremony for the reopening of the newly renovated community center. Who didn't like a good ribbon cutting? I licked the last of the marshmallow fluff off my index finger and gulped the rest of my coffee.

I flung open my window and stuck my head out. It was a bit cool, so I grabbed my brown leather jacket, purchased at a garage sale many years ago for a dollar. I pulled on boots and tucked in my jeans. I decided to walk, since I needed to work off some of the roast beef sandwich from last night. The other two-thirds sat in my fridge for lunch today.

I took the back way instead of walking down Great Road. The road meandered around an odd assortment of houses. Some, like Stella's, had been divided into apartments, although these were a little worse for the wear. Almost all of them were wooden, so different from the stucco homes common in California. The lots here were narrow, the houses were big, and all the curbs were granite—woe to the person who hit one.

A few blocks later, I came to the community center. Local dignitaries were gathered on the porch. CJ was among them. He watched me as I strolled up. Nancy and one of the other council members stood, front and center, behind a big purple ribbon. They whispered to each other. He held the oversized scissors. A nice crowd had gathered, which would make Nancy happy. In fact, she looked really happy, more so than the occasion called for.

I studied Nancy and the town councilman. They were about the same height. Even though they stood side by side, their bodies touched in every place they possibly could without looking like they were touching. Left arm to right arm. Hip to hip. If sparks could fly more than a few feet, we'd be showered with them. I glanced around. No one else seemed to pick up on the chemistry between the two.

Nancy noticed me watching her. I held my thumb up, close to my body where no one else would notice. Nancy looked around nervously, then smiled at me. Now I knew where she was in the middle of the day during the yard sale. A tryst. I don't know why she kept it a secret. The town councilman was a widower and well liked in the community, from what I'd read in the paper.

A few minutes later, the ribbon was cut, and people poured into the community center for refreshments—Dunkin' Donuts coffee and donuts, of course. I headed back to my house. One mission accomplished. Now to tackle the others on my list. CJ pulled up beside me in his official Ellington Police Department SUV. He rolled the window down.

"Need a ride?" he asked.

"Nope. I'm good." I was more than a little mad at him for arresting Carol. I continued walking, and he continued to drive by my side.

"You're mad at me because of Carol?" CJ shook his head. "It's my job."

"I'm well aware it's your job. And well aware that Carol didn't murder Terry, no matter what kind of evidence you think you have." The word *evidence* made me remember I wanted to show him the picture I'd taken in the woods. But that meant dropping my righteous indignation and getting in the car with him. I reminded myself that this was for Carol.

"I need to show you something," I said. CJ stopped, and I climbed into the front seat of the SUV next to him—as next to him as one can be with all kinds of communications equipment separating us, including a computer monitor. That was fine by me. I was still mad enough to appreciate the electronic wall between us. I flipped through my photos until I found the one I was looking for. We leaned together, our heads nearly touching.

"What's this?" CJ asked.

I quickly explained how I'd just happened to be going for a walk and noticed where the fire had been. "I did a little exploring and snapped a couple of pictures. When I downloaded them, I noticed this bit of camouflage cloth tucked back on a branch just beyond the burned area." When I turned to face him, we were almost nose to nose. I thought about how naturally Nancy and the town councilman had leaned into each other, how a year ago that would have been natural for us. Then I thought about how mixed up I was and moved back.

"You just happened to be taking a walk," CJ said, shaking his head. He radioed Pellner and told him to meet him over there.

"Do you want me to go with you and show you where it is?"

"No. We can handle it."

I opened the SUV door and slid out. "No need to thank me. All I did was find what might be a piece of evidence, take a photo, and let you know about it." I closed the door firmly, very firmly.

"Sarah," CJ called after me, but I ducked between two houses, knowing he couldn't follow me.

CHAPTER 27

I spent the afternoon checking more things off my list. I talked to Carol to see how her meeting with Vincenzo had gone. She said fine but couldn't give me any details of their conversation. Apparently Vincenzo wasn't happy we'd listened to the voice mail and questioned Olivia ourselves. Oh, well.

I checked Groton Goods and the thrift shop eBay site. Still no sign of the quilt or the Shirley Temple doll. Then I decided to hit a couple of antiques stores and thrift shops. Tonight Seth and I were going to work on his man cave. I wanted to find something special to add to it, so I drove over to a favorite shop in Concord. It was on Main Street, above another shop. Even though it was in a prime location, I thought their prices were reasonable.

After climbing the stairs and greeting the owner, I roamed from room to room. About a third of the way through, behind a stack of Audubon prints, I found a framed, vintage poster of Fenway Park, home of the Red Sox. It wasn't in perfect condition. It had a few tears and a small piece missing in one corner. But that put it in my price range.

I took it up to the owner and showed her the price. "Can you take anything off?" I asked. I used to find it awkward to ask this question, but now it was routine for me.

She looked the print over. "I'll take ten percent off."

"Perfect," I said. I would have paid full price, so ten percent off made me happy.

Back at home I took the poster out of the frame and carefully cleaned the glass and frame. I made sure everything was dry before I put the poster back in.

I pounded the last nail into the Sheetrock in Seth's basement at 7:30. I stepped back as Seth hung the vintage Fenway poster I'd found for him on the nail.

"You are handy with a hammer," Seth said.

"I am a woman of many talents," I replied.

"Mmm. Yes, you are."

I could tell he wasn't talking about my skills with the hammer. Heat crept from the vee of my long-sleeved black shirt up to my face. I'd tried as hard as I could to keep things professional with Seth. Except for the occasional kiss, I managed that fairly well. I could feel myself weakening, especially after arguing with CJ this afternoon. But I didn't want my being mad at CJ to influence what I did with Seth.

He'd just returned from a workout when I showed up. His Red Sox T-shirt fit him perfectly, not too tight or too loose. His legs were strong and muscled beneath his gym shorts. Even a five o'clock shadow looked great on him.

"That's a great gift," he said, gesturing toward the vintage poster. "Thank you."

I glanced around the room to distract myself from the pull of his personality and physique. Although it wasn't completely finished, Seth's man cave was coming along. The large TV and couch were in place, but I still needed to find him a rug. We'd hung his Red Sox memorabilia or arranged it on shelves. It was the perfect place to hang out and watch a game.

"What's that?" I asked, gesturing to a giant box peeking out from stacks of assorted stuff under the basement stairs.

"It's an old trunk. I guess my great-grandfather used it to travel to Europe."

I went over and started moving the stuff that surrounded the trunk. "Holy crap. This isn't some old trunk. It's a Louis Vuitton." Who had Louis Vuitton trunks sitting around unused in their basements? I looked over my shoulder at Seth. We came from completely different worlds. "I can't believe you never told me about this. It might be the perfect thing to use for a coffee table in your living room."

"I like the trunk you use in your apartment. I never thought about this being down here. Is it too low?" Seth asked as he came over to help me drag it out.

"If it's too low, I can buy bun feet for it at a hardware store. I'll paint them and attach them to the bottom, if that's all right with you." When Seth didn't say anything, I looked up.

He watched me with a grin curving his beautiful lips. "I love how excited you get about things. I've known so many women who seem so blasé about life."

I didn't want to think about the *so* many women. "Let's take it upstairs."

"It's heavy. Are you sure you want to try? I can get someone to come help me tomorrow."

"Of course I can help you. I'm strong." I guess he was used to women like Barbie Doll, who probably couldn't carry more than one pair of stilettos at a time. I'd spent years hauling stuff to and from garage sales. I could lift a lot.

Seth looked unsure, but we hauled it up the stairs and set it down in front of the love seat. He shook his head. "I didn't think it would look good."

It had a couple of small scratches, but to me that just added to the charm, along with the fact that it was a piece of his family history.

I traced a finger across a paper travel tag imprinted with an image of the Eiffel Tower. "It is too low. I'll buy bun feet for it tomorrow."

"Why don't you stay for dinner? I've got a couple of steaks in the refrigerator." It came out "refrigeratah." No matter how long I lived here, the local accent would always charm me. "I can throw together a salad to go with the steaks."

I took a step toward the front door.

"Don't flee. Not tonight. Please?"

Why not? "Okay," I said. "I'll make the salad."

"I'll grab a shower and be right down." Seth grabbed my hand and pressed a kiss into my palm.

I busied myself in the kitchen. The water started in the shower upstairs. I spotted the makings for a salad and started chopping. I found a bottle of champagne vinaigrette in the refrigerator. A decorative Polish pottery bowl sat on the counter. I dumped all the veggies in it and tossed it with the vinaigrette. I found plates and silverware, and carried them into the dining room. The table was covered with folders. I set the plates and silverware, which was actually silver, at one end and started to pick up the folders, humming one of Stella's arias, not that I sounded anything like her.

The domesticity of it all hit me. I sucked in a couple of deep breaths. If this was the life I wanted, shouldn't I be with CJ and not Seth? The folders shook in my hands. Maybe that's why I'd held Seth off all these months. But I did like Seth, too. Could my heart know CJ was the one for me even when my mind didn't? Or was it the other way around? Maybe the problem was I didn't trust myself to choose since I'd misread the situation with CJ so badly last winter. What had I done?

I glanced down at the folders in my hands. One had Carol's name on the label, followed by a long number. I set the others down, staring at it. This might be the case the state had laid out against Carol. If I read it, I might be able to help her. But if I read it, I'd be betraying Seth in the worst possible way. I held it with both hands, debating. A creak sounded behind me.

"I'll put the steaks on," Seth said, coming up behind me. "You didn't need to get the dishes and silverware. I would have done it."

I kept my back to him a few seconds longer and held the folder against my waist. It felt like it was searing my hands. But there didn't seem to be any way to keep Seth from knowing I had it. He nuzzled his lips against my neck, and his wet hair sprinkled a few drops of water on me. I closed my eyes for a minute, breathing in his fresh shower scent, realizing I had to tell him what I was holding.

"What do you have?" Seth drew back as I turned. He wore worn jeans and a cream-colored shirt, sleeves rolled up, showing his strong forearms.

The place on my neck where his lips had been felt cold. I handed him the folder. "I saw it when I came to set the table. I didn't open it."

Seth's face settled into a grim expression as he took the folder from me. A pulse beat madly at his temple. "I think you'd better go."

When I got to the front door, I opened it but turned back. Seth stood there, clenching the folder in one hand.

"I swear I didn't look at it, Seth. I was tempted, but I didn't."

CHAPTER 28

Back home, I turned my grandmother's oak rocking chair to look out over the empty town common. I turned the lights out and opened the window to let some cool air rush in. I tried to sort out what was going on in my mind about Seth and CJ—the alarm I'd felt at Seth's house when the routine of setting the table had confused me. Maybe somehow I liked our clandestine meetings, the risk of getting caught. On the other hand, I really, really didn't want CJ to know I was seeing Seth. Then there was Seth's expression when he saw me with his file. I knew so well how it felt when you thought someone you trusted had betrayed you. It hurt me to see what I'd done to him.

But had tonight proved to me that I belonged with CJ? We'd been so happy for so long. Then when I'd thought he'd slept with his subordinate, I hadn't believed it was just one time, and I'd bolted. To here, my cozy apartment. Part of me

liked being here, being on my own. I'd left my
parents' house at nineteen to marry CJ. The
other part of me missed him on so many levels, I
didn't know what to think.

A car door slammed. I heard Stella and Bubbles laughing as they came up the steps. The
screen door creaked opened and shut. Stella
started singing her aria. It was beautiful. Seth
must be nothing more than a jog off the path of
my life. I cried for a few minutes for all I'd lost
because I hadn't been able to trust CJ or myself.
Then I gave myself a talking to about how if I
didn't like my life I could change it. I rose and
closed the window, closed a chapter in my life.
Next time I got the chance, I'd tell CJ it was
time for us to be back together, where we surely
belonged.

By nine the next morning I sat in Gennie's
fifties room, puzzling over how to price a
boomerang coffee table and matching chairs.
She'd left a note on the door that she was working out in her basement and for me to come
in. It struck me again that she'd left her door
unlocked, this time with a note on it that any
random person could see. I finally decided to
hold off pricing the table and chairs. I needed
to meet with a friend in Acton, an expert in
estate sales and antiques.

After pricing and tagging for another hour, I
heard Gennie come up from the basement. She

leaned against the door, holding a bottle of water. "I don't want to interrupt you, but I have a question about something unrelated to the sale."

That sounded intriguing. "Hang on. Let me put the price tags on these two items." I carefully placed the tags on two pictures of Elvis, making sure they were in a spot where the price would show but the sticker wouldn't do any damage. I stood and stretched my arms up over my head. "What do you need?" I asked when I finished my stretch.

"Want something to drink?" Gennie asked.

"Water would be great," I said.

We headed to the kitchen, my curiosity growing with every step. It seemed like Gennie was putting off asking me anything. I settled on a stool at the kitchen island. Gennie grabbed a bottle of water from the fridge and handed it to me.

Gennie pulled out another stool and sat. "I hate to involve you, but since you're friends with Dave, I thought you might be able to help me out." Gennie took a long drink of her water.

"I'll do whatever I can."

"I know he's probably overwhelmed right now because of Terry's death, but I haven't gotten my monthly statement yet. It's only a few days late, but I like to stay on top of things."

I'd seen Bubbles leaving Stella's apartment this morning, whistling a ditty and tossing his keys in the air. He didn't seem to have a care in the world. Sharing that with Gennie didn't seem wise. "I can call him for you."

"I've left him a couple of messages, but he hasn't returned my calls. I don't want to be insensitive."

"I'll call his cell phone. It's probably just a problem with the post office. Although he did mention the other day that he was looking for help."

I took out my phone and searched my contacts for Bubbles's number. He picked up on the second ring. "Hey, good lookin', what's up? Stella can't get enough of me and wanted you to call?"

I laughed. "No. I'm with Gennie. She said her statement hadn't shown up and was worried."

"Please apologize for me. Or better yet, let me talk to her."

I handed Gennie the phone.

She said "uh-huh" a few times before laughing. "It's okay. Thanks for letting me know." She hung up and handed my phone back to me. "Dave said they went out a day late."

"What about the statements from the fund company? You could look at those."

"Dave gets those directly so he can do a consolidated statement for me."

That sounded a little odd, but it had been years since I was in the business. "But you can look online."

"I didn't ever set up an online account. Dave was always so prompt."

"We could set one up now. All we need is the

account number for the fund from one of the consolidated statements from Dave." It always felt odd calling him Dave, because I'd always known him as Bubbles.

"How do you know all of this?"

"I worked part-time for a small independent financial planning company a long time ago. It wouldn't be that much different than Dave's setup."

"Were you a financial planner?"

"No. I was the assistant to one. But I learned a lot about how the stock market works."

"My laptop's charging upstairs," Gennie said. "I'll grab it and a statement." When she brought it back, Gennie typed in the information. The fund sent her an error message.

"Let me read the fund number to you," I said. "Those things are so long it's hard to type them in accurately." I wanted to believe that was the problem, but concern niggled the back of my head.

I read off the number, but the same error message came back up. "Do you have your other statements? Maybe a number somehow got transposed on this one."

When Gennie went off again, I studied the statement. It looked legit and had everything the Security and Exchange Commission required.

Gennie spread out several months' worth of statements on the granite island. The account numbers were the same on each statement.

"If he entered it wrong the first time, it makes

sense it would be wrong on all of these, right?" she asked.

"Let me call Bubbles, Dave, back and get the right number." I dialed again and explained the situation to Bubbles.

"Terry did the statements. I'm horrified and embarrassed. But you know I can't give you that information, Sarah. Privacy laws."

"I'm still with Gennie, so hang on." I handed the phone over to her.

Gennie listened again and smiled. "Great," she said. She looked at me. "He's getting the number." Gennie held up a finger to me. "Okay," she said into the phone. "Let me know." After she disconnected the call, she looked at me. "The system's down. He's going to call me back."

A system being down when the market was open was almost unheard of. Even if Bubbles's system was down, he should be able to quickly contact the fund and get the information. While we waited, we talked about dates for the yard sale. I needed at least another two weeks to get through everything. As we talked, I kept wondering if Gennie suspected the same thing I did—that something was very wrong. After a half hour, I turned to Gennie. "Could I look at your statements and look up some things online?"

Gennie's eyebrows slanted together in worry, and I was pretty sure my expression echoed hers. I worried about what Terry had done to Bubbles behind his back. Apparently enough to get himself killed. "Sure," she said, "if it will help get this resolved."

I clicked away at the computer for twenty-five minutes, verifying and reverifying what I'd spotted. My mouth settled into a grim line as I worked.

"What is it?" Gennie asked.

"Your statements show a lower profit than the fund actually made on any given day." I pointed to the number on the statement and the number on the fund's website. "It's not off by much, just a few dollars. But a few dollars every month adds up." In my head, I extrapolated that number. If Dave and Terry had one hundred clients, it would be a decent amount of money. If they had one thousand, it would be a jaw-dropping figure.

"What's that mean?"

"I think someone was skimming funds from your account."

CHAPTER 29

I sat in the lobby of the Ellington Police Station, waiting for CJ to see me. I'd come straight from Gennie's house and had tried calling CJ on the way over. Both his cell and office phones went straight to voice mail. I told the person at the front desk it was urgent, but apparently if no one was bleeding, it was kind of like being in the hospital. I was triaged and deemed of low importance. I'd even been desperate enough to ask if Scott Pellner was in, but he was out on patrol.

As I waited, I hoped that all of this was Terry's doing and Bubbles wasn't involved. After all, Terry ended up dead, not Bubbles. I sifted through all the events that had occurred, starting with New England's Largest Yard Sale—fires, the missing painting, a dead body, and erroneous financial statements. Was it possible that Bubbles or Terry was the mystery man who'd commissioned the copy of *Battled*? Carol's painting had been stolen sometime between Friday evening and Saturday evening. That person set the fires as a distraction and switched the paintings during the commotion. But why?

Maybe someone knew that Terry was scamming people. I hoped it was Terry and not Bubbles, but he hadn't returned Gennie's call, which alarmed me. She'd promised to let me know as soon as she heard from him. Maybe one or both of the men came up with the idea to have *Battled* copied and to steal the original so it could be sold to repay the accounts and chalk it all up to a computer glitch. I warmed to that theory.

But I couldn't figure out why Terry had been killed or why at Carol's shop. Terry might have been unhappy that a simple con game had turned into so much more. Or perhaps Terry didn't even know that Bubbles was scamming people. When he found out and wouldn't go along with it, Bubbles killed him. Terry had called Carol that afternoon and said he wanted to meet her. What if someone had overheard the call, followed Terry to the store, and made sure Terry couldn't tell her anything. As much as I didn't want Bubbles to be involved, I hoped this would be enough to get Carol off the hook.

The biggest flaw in my theory, as far as I could tell, was that Bubbles showed no signs of having amassed a lot of money. He drove an old truck, and he lived in simple quarters on the base. It wasn't furnished lavishly. Sure, he had some nice electronics, but as a colonel he could easily afford those. That thought made me feel better. It must have been Terry.

I clutched copies of Gennie's statements. I jiggled my foot and glanced at my phone to check the time again. Just as I was about to blow up with impatience, someone opened the door, and I hurried to CJ's office.

CJ smiled when I came in. It seemed like the first time he'd smiled at me in a long time. It made me happy. "I heard you were about to blow a gasket out in the lobby. What has you so fired up?"

It only took a few minutes to lay out my case to CJ. He'd learned almost as much about the market as I had during the time I worked for the financial planning company. It made explaining my theory to him much easier. "Now you can drop the case against Carol," I said.

CJ leaned back in his chair and studied the ceiling. I waited quietly, knowing how he processed things.

"It's all conjecture," CJ said, leaning his arms on his desk.

"But I have these statements." I handed them over to CJ but didn't tell him I'd kept another set for myself.

"They are so consistently off it could be a glitch in their computer program."

"Bubbles didn't answer my call." It just struck me that I might have alerted him that he'd been caught.

"Bubbles could be at the gym or in the shower.

He might be trying to figure out what went wrong and doesn't want to be disturbed."

"He could be packing up right now."

"Why? He's almost ready to retire. He has a successful business. Everything else is just speculation on your part." He picked up a pencil and tapped it on the top of his desk. "You've forgotten that he was threatened as well as Terry. Maybe someone set them both up."

I had forgotten that. I'd seen the notes myself and their similarity. That cheered me a bit.

"I'll give him a call or drop by his place," CJ said. "I'll let you know what I find out."

I must have given him a skeptical look. CJ hadn't shared any information with me for a long time.

"I promise."

I spotted Vincenzo's car outside Carol's shop. I zipped over. The two of them were huddled together at a table. They looked up, startled when I flung open the door.

"I have news that might help Carol," I said as I hurried to where they were sitting and sat down with them. I explained what I'd found out at Gennie's house.

"Will it help?" Carol asked, leaning forward toward Vincenzo.

Vincenzo stared up at the ceiling. "It's huge. It means every client they have is a suspect. Not to mention Dave's possible involvement. But any good prosecutor would say it was a computer glitch or irrelevant to the murder." He turned to me. "Do you know anyone else who invests with him? One person's erroneous statement could be a fluke. More than one, and it's a trend."

"I might know someone else. I'll call her right now." I called Laura, and when she didn't answer, I left a message. We sat in silence for a moment. Then I couldn't hold it back any longer. "How does your son afford three cars?" I asked, though "asked" might have been a stretch and "demanded" more accurate.

Vincenzo smoothed his purple silk tie and assessed me. His face said "hysterical female alert."

"Do you give him the cars?" I asked.

"I'm not sure which cars you're talking about or which son. I have three."

"I'm talking about Jett, his Mercedes, the red sports car, and the yellow one."

A flicker of doubt crossed Vincenzo's face. "As far as I know, he only has one car. An older Mercedes that I gave him when he returned from the Marines."

"I've seen him driving two other newish-looking cars. And from what I've heard, his income wouldn't support three such cars." I didn't mention that he'd started driving them right after the painting was stolen. The thought that Vincenzo's son might be a thief was awful. I didn't want to spell it out, but I hoped Vincenzo caught my meaning.

Vincenzo looked thoughtful. Carol looked back and forth between us. "Anyone want some water?" she asked. She hopped up and disappeared into her studio.

"Let me call him and see if we can get this cleared up." The normally unruffled Vincenzo looked very unhappy. He made the call and hung up. "He was on his way over with Olivia, anyway."

Carol came out with a pitcher of water and glasses. A few minutes later, a red sports car pulled into a parking spot right in front of the store. Vincenzo paled a bit. Jett held the door open for Olivia as they walked in wearing matching black T-shirts. Olivia wore another tiny skirt with tights, and Jett wore distressed jeans that he'd probably paid way too much for.

"Hey, Dad, what'd you want?" He tossed the keys up in the air and caught them behind his back, executing a snazzy full turn in the process.

Olivia took one look at all the tense faces and bolted to the back room.

"Where'd you get that Mazda?" Vincenzo jabbed a finger toward the red sports car. "And I hear you've been driving some yellow flashy car, too."

"That's what this is about? You think I did something?"

"I know you can't afford those cars on what the family pays you." He blew out a deep breath and took Jett's hand. "If you're in some kind of trouble, I'll help you. I always do."

Jett jerked his hand away. He wheeled toward me, his face red and his nostrils flared. "This is your fault, isn't it?"

CHAPTER 30

Vincenzo leaped up. "Calm down, Jett."

Jett shook his head. "The Mazda belongs to a Marine buddy of mine. He's deployed and asked me to drive it a couple of times a week for him."

My mouth formed a little *o*.

"As for the yellow *flashy* car. The Corvette." He turned back to his father. "You remember Rick Ford? I went to high school with him?"

Vincenzo nodded.

"He moved to California to get an MBA at Stanford. He planned to drive it out, but he got in a bad bike wreck and can't sit long enough to drive that far. So he flew. Rick asked me to drive his Vette occasionally until he can get back out here to pick it up or I drive it out there for him." He lifted his chin. "You don't believe me, you can call them both. Although my Marine buddy is a little hard to get hold of."

The weight of what I'd accused him of and how

wrong I was crashed down on me. "I'm sorry," I said. "I jumped to conclusions with everything that's going on. Please accept my apology."

Jett and Vincenzo exchanged a "what do you think?" look. Jett shrugged and then they both nodded.

I was embarrassed and furious with myself. My zeal for getting Carol off was making me into a crazy woman. I needed to take it down a notch and trust that she was in good hands with Vincenzo.

"But there's something I need to tell you. And you aren't going to like it," Jett said.

Vincenzo kind of braced himself, like he'd heard those words many times and never knew what would follow.

"I got a call a few weeks ago. An old bud." He looked at his father's face, which reddened. "He knew someone who was looking for an expert with ordinance experience."

"I've told you to stay away from your 'old buds,' Jett."

"I do, Dad. I can't stop them from calling me."

"You don't have to answer."

"Will you just hear me out?" Jett asked. His father finally gave a brief nod. "The guy tried to convince me it was perfectly legal. Someone just wanted to burn down an old building on their property. But knowing who was making the call, I said no."

Vincenzo relaxed. "I'm proud of you, son."

Based on the beam on Jett's face, I don't think he'd heard those words very often, if ever.

"It made me wonder if it had something to do with the old chicken coops in Bedford. You know, that developer has been trying to get approval to build low-income housing there."

Vincenzo nodded. "He wanted the tax credit."

"I was thinking maybe he didn't want to pay to have the buildings torn down," Jett said.

"What does that have to do with the other fires that day?" I asked. The two men turned as though they'd forgotten I was in the room. "It just seems too convenient that four fires broke out at the same time." I didn't add "using similar devices." Vincenzo might now trust his son, but I wasn't sure I did.

"We need to go over to the Ellington PD and talk to Chief Hooker, son. Maybe they can find more out through your contact."

Jett didn't look happy as he followed his dad out of the store, but he went without protest.

Carol and I reached for the water that so far no one had touched.

"I feel like a fool," I said to Carol.

Carol sipped some of her water. "But it led to this new information, so it's a good thing."

"I guess. I wonder why Jett mentioned it now and not before?" I asked Carol.

Olivia popped out of the back room. "Because

his buddy called him this morning and said he'd better not mention the first call. Jett was livid. We were headed over to find his father when he called." Olivia moved around the room, setting up for a group that was coming in later today.

"Do you know who the guy was? How he knew Jett?" I asked.

"No idea," she said in a way that made me think that even if she did, she wasn't about to tell me.

I drank some more of my water. "I hope this helps you, Carol."

She sat straight up. "Do you think it could?"

"They took all of those flammable things when they searched here. Hopefully, Jett's information will lead to someone who set up the fires. The fires caused enough distraction that it gave someone the opportunity to steal *Battled*. And none of that would be connected to you."

Carol smiled. "Thank you. Now I'd better get back to painting."

After grabbing a quick sandwich at home, instead of going back to Gennie's as I'd intended, I headed up the 3 to Nashua. Thankfully, at one-thirty traffic was light. Lots of people who lived in Nashua worked in Massachusetts, so the 3 could be slow at rush hour. Bubbles's ex-wife and two kids lived in New Hampshire. While I'd known Bubbles a long time, he was already divorced when I'd met him. Maybe his ex would be able to shed some light on what was going on.

Jill Jackson was a Realtor, and I hoped she worked from home. I'd found her address on the Internet. It's scary how much information is available at a couple of clicks of a button. My excuse for seeing her was flimsy at best. She might slam the door in my face, but I had to try. Thirty minutes later, I pulled up in front of her house.

It was nice-looking, newish, built to look like a bigger version of a wood-framed saltbox house. The roof had a steep pitch. The style was original to colonial New England and called a saltbox because the structure resembled the wooden boxes salt was kept in at the time. The original saltbox houses were two stories in front and one story in the back.

A silver Mercedes SUV sat in the driveway; magnetic signs on the car's side displayed the name of the realty company. I rang the bell. A nicely groomed woman who looked to be in her early forties opened the door. Her dress, haircut, and makeup looked expensive. I'd trust her to sell my house, if I had one.

"Can I help you?" She smiled a friendly smile.

"I'm a friend of Bubbles, Dave."

"Are you his latest fling coming up here to cry on my shoulder?" She shook her head, her hair's subtle highlights catching the sun. "Come on in."

"You have a lot of his exes showing up here?" Maybe I needed to mention that to Stella.

"Showing up, calling, texting. I'm easy to find since I'm a Realtor. I guess Dave talks about me. After he moved back here, he wanted to get back together. But I told him 'been there, done that.'"

We walked into the living room. "Have a seat."

The room looked as though it came out of a page of a Pottery Barn catalog, though some of the pieces were higher end. Everything was in its place, but none of it looked very personal, kind of like a Realtor had staged it to sell. I settled onto a couch after moving a couple of plump pillows out of the way. Jill sat in a chair opposite me.

"I'm not one of his exes," I said. "We're just friends. My husband, ex-husband, and I met him a long time ago at one of our assignments."

"You're an air force wife?"

I nodded, not wanting to take the time to explain my long, involved story.

"I didn't like the life. We were high school sweethearts. Married right after. I worked and had our two kids while he went to college on an ROTC scholarship at the University of New Hampshire."

Some people couldn't adjust to all the moves. "It can be hard," I said.

"Once Dave's dream of being a flight test engineer fell apart, they sent us to Cheyenne, Wyoming. I hated it there. No trees and too far from our family. Too windy." She shook her head at the memory. "I always felt like grit was blowing into my mouth."

We'd never been stationed in Cheyenne, but most of the people I knew who'd lived there had liked it. "So what happened?"

"He put his twenty-four-hour shifts in the launch-control center to good use."

Lots of guys worked on master's degrees while they were on crew. "He studied?"

"I wish. He had an affair with his crew partner, Anna Sweeney. Dave swore it wouldn't happen again, but I packed up the kids and came back."

Could Anna Sweeney be Anna McQueen? "I'm sorry. I know how difficult being divorced is."

"Don't be. He actually ended up being a pretty good father. Always sent more than his allotted child payments. Saw the kids as often as he could. He's been up here a lot since he got stationed at Fitch. He's paying for their college. Dave couldn't be prouder—one at Dartmouth and one at U-Mass Amherst."

A private college for one and out-of-state tuition for the other. That had to be expensive.

"I'm rattling on. Why'd you come?"

"I've been worried about Bubbles with all that's going on."

"I'm glad he has someone who cares about him."

"Did you know Terry McQueen?"

"No. I only know him because Dave mentioned him."

"Did Anna Sweeney marry Terry?"

"No idea. Like I said, I left." She glanced at her Rolex.

"Nice watch," I said as I stood. She was probably busy.

"Dave gave it to me. He hasn't given up on the concept of us." Jill stood, too. "Thanks for worrying about Dave. He's very good at picking the wrong people to trust."

CHAPTER 31

Laura lived in the newest housing section on base; the lawns were broad, toys were scattered, and kids ran loose. Tot lots and basketball courts dotted the open spaces. I pulled into Laura's driveway. It was a wood-frame like Jill's, but more Craftsman style than saltbox. I'd called her, for a second time, on my way back from Nashua and said I needed to talk to her privately. Even though CJ had assured me he'd look into this, I wanted to follow up on my own. He already had a suspect and knew there was a fairly solid case laid out against Carol. CJ had lots of balls in the air. I had one—helping Carol.

I got out and rang Laura's doorbell. The wing commander's house was bigger than most of the houses on base, not only because of the rank and position of the person who lived here, but because it was also used for entertaining dignitaries who visited the base. It was a home and a place of business. We'd been here many times for official functions.

"What's going on?" Laura asked when we'd settled into her family room. You'd never guess this was a base house and not her own home. It was beautifully decorated, from the curtains to the rugs to the paintings on the wall. The house looked like they'd lived here forever, not just a year and a half. I'm guessing all of her homes over the years had looked this way.

It wasn't easy asking to look at someone's financial information. But I needed to know if what had happened to Gennie was or wasn't a fluke. "I know I'm imposing, but could I look at the most recent statement you got from Bubbles and Terry?"

Laura's eyebrows shot up. "Why would you want to see that?"

"You have to swear to me you won't let anyone else know what I'm going to tell you."

Laura nodded, and I explained, without using any names, that Gennie's statement had an error. I didn't mention going to CJ. "I thought if yours had the same error I'd better let Bubbles know right away so he can get it fixed." I didn't want to throw Bubbles under the bus if CJ was right and this was a glitch or if someone was setting Bubbles up.

Laura left and returned with a statement. It was dated about the same time as Gennie's last one, and another should have arrived. "You're sure this is the most recent one?" I asked.

"Yes. I always enter the numbers on our computer when the new one comes in."

"Do you have the statements from the funds company?"

"No. Dave and Terry kept them to consolidate the information into one statement for us."

At least that story was consistent. I compared the numbers on Laura's statement to the funds company. There wasn't any difference between the numbers the company had and the ones on her statement. I was disappointed, not because I wanted Bubbles to be a bad guy but because I thought this might help Carol.

"Yours looks fine," I told Laura.

"Whew. I'm sure Bubbles will get it straightened out for your friend."

I hoped so. "I think I'll drop over and see him on my way home."

I tried to figure out what was going on as I walked up to Bubbles's front door. Could Gennie's statements really be a fluke, or was Bubbles smart enough to know that ripping off a wing commander would land him in hot water fast.

I knocked on the town house door and waited. Tux meowed on the other side of the door. I pounded harder, but Bubbles didn't answer. His truck wasn't out front, but I knew he had a garage around back. I headed back to the row of garages. Bubbles's garage door was down. I looked around before hefting it up. The garage was empty. I started pulling the door back down.

"Can I help you?" a female voice called.

I jumped back, letting the garage door crash closed. A woman stood on the back porch of her town house. This is why there was so little crime on base: people watched out for each other.

I smiled my best "I'm not doing anything" smile. "Bubbles told me he had a ladder I could borrow and to just drop over and get it." I tried to relax my shoulders, which wasn't easy with my pulse racing. "I didn't see it in there, though."

I walked over to her. She must have moved onto the base after I left. I didn't recognize her. I stuck out my hand and introduced myself.

"Dave left a few hours ago," she said. "I'm watching his cat for him."

"You didn't happen to notice a ladder in his house, did you?"

She shook her head.

"Maybe in the basement?"

"I've never been down there. I have to go over to feed Tux. You can come with me and take a look." And this was why there was crime on base: everyone was very trusting.

While she went upstairs to feed Tux, I rushed down to the basement; fortunately, there wasn't a ladder in sight. I didn't want to have to haul one to my Suburban. But there also weren't any computers or statements lying around for me to peruse. I darted back upstairs and looked around the first floor. Not that it helped. It looked the same as the last time I was here. The only difference was that Bubbles's laptop was gone from the desk in his living room. But if he'd left for a few days it would make sense that he'd taken it. I didn't spot any signs of recent conspicuous consumption nor any indications he'd fled the country, or even the base, for that matter. Another flutter of hope went through me. It wasn't Bubbles; it was Terry.

When the woman came back down, I thanked her. "No luck with the ladder. I'll check back when he gets home. How long did he say he'd be gone?"

"Just a couple of days."

"Did he say where he was off to?" I asked as we walked out and she locked the door.

"A business trip somewhere for a few days."

Since she started to look suspicious, I left with a wave and a "thanks."

I knocked on Stella's door when I got back to Ellington. She opened it, dressed in a beautiful black cocktail dress. But she didn't look happy; in fact, if it were possible for steam to come out of ears, hers would be blasting.

"It looks like you're headed out," I said.

"I thought I was. Dave was supposed to be here thirty minutes ago." Stella tapped her watch impatiently and then looked back up at me.

My unease came back. "You're planning to climb into Bubbles's old beat-up pickup in that gorgeous dress?"

"I hope not. I assumed he'd bring his Porsche."

"Bubbles has a Porsche?" I remembered my conversation with Lindsay. She'd said the McQueens' fight ended when some old guy in a Porsche showed up. I'd been thinking white hair and stooped. But of course to a teenager someone in their forties would seem old.

I wondered why no one had ever mentioned Bubbles having a fancy car, not that he couldn't afford it as a single colonel. "I wonder where he keeps it since he has only a one-car garage."

"He doesn't drive it all the time. And he keeps it garaged at his place in the Back Bay."

"Back Bay?" I squeaked out. It was one of the most exclusive neighborhoods in Boston.

"It's stunning. Great views. I'm surprised you've never been there. He said lots of guys keep two places so they don't have to commute—one in the city for the weekends, and one on base."

"No one keeps two places. You can't on a military salary."

"What?"

I'd been working hard at maintaining what I thought was a neutral expression. "I'd better come in."

"Is this going to require scotch?"

"It might." *For you, anyway.* It seemed unlikely that Bubbles was off on a business trip if Stella was sitting here waiting for him to pick her up. While Stella got the scotch, I thought over how things in Bubbles's life weren't adding up, unless he came from a very wealthy family. I'd never heard anyone say that. In fact, his ex-wife said he'd gone to the University of New Hampshire on an ROTC scholarship. That didn't sound like he came from a family with money.

I sat in Stella's living room. Her apartment had a bump out on the back, which added an extra room. But I liked my bird's-eye view of the common better. Stella grabbed a bottle of scotch and two rocks glasses off a dry bar. She poured. If scotch is measured in fingers, she had a fist and I had a pinky. Stella knew it wasn't my favorite. After we clinked our glasses, she tossed some back and shook herself. "Tell me."

I took a small sip, feeling the burn all the way down. "I was just over at Bubbles's place. He wasn't home, and his neighbor said he'd left on a business trip this afternoon."

Stella knocked back some more of her scotch.

"Have you eaten anything?" I was worried about what that much scotch could do on an empty stomach.

"I had a sandwich before Dave was supposed to get here. I didn't want to drink on an empty stomach at the event we were going to."

"Where were you going?" I asked.

"Some kind of promotion party at Gillganins."

Usually promotion parties were held at the

Club on the base, but it was closed for renovations. Stella would have been overdressed for the occasion, but it didn't look like that was going to be a problem.

"So he stood me up and didn't call." Stella thought for a moment. "It could be worse."

"It might be worse," I said. Then I plunged into a description of what had happened to her Aunt Gennie, without telling her it was her aunt. And I talked about Laura, again without mentioning any names. Stella's rigid posture made me sad. "Did you invest any money with him?"

"I did," Stella said; the words came out from between clenched teeth.

I sighed not wanting to go on. "Have you received your latest statement?"

Stella reddened, this time not from the scotch. "I don't know. I'm not that good with investments. I trusted Dave and Terry to take care of things for me. I'll see what I can find."

"Bring your laptop too, please. We're going to need it."

When Stella came back with the statements, she'd changed into jeans and a long-sleeved, loose-fitting shirt. She handed me a couple of statements and her laptop. As I worked, she sipped her scotch.

I typed in her account number and got an error message, just as I had when I'd typed in Gennie's. I started the tedious process of comparing the numbers on the statement to the numbers on the fund's website. I felt that grim line settling in on my mouth again. Stella just watched.

I finally looked up. "These numbers don't match the fund's numbers. Stella, Bubbles was stealing from you."

Instead of looking furious, she just looked sad. "I have to call CJ. He thinks this is a fluke. That someone set Bubbles and Terry up."

Stella looked up hopefully. "CJ's right. That must be what happened."

"Why hasn't Bubbles called you, then?" It sounded harsh, but I couldn't believe that someone had set up an elaborate scheme and hacked into Bubbles's computer system and that neither Bubbles nor Terry had caught it. "Why'd he leave town?"

I called CJ and got his voice mail. I laid out my case again. One statement could have been a fluke, but two made that less likely. I thought about the two wives I'd overheard at the garage sale on Saturday. They'd talked about their husbands investing with Bubbles. It had sounded like they lived on Fitch.

"Want to go to a party?" I asked Stella.

She threw me a look like I'd lost my mind.

"The promotion party at Gillganins will be the perfect place to find a lot of military people who might have invested with Bubbles."

CHAPTER 32

We walked into a packed Gillganins. I'd changed into a sparkly top and designer jeans. Beer was on the house, paid for by the new colonel selects. I waved to Laura across the crowd, and she lifted her glass in acknowledgment. Stella and I fought our way to the bar for a beer. After we were served, we leaned our backs against the bar, studying the crowd.

"Some part of me hoped Bubbles would be holding court at a table in a corner, that everything I've been thinking this afternoon was wrong," I said.

"We're not going to find anything out by standing here. Let's mingle."

I asked a couple of people I knew if they'd seen Bubbles. The third time I asked, a man, still in his uniform with eagles on his epaulets, turned.

"Bubbles isn't here. He should be. I made the boy what he is today." The man's beer breath wafted over me. He threw an arm around Stella and me and pulled us into his group. "They're asking for Bubbles," he told the group. "Did I ever tell you how Bubbles got his call sign?" he asked them.

From their looks, I'm pretty sure they'd heard the story more than once, but since he was their senior officer, they felt obliged to listen again.

"Dave was a second luey and wanted to be a test engineer on a flight crew." The guy still clung to Stella and me. We were more or less holding him up. When he swayed, so did we. "Everyone who wants to be on a flight crew has to go in the high altitude chamber so they know the signs of oxygen deprivation in flight."

The guy unwrapped his arm from around Stella's shoulder to take a drink of his beer. He barely missed sloshing it all over her when he put his arm back. "Dave got nitrogen bubbles in his blood while he was in the chamber. Almost died. That's when I gave him the call sign 'Bubbles.'" He threw his head back and laughed. Most of the crowd joined in. Stella and I looked at each other. All those years I'd believed the swimming pool story. Bubbles must have wanted people to believe that version.

But he'd lived with a daily reminder that he'd almost died. Cop humor could be morbid, but this was right up there. I tried to duck under the colonel's arm, but he tightened his grip.

"Don't you worry," he said to me. "I took care of that boy even after his dream of being on a flight crew died. I got him into the space career field. Made sure he got his dream job in England, a peach of a special-duty assignment. And when he was going to be deployed to Iraq, I made sure he knew how to set up an IED and spot one from a good safe distance so he'd make it out alive."

"Bubbles has a way with fire," one of the other guys said.

I froze. "He knows how to make incendiary devices?" I tried hard to keep my voice casual and hoped the colonel didn't know about what had happened in Ellington.

"Of course." He pointed at the crowd. "Bubbles is a genius, not only with IEDs but also with investing. Best returns I've ever had. You all can thank me." The group nodded.

This time I did manage to slip out of his grasp. Stella followed suit. The colonel swayed a bit, and someone pulled out a chair for him. "Forty percent is a damn good return on an investment."

I wanted to smack my hand to my forehead. I never understood people who fell for financial schemes. It should be obvious that if one guy could make forty percent in the market, everyone else should be able to do the same. Forty percent profit was way more than Bubbles had shown on Gennie's and Stella's statements. Their statements showed a small profit, not a large one.

I'd love to get my hands on the colonel's statements, but I didn't see any way that was going to happen. I guessed one of two things: either the colonel's profit was only on paper, or he had wanted to cash in part of the profit. In that case, Bubbles would had to have pulled money from other accounts or done something even more desperate, like steal and sell a painting.

In some ways, people that went to garage sales were the same. They too wanted something for nothing. Everyone loved a good "I paid fifty cents for this, and it's worth fifty thousand dollars" story. But at least at a garage sale, the playing field was level.

I mingled in the crowd, working Bubbles and their investments into the conversation under the guise that I'd been thinking about investing with him. Bubbles had convinced some of the guys to take out loans to invest with him. Most of them hadn't shown the same profit margins as the colonel had. I wondered how many he'd stolen money from, if anyone had figured it out, or if one of them had killed Terry. Maybe they'd left the frame around his neck as a threat to Bubbles. Or maybe they were trying to frame him. While it looked likely that Bubbles killed Terry, I still had my suspicions about Gennie.

An hour and a half later, I met up with Stella again. She'd heard similar stories. We took off. When we pulled up to the apartment, we could see a man sitting in the shadows on the porch.

Stella grabbed my arm. "It's Bubbles."

I peered as the figure stood. "It's CJ. He told me he'd come by with news."

"I'll leave you to it, then," Stella said. "I'm too tired, and I've had too much to drink. Whatever you find out tonight isn't going to make any difference in my life."

We walked up to CJ together. Stella looked so sad I gave her a hug.

"What was all that about?" CJ asked as Stella went into her apartment.

"Bubbles was supposed to pick her up for a date, and he never did. But even worse, he stole from her, too," I said as I climbed the stairs to my apartment.

We settled on the couch, knees almost touching. "Now do you believe me?"

"Because Bubbles stood Stella up? No." He rubbed his face. "But I do know that Bubbles didn't show up for a meeting he was supposed to be at on base this afternoon. But it still isn't proof."

"His neighbor told me she was watching his cat because he'd left on a business trip for the next few days. What about the piece of camouflage I found in the woods?"

"All it tells us is that someone at some point was in the woods wearing camouflage. We didn't find anything else out there."

I filled him in on what I'd found out at the promotion party.

"It sounds damning," CJ admitted. "But again, it's not proof."

I filled him in about Bubbles being good with fire.

"So are half the guys in the military. It doesn't mean he set the fires."

"But he could have. Did Jett get hold of you?" I asked.

CJ nodded after a pause.

"Maybe he and Bubbles knew the same people."

CJ just shrugged.

"What about the message that was left on Bubbles's home phone? Did anything come of that?" I wasn't sure CJ would answer me.

"What are you talking about?"

"Bubbles told me someone left a threatening message on his home phone. That he told you and you were going to run a trace."

CJ narrowed his eyes. "First I've heard of it."

"Bubbles is telling a lot of lies."

"He is, but lying isn't a crime. There's still the threats against him and Terry."

"Wait." I ran over to my computer and fired it up. I carried it back to the couch and set it on the trunk I used as a coffee table. "I have photographs of the notes Terry got and the one from Bubbles's house." I showed them to CJ one by one, our heads nearly touching. My heart pounded a little harder.

"They all look like they're written by the same person," CJ said.

"I know, but look at the condition. The ones Terry received were creased or smudged from being stuck in the door or on a windshield."

"How did you get these?" CJ asked and not with a happy "wow, you've solved my case" tone.

"I got Terry's notes from Anna. And I snapped the other one when I was at Bubbles's house.

The two Bubbles claims he received are pristine, like they'd just come out of a file folder. CJ, Bubbles wrote these. No one saw the note on Bubbles's windshield. We just believed what he said was true. But it should have been wrinkled or dirty if it was tucked under the wipers. You saw his truck. He rarely washes that thing."

CJ studied the pictures, a pulse beating on his temple. "Bubbles had no way of knowing that you or Stella would find the photo."

"It doesn't matter; if we hadn't, he would just have called it in himself when he got home."

CJ nodded. "I'll do what I can to track him down. It doesn't mean he killed Terry, but he has some explaining to do."

He stood and headed for the door. I took a deep breath. "Wait, CJ. There's something else." I fiddled with my hands, feeling shy all of a sudden. "I've been foolish. Stupid." I managed to look up at CJ. "Charles James Hooker, I think we should try again. To be together."

CJ met my eyes. I smiled at him.

"I can't, Sarah. I'm seeing someone." He turned and left.

CHAPTER 33

At nine on Thursday morning, I headed to the one place I always went when I felt blue—DiNapoli's. Even though they weren't officially open, I knew they'd be there doing prep work. The door wasn't locked, so I went in without knocking. Rosalie looked up and dropped the rag she was scrubbing tables with.

"Angelo, we need coffee."

"Coffee?" Angelo turned from the stove and saw me. He lowered the flame under the pot he was cooking something garlicky-smelling in, washed his hands, and filled three mugs with coffee. He loaded a tray with the mugs and some cookies and set it on the table Rosalie had just cleaned. I flopped in a chair while they sat across from me, pushing coffee and cookies toward me.

They watched me with concerned expressions as I sipped the coffee. I took a cookie but ended up crumbling it.

"CJ's seeing someone," I said. "I thought I was done with Seth and ready to go back to him. But he's seeing someone."

Angelo frowned and folded his arms over his chest—a sure sign he was mad, but I wasn't sure if it was directed at CJ or me. Rosalie reached across and patted my hand.

"I shouldn't be surprised. CJ's a great guy. I'm the one who told him we needed to see other people. I didn't think about how I'd feel if he did." I took another gulp of my coffee. It was strong, unlike the sweeter stuff I usually drank. "And when I think about it, maybe I told him I wanted him back because Seth is mad at me."

I slapped a hand over my mouth. "Oh, no. What if I'm one of those women who can't be without a man?"

Rosalie patted my hand again. "You've been through a lot, Sarah. And you didn't rush into a relationship with Seth. If anything, you've kept him at arm's length."

"So I'm a tease."

"No. You were giving yourself space to work things out." Rosalie pushed back her chair. "But it isn't fair to CJ if you went to him because of Seth." She headed back to the kitchen.

Was I doing that? I was so confused. I'd spent half the night trying to puzzle it out. Obviously, that hadn't worked.

"Did you know that when I was growing up in

Cambridge there wasn't a single dandelion on MIT's lawn," Angelo said.

I shook my head to indicate I didn't know anything about the history of dandelions at MIT.

"We were so poor my mom went over to MIT to dig the dandelions up for our dinner." He stood. "I've gotta get back to my marinara sauce. Eat a cookie. You'll feel better."

I finished my coffee and ate a cookie. Angelo told me stories for one reason, to remind me that my life wasn't so bad. I smiled. It was time to quit feeling sorry for myself and get some work done.

At ten o'clock, I sat across from Missy Tucker in a beat-up recliner that looked like she'd used it as a punching bag. Most of the things in her house didn't look much better, even though it was a Cape with dormers in pricy Concord. Missy seemed run-down too and a lot older than Gennie. But she still looked strong enough to throw a few punches. I just hoped they wouldn't be aimed at me if she didn't buy my story about being a freelance writer.

I whipped out a recorder, with Missy's permission. Her eyes glowed as she regaled me with stories of the early days of female cage fighting. It was surprisingly entertaining.

"I read you were the only one who ever knocked out Gennie 'the Jawbreaker' Elder." I watched her closely.

She nodded, sending her salt-and-pepper hair flying around her ears.

"There were rumors the fight was thrown," I said.

"It's nonsense," she said a bit too quickly, her voice louder.

"Did you know Terry McQueen, her agent at the time? He was murdered in Ellington just last week."

"Of course, I knew him." She shifted in her seat as if the springs had all started popping out at once. "I read about his murder. Terrible way to die."

That at least sounded sincere. "Do you know anything about the falling-out they had?"

"Happens all the time." Missy's voice rose again as she said it. "Why are you asking me all these questions about Jawbreaker? I thought you wanted to know about my career."

"Her last fight is coming up, and you were the only one to knock her out. It's a great story." At least all of that was true.

Missy stood. "We're done."

I sat in a booth at Dunkin' Donuts, waiting for Gennie. Two cups of coffee sat on the table. I'd barely touched mine. Since I'd left Missy's house, I'd put together a pretty good scenario, in my head, that said Gennie had killed Terry. But with Carol's arrest, I couldn't sit around wondering if Gennie might be involved, I had to find out.

"Sarah, what was so urgent that you needed to meet me?" Gennie asked as she sat down across from me. She was dressed in a black skirt and a white button-down shirt. She even had on black tights and red pumps. Gennie studied me for a minute. "Something on your mind?"

"Yes. The paintings. I know you and Carol know each other. I can't figure out why both of you are lying about them. She's in trouble, and I'm going to do whatever it takes to help her."

"You saw the paintings in my closet?"

"Yes. The paintings from Carol's shop."

Gennie sipped her coffee, studying me over the cup. "I hope you're good at keeping secrets."

"I earned a merit badge in Brownies for secret keeping."

"I'm opening an art studio in Dorchestah."

I almost fell out of the booth. "I thought you were opening a mixed martial arts training facility to keep kids off the street."

"That's what I wanted you to think. What I wanted everyone to think. But fighting's difficult. It's hard on the body. Painting allows people to express themselves."

"Why didn't you just tell me?"

"I'm trying to keep it quiet until after my last fight. I have to keep up my tough girl image."

"What's Carol got to do with this?" I drank some of my coffee.

"I always loved art as a kid. When Carol opened her shop, I dropped by. I've been taking private lessons from her ever since. I swore her to secrecy."

"She's very good at keeping secrets too, apparently," I said. "Your name doesn't even show up in her client records." I finished my coffee and worried about what other secrets Carol was keeping from me. "There's more."

Gennie raised her eyebrows at me.

"I know you threw your first fight. I'm guessing Terry talked you into it somehow."

Gennie looked down. I waited. She finally raised her head and met my eyes. "You're right. I did throw it."

"And Terry was involved."

"He talked me into it. I was young, in love." Gennie shook her head. "He filled my head with nonsense about how everyone did it and we could make a lot of money. Afterward we argued when I refused to do it again. He'd made a small fortune off that fight and wanted more. He threatened me."

"What did you do?"

"I broke up with him. Then I called his dad and told him what had happened. His dad said no one would ever find out. And then Terry left the company and moved away." She drummed her fingers on the table. "Someone's been threatening to expose me. And trying to get me to throw my last fight."

"How?"

"Some notes in the mailbox, voice mail, even a couple of e-mails."

"Who?"

Gennie shrugged. "I thought it was Terry and told him to shove it. If it gets out, it will put a shadow over my entire career. No one will believe I only did it once."

"And now that Terry's dead, the problem's gone away?"

"I haven't heard a thing since the day he died."

I stood. "You need to tell the police. His attempt to blackmail you might be the reason he's dead."

Gennie shook her head. "I can't. I won't. I didn't kill Terry."

"You have to."

CHAPTER 34

I headed over to Acton to talk to my friend who owned the estate-sale business. She was going to help me price things. Part of me wondered if I should even proceed with Gennie's sale. My mind whirled around what I'd found out about Gennie as I drove down the 2 through the rotary by the prison in Concord and on to Acton.

She could have murdered Terry. He'd been blackmailing her. She had a secret she didn't want to get out. A chill went through me as I thought of all the time I'd spent alone with her at her house. If Nancy was as protective as I suspected, it gave her a motive too. But it was harder for me to believe she had murdered someone.

The GPS said I was close, but the area was still fairly commercial, and my friend worked out of her home. A few houses sat between strip malls. As I passed a one-story, rambling motel, I did a double take. Anna McQueen was going into one of the rooms.

I pulled into the cracked paved driveway. A neon sign said ACANCY, which wasn't surprising, given the run-down appearance of the place. Only five cars sat in the lot. I parked near the door I'd seen Anna go in. I *bam, bam, bammed* on the door a little harder than I intended to. When she opened it and saw it was me, she stepped back. I took that as an invitation to enter, though she tried to close the door.

"Anna, what the heck are you doing here? You could have stayed on base," I said.

The room was cramped, more so because it was filled with file and moving boxes stacked almost to the ceiling. A couple of computers were open on the desk. It smelled a little musty, and I wasn't sure if it was the boxes or the dingy, stained carpet.

"How did you find me?"

"Were you hiding?" I joked.

Anna laughed. "Just from all the helpful neighbors ringing my doorbell to make sure I'm okay. I couldn't get any studying done."

That made sense. Everyone on base wanted to pitch in and lend a hand. It's what military folks did for one another. Anna looked more rested than the last time I'd seen her. Her red hair fell in shiny waves around her shoulders. So maybe it worked for her. But how could she study here when she could barely get by the bed to the bathroom? The large number of boxes made the room claustrophobic. I could hear traffic through the thin door. It didn't seem that much quieter with it closed.

"Surely you could have found a better situation than this?"

"I suppose, but I took this so I'd be out of the way. It's only for another week. Then I'll be moving back to Oregon. Near Terry's family. It's what he would have wanted."

"What about your family?"

"I don't want to move back to Kansas. And we aren't that close anyway."

"I have some bad news." It sounded trite, considering her husband had just died. But I knew sooner or later the skimming scandal would come out. It was better for her to hear it from me than on her car radio. I quickly filled her in but left out the part about Dave's disappearance or my suspicions that he had murdered Terry.

Anna gasped and got continually paler as I told her the story. "Terry would never have been involved with something like that."

She sounded so confident I almost believed her. But I didn't want to. Even after all I'd learned about Bubbles, part of me still didn't want to believe he'd done anything wrong.

"Dave gave Terry the figures to input," she said. "He must have been the one doing it. Terry was too honest." She sounded like she was

pleading with me to believe her. "He trusted
everyone." Her eyes filled with tears.

She must not know about his days as a sports
agent. I didn't plan to fill her in on them, or on
Gennie's assumption that he was blackmailing
her again. "I really hope all this is resolved
quickly and that the police have it right and it's
only a glitch in the system. Have you seen Dave?"

"Why?"

Rats. "He's dating my friend Stella and he
stood her up the other night. She's worried
about him."

"I'll be sure and tell him to call her." Anna
opened the door. "I have to get back to studying."
She gave me a little shove toward the door.

"Call me if you need anything. I hate to leave
you here." As the door closed behind me, I heard
a few choked-back sobs.

"Damn it. What have you done?" Anna said.

I froze. Could Anna have called someone on
her phone that fast? I pressed my ear to the
door and heard the murmur of someone else's
voice. Someone had been in there the whole
time I had.

I hurried to my car, scanning the parking lot as
I went. I didn't recognize any of the cars, but that
didn't mean anything. I knew very little about
Anna except that her husband had died and
she was studying for her CPA exam. Really, what
she did and with whom was none of my business.
Unless . . . Anna was involved in the scam too.

THE LONGEST YARD SALE   327

Instead of heading down the highway I drove around the back of the motel. There were rooms on this side, too. Parked in front of another door, a room that must be opposite Anna's, was a shiny, black Porsche.

Could it be Bubbles's car? Thoughts swirled in my mind as I looked around. I thought about Bubbles's affair with someone named Anna. Could it be Anna McQueen? Were they still involved? The Porsche looked out of place at this seedy motel, like a diamond in a flophouse. I parked beside it and climbed out. I tried to peer inside, cupping my hands to cut the glare, but the tinted windows were too dark. I tried the handles, but the doors were locked. I leaned in to look through the windshield. There wasn't anything on the seat to indicate it was Bubbles's car.

I climbed back into my Suburban. Anna had seemed sincere when she'd said Terry was honest. Then she'd added that he was too trusting, which was almost exactly what Jill had said about Bubbles. Maybe Anna, not Terry, had helped Bubbles with the faked statements. He'd found out. But why call Carol? Why did he want to meet with her? If he somehow knew Bubbles was planning to steal the painting and didn't know he'd already taken it, Terry might have wanted to warn her. He might have thought she was in danger.

According to Gennie, Terry was no innocent, even if Anna proclaimed he was. I could be way off base; Terry might have been up to his neck in all of it. At some point, something had gone horribly wrong, and Terry had ended up dead. As I thought over my conversation with Anna, I realized she'd said, "I'll be sure and tell him to call her." Anna didn't say she wouldn't hear from him. She more or less admitted that she'd be in touch with Bubbles.

I called CJ. After a quick explanation, I convinced him to run the license plate number and read it off to him.

"Get out of there," CJ said. "I don't know what's going on with Bubbles, and I don't want you anywhere near him."

"Okay," I said. "I'm starting my car and leaving." The only way out of the lot was to go back around the front. I spotted a convenience store across the street from the motel and headed over.

"I mean it, Sarah. Don't hang around there."

"I left. I have an appointment with an antiques appraiser anyway," I said as I drove into the convenience store lot. "Have you run the plate?" I backed into a space, so I had a good view of not only Anna's room but also the entrance and exit to the motel.

"Not yet."

"Will you call me when you know?"

"Worry about your own life, Sarah." CJ disconnected.

I tapped my finger on the steering wheel. First, CJ had sounded concerned about me being at the motel, which had made me think he still cared about me. Then he'd told me to mind my own business, but maybe that meant he cared about me too. I sat a few more minutes, debating whether to stay or go.

I sent a quick text to the woman I was supposed to be meeting with and told her I was running late. She sent back a message that said "obviously" and asked if I could reschedule. Before I could answer, the Porsche careened around the side of the motel. It slid onto the 2 and headed west. It moved fast, cutting in and out of traffic, which was not that unusual considering the way people drove around here. I thought about trying to follow the car, but it was already a tiny dot. There was no way my Suburban could keep up.

Instead, I called CJ again. I told him what I'd seen and then hung up before he could lecture me. I was tired of being lectured. Bubbles must have killed Terry and left the frame around his face to throw off an investigation. Then he'd sent the notes to himself to make it look like he was a potential victim, too. All the while, he continued to steal from his investors, people who trusted him. Bubbles wasn't the man I'd believed him to be. He was a liar, a cheat, and probably a murderer. But instead of feeling sad, a slow anger built in me.

I decided to go back over to the motel. In my brief glimpse of the Porsche, it didn't look like anyone was in the passenger seat. If that were true, Anna was still over there, and I wanted to talk to her before she fled. If she didn't answer, I'd ask the manager to open the room to make sure she wasn't dead on the floor.

I parked a couple of doors down from her room and knocked. The door flung open. Anna stood there, looking hopeful even though her face was streaked with tears. Before Anna could register it was me, I grabbed her arm and hauled her out.

CHAPTER 35

I wasn't about to go into her room again. Who knew what or who was hiding in there.

"Let's go sit over there." I pointed to a couple of rusted lawn chairs sitting in front of the manager's office. By the time we sat down, tears were flowing down Anna's face again.

"I can't believe he was dating someone," Anna said when we sat down.

"That's what you're worried about?" Good heavens, and I thought my personal life was a mess. I started to feel better about myself. At least I wasn't *that* stupid. "Shouldn't you be worried about jail time? Mail fraud? Murder?" Those were just the crimes I could think of off the top of my head. I figured there were more. Lots more.

"It was all Dave. He came up with the idea to rig the statements. And to sell *Battled*." She gripped the arms of her chair. "How long has he been seeing her?"

If this was the way to get information out of

her, I'd answer. "A few months. Did he set the fires?"

"Yes. Just to make sure there were plenty of distractions."

"So you could steal the painting?"

"Most of the librarians were outside selling books. I made sure the one inside was busy. But Dave made the switch. Is she pretty?"

I thought about Stella. *Pretty* wasn't a good enough word to describe her, and yet *beautiful* seemed too much. She was intriguing, interesting, and smart, but for Anna, I'd keep it simple. "Yes. She's pretty. Why'd he steal *Battled*?"

"For the money." She said it with a tone that implied I was stupid. "The black market for art's always booming. Please tell me she's fat."

"Sorry. She's got curves where every woman wants them." I worried Anna was going to run out of questions for me before I did for her. "How did Terry end up dead at Paint and Wine?"

Anna released her grip on the arms of the chair. Her hands were covered with bits of rust and paint. She flicked a few off. I was afraid our conversation was over.

"I overheard Terry call Carol and ask to meet her. I told Dave." Anna looked at me. "Dave said Terry's death was a horrible accident."

You don't accidentally strangle someone. "How'd he get into the store?"

"Dave knew a girl that worked there."

I wondered how Bubbles knew Olivia. Then I remembered she'd mentioned karaoke at

Gillganins and that Bubbles hung out there too. "She let him into the store?"

"No. He slipped her key out of her purse one night at Gillganins. I took it and made a copy."

I shook my head. "Is your maiden name Sweeney?"

Anna jerked up. "How'd you know?"

"You and Dave were missile crew partners and had an affair."

"We've loved each other for years and saw each other when we could."

There were so many things I wanted to ask her but had to choose wisely. "Why'd he steal the money from his clients? People who trusted him."

She looked out over the parking lot, like she hadn't thought about this before. "Broken promises. He should have made general. They shouldn't cut so many benefits to veterans. It's only going to get worse, you know."

"But Dave was taking money from the very people affected by those same things."

"Not all his clients were in the military." She turned in her chair to look at me. "Did Dave seem happy with her?"

I thought about the times I'd seen Stella and Bubbles together; there'd been a lot of laughter. "He did."

"I'd punch her in the face if I could."

I never understood women who were mad at the other woman when their man dallied. I called CJ and sat with Anna until the police arrived.

* * *

Laura called me as I was headed back to base. "It's Beverly. I think she's moving some of the stuff."

"What makes you think that?" I asked.

"She said she wanted to leave early so she could drop off some old clothes she'd stuck in the storage shed at Goodwill."

"Are you at the shop?"

"Yes."

"Did you call base security?"

"Of course."

I wasn't that far from the back entrance to Fitch. "Sponsor me on. I'll be there in a few minutes."

As I drove to the base, I called Carol. "It looks like you will be a free woman," I said, and then I filled her in on my conversation with Anna.

"Now Brad's mom can go home. Just as soon as I finish this painting."

"Why are you going to finish it? There's no client. There never was."

"I put my heart into this painting. It's almost done, and it's even better than the first version. If no one else wants it, I'll keep it."

"I wonder if they'll ever find the original."

"I hope so. I can't believe your friend did all this."

"Neither can I. I don't know who to trust anymore," I said.

"Trust yourself."

* * *

Fifteen minutes later, I walked through the front door of the thrift shop. All was calm. Laura stood behind the counter, helping someone check out. Beverly sat in her office as though she didn't have a care in the world. She waved and smiled when she saw me. I poked around a couple of racks of clothes before moseying out to the shed at the side of the shop. All the bags seemed to be in place, untouched since Sunday night. I looked up at the cameras. They weren't that easy to see. A security police car drove by as if it was on a routine patrol. I spotted another one parked down the street.

I went back into the thrift shop. Laura waited for me in the sorting room.

"So what's the plan?" I asked.

"We can't actually do anything until she takes the stuff."

"Hey, girls. I'm heading out."

We jumped apart at Beverly's voice.

"Want me to help you move the stuff from the shed to your car?" Laura asked.

"It's only a couple of bags, and you shouldn't leave the register uncovered. Someone might try to steal from us."

Laura and I nodded like a couple of bobble-head dolls. The nerve of that woman astounded me. I followed Laura to the front. She called the security force squadron again. We watched as Beverly drove by the front of the shop. We rushed out to the shed and flung open the doors. It was empty. Out front tires squealed. We ran to see what was going on.

Beverly was out of her car, yelling at James. "You almost caused a wreck. I'm going to report you."

"Open your trunk please, ma'am," James said.

"Absolutely not." Beverly spotted us. "Laura, call your husband. I'm being harassed."

"Just open your trunk, Beverly," Laura said. "We know you're stealing from the thrift shop and selling things on eBay."

Beverly tossed her hair as she clicked open her trunk. She held her head up as the bags came out. The first ones were all of the old clothes.

"See. This is clothing that's going to the recycler."

But the next bags held the dolls, quilts, and purses. Even after she'd been caught, she stood there, as haughty as ever.

"Why would you do this?" Laura asked her.

"You don't pay me enough, and there's plenty to go around."

CHAPTER 36

By ten that night, I was still too keyed up to even think about going to bed. I'd been waiting for CJ to call with word about Bubbles. While I waited, I scrubbed, dusted, or straightened every surface in the apartment. And Beverly's comment "you don't pay me enough" stayed with me. Bubbles must have felt the same way. He'd almost died as a young lieutenant, and his nickname had been a constant reminder. Then after the mess with the missiles, he knew he'd never make general. It dawned on me then. Terry's blackmailing Gennie might have put Bubbles's scam in jeopardy. They were two criminals with two different agendas, neither knowing the other's secret. If Bubbles managed to evade the law, we might never learn the full truth.

I'd made my own mess of things with Seth and CJ. My apartment seemed small and hot, so I flung open the window. Cool air rushed in. I leaned on the sill. The town common was quiet, and Great Road was empty. Lights were on in Carol's store. Her car was parked out front. I knew she'd almost finished her second copy of *Battled*. Maybe she needed some company to keep her going.

I chuckled at that thought as I threw on my leather jacket. Carol would know I was the one who needed company. I grabbed my cell phone and my key to Carol's store. Stars popped in the dark sky. The scent of fallen leaves spiced the autumn air.

As I approached the door to Paint and Wine, something crashed inside, and I heard a muffled scream. Carol. I ducked below the wooden half of the door and peeked in. Someone stood beyond the studio door behind Carol. All I could see was a man's hairy arm wrapped around Carol's neck, choking her. The dark shadows of the studio hid all but a bit of his face. Bubbles. She pried at his arm, scratching it. He dragged her into her studio. Her legs kicked out in front of her until he hauled her out of my sight.

I called 9-1-1 as I ran around to the alley, filling in as many details as I knew. "Get someone here now. I'm heading down the alley to the back door."

The dispatcher advised me not to do that and asked me to stay on the line. I agreed but put my phone on silent and tucked it in my pocket. I didn't plan to do anything stupid, but if there was something I could do to help Carol, I would. I hurried down the alley, making too much noise. I slowed behind DiNapoli's, wishing it was open and someone was in there to help me. I glanced at Herb's house. No lights were on, and no curtains twitched.

I hesitated at the back door of Carol's shop. I turned the knob. The door was locked. My hand shook. I stuck the key in the lock, turning it ever so slowly until I heard the lock release. Should I risk opening it or wait? Sirens wailed in the far distance. I hoped they were racing here.

Inside someone yelled out in pain. I eased the door open and slipped into the supply room. The curtains between the supply room and the studio stirred. I held my breath as I inched the door closed. After picking my way around boxes of Carol's supplies, I peered through a crack in the curtains. Dim light from the skylight streamed down on Bubbles's and Carol's silhouettes. He yanked up on a frame around her neck. Her breath came out in short pants as she clawed at it.

I looked around the storage area. The box of frames Carol had bought at New England's Largest Yard Sale sat in a corner. I slid a heavy frame with sharp corners out of the box. I stepped through the curtains. Carol's hands dropped from the frame to her sides, limp.

"Bubbles!" I yelled. As he turned, I lobbed the frame at him boomerang style. The sharp corner struck his temple. He dropped to the ground, and his head thunked against the floor. Carol crumbled to the floor next to him, the frame hanging around her shoulders. I was stunned I'd hit him. I'd only hoped to distract him long enough for the police to arrive.

Bubbles moaned as I heard the screech of tires at the back door. Glass broke out front. Police burst into the room from both sides.

Pellner kneeled beside Bubbles, flipping him over and cuffing him. I ran over to Carol. Her eyes opened.

"We need an ambulance," I shouted. I slid down beside Carol and removed the frame from around her shoulders.

"One's on the way," someone said.

Pellner yanked Bubbles up. Blood dripped from a cut on his temple. A bruise blossomed around it. Pellner handed him off to someone. "Get him to a hospital." He looked at me. "What happened here?"

I told him as much as I knew. "Did Bubbles come back for the second painting?" I asked Carol. I bet he wanted to con someone with that one, too.

"Yes." Her voice rasped out. I helped her sit up, bracing her against me.

I shuddered as I realized how lucky Carol was to be alive. The EMTs arrived and loaded a protesting Carol onto a gurney.

I called Brad to let him know what had happened and that Carol was heading to Lahey in Burlington. Pellner stood over me until I hung up.

"Chuck's going to have a fit when he hears you came in here."

"I couldn't wait. He'd have killed her."

Pellner patted me on the shoulder. I waited for another lecture.

"You saved her. Good work." He flashed his dimples at me before he turned and started talking to another officer. I gaped after him. Then I smiled to myself. Good work.

The next night, Stella and I sat at the window table of DiNapoli's. We'd gone to Gennie's last fight. Right before the fight the promoters had conducted a huge ceremony. They showed a film of her illustrious career. Gennie announced to the world that she was opening an art studio in Dorchester. For a moment, there was dead silence in the arena. Her opponent sneered. Then a thunder of applause broke out. Gennie beat the sneer right off of her opponent's face and won her final fight.

The remains of a celebration pizza sat in the middle of the table. Angelo had whipped it up just for us, trying out a new recipe with blue cheese, grilled red peppers, and baby portobello mushrooms. Plastic kiddie cups with lids and straws sat in front of us filled with Chianti. We were on our second round. Since all we had to do was walk across the town common to get home, we could drink our fill tonight. Of course, it would be my luck that some overeager Ellington police officer would be out there and arrest us for being drunk in public.

"So, Stefano bought Carol's copy of *Battled*?" Stella asked.

"He did. Not for as much as Bubbles had promised her, but for a very nice sum."

"At least Stefano didn't have the real one."

I glanced over at Angelo. "I know Angelo was relieved when they found the original in Bubbles's Porsche. He never said it, but I think he was worried Stefano might really have had it."

"Here's to us," Stella said, picking up her cup.

"To sucking at relationships." I held up my cup.

"To always picking the wrong man. I've outdone myself this time," Stella said. "He not only stole my heart, but he stole my money."

We drank to that.

"It's hard to believe he was using the money to pay for his fancy car and penthouse," Stella said.

"Along with his kids' education and his wife's Rolex," I added. "But at least you have a new man in your life."

"Tux." Stella smiled. "He's already captured my heart."

"Won't he be a constant reminder of Bubbles?"

"With Dave in jail and no bail, I couldn't let Tux go to a shelter." She paused and grinned. "Or let him think I was a mean landlady."

I laughed.

"Maybe *your* problem is having two right men," Stella said.

"Not anymore. To singledom," I said as we smacked our cups together again. We took another sip in solidarity.

Stella looked out the window as I studied the dessert menu.

"What do you think about sharing a chocolate mousse cannoli?" I asked. "Or tiramisu. Theirs is the best."

"I think you have a problem. And it's not from the fat and calories in the cannoli."

Not another one. I glanced up at Stella. She pointed out the window. I was almost afraid to look, thinking of my car being towed or booted for some infraction I wasn't aware of. I looked anyway, ready to call Vincenzo for representation, if necessary. Across the town common, walking down the sidewalk toward each other, were Seth and CJ. Both carried bouquets of flowers. I dropped the menu. They stopped under the streetlight at the bottom of the steps to my apartment and stared at each other.

I turned to Stella, eyes wide open.

"Like I said, to two right men." Stella grinned.

I grinned as we touched our cups together again.

Garage Sale Tips

Tips for Sellers

- Use tags for pricing that will stick to the item but won't damage it with residue.

- If you don't want to tag each item with a dollar amount, use different colors for different prices: orange for $1, blue for $5, green for $10, etc. Post signs that show what color corresponds with what price.

Tips for Buyers

- Don't overestimate your ability to fix things or underestimate the cost of having something fixed. Some bargains just aren't worth it.

- Always check the backs of rugs for stains; sometimes they don't show on the front.

- Always ask for a better price, whether you're at a garage sale, a flea market, or an antiques show. The worst that can happen is someone will tell you "no," and that's rare.